LEARNING TO DANCE

SUSAN SALLIS

ISIS
LARGE PRINT
Oxford

First published in Great Britain 2013
by
Bantam Press
an Imprint of Transworld Publishers

Published in Large Print 2014 by ISIS Publishing Ltd.,
7 Centremead, Osney Mead, Oxford OX2 0ES
by arrangement with
Transworld Publishers
a Random House Group Company

CIP data is available for this title from the British Library

ISBN 978–0–7531–9276–4 (hb)
ISBN 978–0–7531–9277–1 (pb)

Printed and bound in Great Britain by
T. J. International Ltd., Padstow, Cornwall

LEARNING TO DANCE

For my family

CHAPTER
ONE

The discreet advertisement in the local paper announced: "Unique opportunity for art lovers. Four nights at Castle Dove. Final week of Robert Hausmann's retrospective exhibition. Somerset's much-loved landscape artist will be in residence to talk about his work. Luxury mini-coach. All inclusive. Telephone . . ."

Judith squinted slightly as she printed the eleven digits on the side of the paper with a pencil she had dug out of the garden that Sunday afternoon; her glasses were probably upstairs. She dreaded Sundays: in spite of the supermarkets opening practically all day, Sundays still seemed shut down. Internalized. An exclusion zone around each household.

She spotted her glasses on top of the television, discovered that she had reversed the digits, scribbled them out and started again. Was there such a thing as dysnumeracy? Well, it was probably better than dyslexia anyway. She checked again, tore the edge off the newspaper, and stuck it behind the clock on the mantelpiece. Then she returned to the paper and her après-gardening cup of tea and read the local football results so that she could pass them on to the boys in Australia; then the obituaries.

Arnold McCready had died; she was shocked. He was a regular golfer, retired for some time, so older than Jack. She had met him in the clubhouse and had a nodding relationship with his wife. Beattie, presumably Beatrice. Called herself a golfing widow. Well, she was a fully-fledged widow now. Sympathy cards, flowers, lots of callers. Judith tightened her mouth against unexpected tears. He had been a nice chap. He had spotted her in the library a week ago and hadn't pretended not to see her. He'd come up, half-a-dozen books under one arm, free hand held out. "Judith! How are you? Sorry, stupid question. Listen, if you're stuck for a strong, long arm — light bulbs, exploding washing machine — you know the sort of thing, our number is in the book. I'm no do-it-yourselfer, but it's worth ringing me before you go to the Yellow Pages. OK?"

She had smiled gratefully, knowing that she would not take advantage of the offer simply because Beattie wouldn't like it. Surprisingly, other wives were highly suspicious of women who no longer had husbands. Naomi had told her that; she had known from personal experience.

She closed and folded the paper neatly, not allowing herself to think about Naomi. Death was so . . . final. At least Jack was alive, even if he had deserted her. And that's what he had done. Incredible, really. Jack. A deserter. He would have been shot in the War. And serve him right, too.

She tried to whip up her anger. The divorce helpline had told her that anger was good at first, it was a source of energy. But underneath the whipped-up anger were other much less positive emotions. Bewilderment. Absence of confidence. A feeling of standing on the edge of a precipice. And now . . . these damned tears. For Arnold McCready, yes. But also for Jack.

She ripped off her specs and scrubbed her eyes with a tissue, then went to the kitchen for more tea. Dammit, she would go on this trip in this damned minibus. She'd always liked art exhibitions and had been within six months of completing a two-year course in visual art when she'd been nineteen. Then Jack had come along and a year later she'd been an old married woman with twin boys. And now she was forty-eight, both sons doing well in Australia, nice home, fairly new car, no husband.

She stared out of the window, waiting for the kettle to boil, admiring the long flower border she had spent the afternoon clearing. It was September, and she was already "putting the garden to bed" as she called it.

Jack had not approved wholeheartedly of gardening as a hobby.

"Too solitary," he had said — not long ago. "You should join something. Make friends."

She'd had a good friend, Naomi Parsons. She allowed herself — just while the tea brewed and she refilled the kettle — to think of Naomi.

Naomi had been one of the local librarians, and had suggested books that Judith's mother might enjoy. She had always been cheerful; she had made sure that the four high window ledges in the old-fashioned building had held fresh flowers. Judith remembered hearing her in the children's corner, talking about a vase of cowslips

3

she had picked and brought in that morning. "When I was a little girl like you," she'd been saying, "I used to pull out one of these tiny trumpets, very gently, and taste the nectar." She had laughed, lifting her head slightly. "Then I could understand just what the bees and other insects enjoyed for their breakfast every morning!"

Someone — the child's mother probably — had laughed too, but said, "Don't you try that, Beverley! You're likely to poison yourself with all the traffic fumes we get these days!"

Judith had thought how much the twins would have enjoyed Naomi, had they known her when they were little. She began to notice little things about the tall, rather gangly librarian. Her laugh was infectious and bubbled somehow — she lifted her head to let it out; she wore a wedding ring and Judith had heard her turn down an invitation to attend a library meeting after-hours. "I'm really sorry — you know I have to get home for William." Was William the husband or a child?

Then two things had happened: firstly, Judith's dearly loved mother had died, and then Judith had stopped going to the library for a whole month. Jack had said, "Listen, love. We have to do something to . . . to break through . . . this time. Let's go off and see the boys. Or just have a holiday."

She was surprised. "I'm all right, Jack, honestly. I need to be quiet —"

"But you're so rarely quiet! You've gone inside yourself somewhere — I can't find you!"

4

She tried to grin. "So, I really am a dumb blonde, as you once so charmingly called me!"

"I've never called you that!"

But he was right, she couldn't talk about her mother to anyone, not even Jack. Everything she did emphasized the fact that her mother — Eunice Denman — was not there any more. She read articles, watched programmes, so many of which portrayed this remarkable closeness between mothers and their children. The awful thing was, she did not want it any other way. She did not want to leave the house where for so long she had nursed her mother; a holiday would be a penance not a joy. Of course she and Jack would go and see their sons; but not yet . . . not yet . . . it was too soon.

Then, when Judith finally went back to the library, because it was what she did each week, Naomi was not there.

One of the others said, "Dark hair — tall? Mrs Parsons, it must be. She's lost her husband, I'm afraid. But she will be back next week, we hope."

She had been. And Judith had asked her whether they could have a cup of tea together one afternoon.

Suddenly it was as if Naomi was there, in the kitchen, reaching for the biscuit tin. She turned to look at Judith and there was her long face framed in a marvellous hairdo rather like a black satin bonnet, the ends almost meeting beneath her chin. Brown eyes, clear as milkless tea, long uncontrollable legs that made her ungainly at times. Judith closed her eyes, opened them, poured the tea, and went back to the living room.

5

She collapsed on to the sofa and stared out of the window. It was getting dark and the glass showed a shadowy reflection; not Naomi any more, just herself. Her stupid self. Because two months ago, at the beginning of July, Naomi had gone to London to meet someone — Judith never discovered who it was — and had come out of her hotel at exactly the same time as a car driven by a man over the limit had mounted the pavement. Judith dropped her head, held her cup in both hands, and squeezed her eyes shut.

Physically, they had been complete opposites. Judith was short, rounded, blonde and blue-eyed. She had hardly changed from the nineteen-year-old who had so very much enjoyed being swept off her feet by the visiting cartoonist, Jack Freeman. She sucked in a deep breath, opened her eyes and forced herself to drink some of the tea. She must let Naomi go. Jack had said that. He had encouraged her to make a friend, and then had told her to let Naomi go.

"Let Mum go, too?" she had asked without bitterness.

"Yes. Otherwise you are blind to all the lovely memories you shared — we all shared."

She had seen his point, of course. And she wasn't blind to the fact that he was looking gaunt, almost haggard, himself. He was right: there had been lovely memories and they were being blocked by the bitterness.

She had made an enormous effort. In her mind she had cocooned both her mother and Naomi in a kind of silk robe, and said goodbye. Then she had suggested that they should have the whole of September with the boys in Perth.

Jack had stared at her, immobile, looked at her outstretched hand, then turned and walked to the window and gazed out at the garden. She joined him. She had no inkling that things were terribly wrong until she glanced up at his face. Tears were gathering along his eyelashes; even as she saw them they overflowed.

She made a choking noise and took his hand. Then he asked her to let him go, too. She waited for more: an explanation of what he had really meant. And, if he had meant what it sounded as if he had meant . . . some kind of discussion?

There was none. He withdrew his hand and went to their room. She discovered he had packed everything he needed while she had been in her mother's old room, sorting through the bookshelves.

She followed him around while he gathered up some files. She kept asking why, what had happened? And eventually, was there someone else? He looked at her as if she had attacked him physically. He said, "Another woman? I don't know. Yes, I suppose that's what it was. It's over, of course." Then he opened the front door. "I'm not worth anything, Jude. Just let me go. Forget me. I'm sorry."

He had gone. But after the long bewilderment and sheer disbelief, the bitterness had come back. She could taste it in her mouth right now. Gall. Her memories of her mother, of Naomi, all tainted. She had not allowed herself to remember Jack.

She swallowed chokingly on the gall and looked again at the darkening window. Her reflection was blurred by the steam from her tea. But she knew full well what she looked like. She looked like Doris Day playing Annie in *Annie Get Your Gun*. Only her curly hair was no longer blonde, it was colourless, and her well-rounded figure would become plump if she so much as looked at chocolate. She had discovered that over the last two months, when her frantically busy life had slowed abruptly, and she really had not had enough to do. Jack had been gone for two months; she couldn't believe it. No word, no divorce papers, no phone calls. He could be dead. Her heart twisted inside her chest cavity, and she gasped audibly. She put her cup on the floor, ready to leap to her feet and get on with something, anything. And then she subsided. Of course she would know if he were dead. She was being ridiculous. She forced a smile and caught sight of it in the window. And then, suppressing the bitterness with the cold dregs of her tea, she began to remember Jack.

He had come as part of their six-week taster course in graphic design. It was the first time her art college had ventured into any kind of pop art; they had looked at lampoons, and someone had asked about Andy Warhol, and the college had responded by inviting Jack Freeman to give the second-year students a lecture. His visit had been like a bomb exploding in the middle of the lecture room, where such names as Constable, Reynolds, even Picasso were spoken with reverence. This man had talked to the students about the imminent arrival of the graphic novel. He had used words like "vivid", "vibrant", "vivacious". They had all been "fast words". The vision, and the execution of that vision, had to be quick. Brain, eyes, pencil, paper.

Words came from him like bullets. Questions from the students flew around the room. He had a stack of their work on the table in front of him, and he picked out two or three and talked about less being more. "Never use two strokes of the pencil when one will do." By now, the students were almost at the end of their six-week taster and they all were hooked by what Jack Freeman was saying, all except for Judith Denman. She loved colour, consideration and then total immersion. Irony and satire had nothing to do with it. But she could not take her eyes off this lecturer. She had never seen anyone so . . . alive.

When the other students left at the end of the lecture she remained behind speechless, her eyes never leaving him. He flicked through the work on the desk and pulled out one of her watercolours.

"Are you Judith Denman?" he asked.

She nodded.

"Do you know my name?"

She cleared her throat. "Of course. Jack Freeman."

"Interesting. We share the 'man'. But I am 'Free' and you are 'Den'. That says something to me. Do you see it, too?" She nodded. She had understood everything he had said. And more.

He persisted. "I mean, do you see it rather than hear it?" She nodded again, and he said, "Tell me what you see."

"I see two birds in a nest. And one flies. Up and away." She almost choked with embarrassment, and thanked God that no one else was in the room.

"I see that, too." He tapped a pencil on the pile of drawings. "How serious are you with your landscapes?"

"Very. I love what I see out there." She shifted her eyes to the windows.

"Do you want to produce them commercially? Postcards? Watercolours for tourists?"

"Not really."

"That's good. And you're not interested in anything else — my stuff, for instance?"

"Not really," she repeated.

"OK." He sighed, replaced her painting and seemed to surrender to something. Then he lifted his head and looked at her as she had been looking at him all afternoon. It went on and on. At first she thought she might be going to faint; but she had never fainted, so wasn't quite sure how it started. And then a calmness washed through her and she no longer tried to break away. He stayed where he was, hand on top of the stack of drawings, weight on his left foot, right leg slightly extended. He was nothing much to look at really; she realized that with surprise. Fair, just as she was, but his hair was like damp straw across his forehead and his eyes were a bit too solidly blue. His nose was too small for his long, thin mouth and — oh dear — his ears protruded.

He cleared his throat and she smiled slightly as some of the afternoon's dynamism returned. She had not been mistaken, he was beautiful. Lit by fire.

10

He said, "I did not dare see you. But I must have perceived you somehow because I knew you were there. All the time. I could not pull out any of your work because it would have meant looking at you. And I wasn't sure whether I would be able to look away. Do you understand?"

She did not have to clear her throat; she had been looking at him all afternoon. All embarrassment had gone now. She simply nodded. They were both on some kind of baseline where truth was the only language possible. It was so — so absolutely *factual*. Not even romantic then. Just plain and frighteningly honest.

He said, suddenly humble, "I'm sorry. You had more courage."

"I had no other options." She tried to smile. She wanted to reassure him. She was overwhelmed by an enormous tenderness.

He drew in his right leg and stood away from the desk.

"Let's look at this sensibly. I am twenty-eight. You must be still a teenager. I am a freelance political cartoonist. Your adult life, your career, is still to come. We are experiencing a rather strong physical attraction. I think it might be a good thing if you left. Now."

She clenched her hands; she did not know whether she was courageous or not. She was terrible about all dental treatment. And heights. No, she wasn't courageous at all. But . . . she had been strong when her father had died; her mother had said often, "I couldn't do this without you, Jude." Anyway, now, at this moment, she had no choice because her legs would not move. She could not leave the lecture room. Not yet, anyway.

This time she did clear her throat before she spoke.

"It's not only physical attraction. You know that. Because of the birds in the nest. You said you saw the same thing."

"No, I didn't see the same thing."

"You said you did."

"I saw two badgers in a sett. One of them stayed, one of them left."

There was a pause; the almost-rhyme had been unintentional, their connected gaze changed slightly, and then they both started to laugh. They walked towards each other and reached out. His hands were warm on hers; rough, too. He was much more a badger than a bird.

He shook both her hands, and gradually they stopped laughing. She knew he was going to tell her to go away and ring him in three years' time. She held on to his hands fiercely. She knew this had to happen. And then he knew it, too. He sighed.

"So . . . you want a den. And I want to fly. I don't see why it shouldn't work. Anyway, let's see how it goes. I'm going to Paris tomorrow. New exhibition on the Champs-Elysée, lots of interesting things. How would you feel about coming with me?"

She wanted to go, but she said nothing and went on looking at him. He shook her hands again, knowing.

"Fine, I'll see to your ticket now and pick you up at seven thirty tomorrow morning. We'll fly together."

12

He turned her around, put his hands on her shoulders and propelled her to the door. He did not ask her anything about her circumstances, and she asked him nothing about his. Just before the door closed between them she turned and said, "I live at forty-seven Meadow Road."

"Right. If you change your mind, don't answer my knock."

Her mother was appalled. "Marry in haste, repent at leisure," she intoned like her mother before her. Judith could tell that — beneath the shocked surprise — she was intrigued.

All through their evening meal Eunice Denman voiced rhetorical questions and answered them herself with words like "unwise" and "foolhardy". Then she changed tack slightly and said that if someone was paying for him to lecture at the art school then he must have some standing, which of course he couldn't afford to jeopardize with such an obvious seduction scenario.

Judith said nothing about his brief "let's see how it goes". Instead she reiterated her first argument: that he obviously thought the exhibition at such a prestigious gallery on the Champs-Elysée would be well worth her seeing. She began to believe it herself. He hadn't been very complimentary about her watercolour, but now she said, "Perhaps he really thinks I've got something, Ma. Dad always used to say I was a natural-born painter —"

"He said you were a natural-born woman, Jude. There was a song around at the time. Dad knew nothing at all about painting."

Judith tightened her mouth with disappointment. Yes, that was what Dad had said; typically kitsch. She had loved him saying it, it had made her feel confident. It was the reason she had left off the gripper-knickers that Joyce Belling had said held in stomachs better than anything. She had been pathetic. Just pathetic.

She thought of Dad and his spurious charm, and said suddenly, "Actually, Mr Freeman reminds me of Dad. How strange. He's not a bit like him really, no compliments — can't imagine him bringing me any flowers like Dad did with you. But there's just something."

"A dozen red roses, every day for a month. Until I said I'd go out with him." Mum's eyes were watering and her chin was trembling.

Judith said quickly, "One of the things Dad used to say was about seizing opportunities. I think I should seize this one, Ma. I really do."

There was a sniff, then a scrabbling up the cardigan sleeve for a handkerchief, then a mixture of sniffs and blows, and eventually Eunice sighed deeply and acknowledged it might be silly for Judith to miss "an outing with her teacher".

So, on the basis of it being a school trip, Judith set her alarm for six thirty the next morning, packed the knapsack she had taken to guide camp five years ago, and was waiting by the gate at seven twenty. She never doubted he would turn up. She never ever doubted his wholehearted love for her; he felt as she felt. There were no options. Her mother stayed by the front door, as her dressing gown was not suitable for public viewing. She kept calling Judith back for yet another piece of advice, but when the Armstrong Siddeley appeared at the mouth of their cul-de-sac she closed the door to a mere crack and peered through it with one eye. She did not notice the rust, nor the fact that the rear of the car appeared to be used as a litter bin.

Judith noticed, but rather liked it. Even more she liked the way Jack shot from the driver's seat, his face split by an enormous grin, grabbed her knapsack and hurled it in with the rest of the stuff, before handing her into the slippery polished seat as if she were royalty.

He settled himself next to her, did a noisy three-point turn, and they were on their way. She remembered very well what he had said.

"My God, this is great. Never thought you'd come, of course. Never thought I'd go crazy for a girl like you — blonde bombshell. I don't know how I'll wait till we get to the hotel."

She had suddenly felt the smallest affront. She translated the "blonde bombshell" into "dumb blonde" and saw them scurrying up a winding staircase in a rather seedy hotel in Montmartre. But the hotel was not far from the Tuileries, and only a walk from the gallery on the Champs-Elysée, and they had separate rooms, but with only a low rail between the wonderful wrought-iron balconies. And when he clambered over the railing he was suddenly diffident.

He said, "I should know how to go about this, Judith. I'm almost ten years older than you, and you're so — so blessedly ordinary. Not edgy and clever-clever. You really are the nesting type, and here I am dragging you on one of my flights!"

And all doubts left her. She spoke calmly. "But now, at this moment, we are in my nest. And you are with me. If you weren't, I would be terrified. When my father died he seemed to take away . . . so much. And you are giving it back!"

It was simple, direct. Afterwards he had cried and she had not. She remembered the passion, yes. But more she remembered the warmth and total safety of being with him.

He had always been with her. Through the birth of the twins . . . when Toby's tonsillitis had proved to be meningitis . . . when Matt had won a scholarship to the grammar school and Toby had not . . . and then, when Jack's brother in Australia had offered the boys "a kind of apprenticeship" with his air-delivery service, Jack had gone with them to Perth to investigate the whole idea and had returned full of enthusiasm but without the boys.

That had been hard. She had pretended it was better that way, but she had felt she was making excuses for him. They had gone out with return tickets and should have come back to be hugged and instructed on every detail of life in the outback — she had read it up in the two weeks they had actually experienced it. And when he had grinned and said, "It's one way of getting you to fly the nest, Jude! I've said we'll go and see them in the autumn," she had managed a little smile and a nod. But somehow the safety net had suddenly revealed a small hole.

Jack was twelve years younger than Len. Their parents had died in a road accident when Jack was six and his brother was eighteen. Len had stepped into his father's shoes; he had already been well into the third year of his engineering apprenticeship. With the help of his mother's best friend he had provided everything Jack had needed, and had always recognized his young brother's talent and fostered it carefully.

And then, when Jack was thoroughly enjoying his own training in a local newspaper group, Len took over the job of servicing a group of private helicopters stabled at Filton Airfield. One of the helicopters belonged to William Whortley, the owner of a prestigious weekly newspaper. Len labelled him "old-school-tie" and found him easy-going and laid-back. One day, they shared sandwiches over the wonderfully intricate engine, which Len had winched on to the wide inspection bench. William Whortley seemed to understand Len's "guided tour". At the end of it he nodded.

"You know, Freeman, what really interests me is that this is one of the many places where art and science meet. It's the sheer precision, I think."

Len was doubtful. "Yes . . . I know what you mean. Anything that is out of place or alignment would spoil it as a work of art. But also — as an engine — it might still work. The only trouble is, if it packs up mid-flight you lose lives."

"And a wrong line in a painting would not lose lives? Ah. I wonder. No statistics for it, but I think it could happen. I've seen one wrong line wreck the painter who made it." He peered down into the neatly packed cogs and levers. "I still think this is a work of art. There's a sculptor I know of who works in small metal objects — intertwining angles all interdependent and evolving from a single cube." He looked up, smiling. "I reckon you're an artist! Can't remember the chap's name, but he could easily have made this!"

Len laughed. "You should see some of my brother's stuff — he's the artist."

The discussion went on amiably, and the next day Mr Whortley came again and brought with him the previous evening's *Bristol News.* "Is this your brother's work?" he asked immediately.

When Len nodded cautiously, ready to defend Jack's cartoon as a work of art, Mr Whortley said directly, "Would he consider coming to work for me?"

So, at the age of twenty-four, Jack had joined the staff of the *Magnet,* and Len, suddenly free, had gone to Australia and started a private rescue company with one helicopter and an emergency medical team. Twenty-three years later he had offered jobs to his two young nephews.

Jack had been over the moon. Judith had shown her surprise, and he had said straightly, "They don't know what they want to do — all these odd jobs in the city are not taking them anywhere. Len is offering something special here, Jude. The boys will see it as an adventure — they'll love it — well, they will soon tell us if they don't! And we can visit them." He took her hand. "Darling, do you realize I am almost fifty?" He enunciated disbelievingly, "Fifty years old, Jude!"

She remembered thinking that she would be forty soon. Forty years old. But what had that got to do with the boys being hijacked by Len?

They had gone to Australia together, and it had been wonderful. Two months later Eunice Denman had had her first stroke. It was Jack who had leaned over her in her hospital bed and whispered, "I can't cope with all the housework any more, Eunice. You'll have to come and live with us and take some of it off my hands." Judith had wept then, because it was the first time her mother had smiled since they had found her on the floor of her bathroom a month before. He had loved and helped to nurse Eunice over the next nine years; he had gone to Perth every year, and the boys had come home each year, too. Eunice could not be left, and Judith could not bear to send her to a nursing home, so Jack had looked after the "home front", as he called it, while she went to see the boys. She always thought they would come back home, but they loved it in Perth. So life gradually shook into a new pattern; the good days were when Eunice managed to come and sit with them in the conservatory and look at the garden. Jack had always worked from home with forays to London to discuss his work. They were a tight-knit trio. Stupidly, Judith thought it would never change.

For some reason, Jack worried about her and could only explain it by saying she had "nothing for herself". At his suggestion she took up her painting again and he refurbished one of the bedrooms, filled it with artists' materials — even an easel — and called it "Jude's stude".

And now . . . Now he had left her.

CHAPTER
TWO

There were six other people on the minibus: two married couples, a single man, and another single woman. The man was courtly; no other word would do. He was taller than Judith, but that was because she was so short. He was much shorter than the other woman. She was probably only just under six feet. She reminded Judith of Naomi. She followed Judith to the back of the coach and asked if she could sit with her. Judith smiled and nodded gratefully. It was immediately established that neither of them was the odd one out.

The man took the seat in front of them and watched while the couples chose where they were going to sit and struggled out of their topcoats. The weather called for topcoats; it might be September, but the seasonal mist that morning was damp and cold.

The man leaned over the back of the seat. "I expect we'll all be introduced in a moment, but may I say what a pleasure it would be if you two ladies would look on me as your escort during this holiday?" He smiled benevolently. Both women stared up at him. He said, "I am Nathaniel Jones, and Robert Hausmann was my neighbour in Cardiff when I was a boy. I've never kept in touch, but as my own work is to do with printing, I thought I would look him up." He paused, then widened the smile.

Judith glanced at her neighbour, and seeing a kind of numbness there, said quickly, "I'm Judith Freeman. I don't know anything about the artist, but he does landscapes and I used to . . . when I was a student . . . myself . . ."

Her voice petered out, and luckily the other woman carried on almost seamlessly. "I'm Sybil Jessup. I used to be a painter, too. I know Hausmann's work. That's all." She looked embarrassed. "I think, if you don't mind, I'd prefer to be on my own, but if the occasion arises . . ." She petered out, too.

Another man leaned out of his seat. "We're the Olsens. Margaret and Sven." He shook hands all round. "And these are our friends. We stay with them every year. Jennifer and Stanley Markham." All six of them smiled, nodded, murmured things. Judith felt grateful that Sybil had said nothing about her personal history; she had no wish to tell everyone she was waiting for her divorce papers to come through and this long weekend would help the time to pass. She turned and smiled at the Markhams.

The woman, Jennifer Markham, said, "Margaret and I are school friends, we go back nearly thirty years."

Margaret Olsen pushed up a sleeve and thrust her arm into the aisle. "That scar — you can only just see it now — is where we became blood sisters at the age of ten."

The driver loomed behind Nathaniel Jones.

"Doing my job for me? Excellent! Excellent! You all know that I am Martin Morris — also from Cardiff, Mr Jones. I, too, am acquainted with Robert Hausmann and have done this trip several times. I'm sure you will enjoy the exhibition as well as the glorious countryside around." He flapped open a folded sheet of paper. "You all have copies of the itinerary, so I need not go through it too thoroughly. Our first port of call will be Taunton — a convenience stop, but time enough for coffee if you wish. And then we wind through the villages of the Blackdown hills, taking in Dunster and its castle, Blue Anchor, Minehead and then up into the Quantocks and beautiful Exmoor to Castle Dove." He folded the paper, looked round with a beaming smile and rallied them all. "So here we go. Is everybody ready?"

Both couples responded enthusiastically. Nathaniel Jones lifted a newspaper on high and waved it like a flag. Judith and her apparently shy companion smiled slightly, though Judith was already wondering whether she had done the right thing in coming.

Martin Morris slid into the driving seat and switched on. They eased out of the park-and-ride and joined the traffic going to Weston-Super-Mare. Judith glanced sideways and saw with enormous relief that Sybil Jessup had her head back and her eyes closed. She did the same.

Castle Dove was situated on a headland between Porlock Weir and the sweep of sandy beaches which included Croyde and Woolacombe. At one point its grounds actually straddled the Somerset-Devon border.

It was Victorian Gothic, with turrets sprouting everywhere like giant pimples, and a conservatory almost overhanging the drop down to Dove Cove — where the River Dove emptied itself into the beginning of the Atlantic. Lundy Island was visible when the mist lifted, Martin Morris assured them. He pointed out a table with booklets about Lundy and its history and underwater gardens. The Lorna Doone trail map was of interest to the Olsens, they were walkers. Jennifer might go with them on their shorter hikes; Stanley would not. Nathaniel — "I really would prefer the full name, Nat sounds a bit trendy for me!" — was keen to meet Robert Hausmann. The housekeeper said he would be in the Long Gallery from midday, but he liked to go out looking for local colour most evenings.

Martin Morris guffawed. "You can find Robert Hausmann at the Dove Inn if you fancy a walk after dinner."

"Ideal. Would you ladies care to accompany me? A quiet stroll, perhaps a sherry or a soft drink?"

Sybil Jessup managed a smile. "I would like an early night."

Judith followed up quickly. "Me, too." She worked out as they were shown to their rooms that Sybil had said six words and she had said two. Brilliant. It was a shame their rooms were on different floors, they could learn from each other. In fact all seven of them were scattered about the castle, apparently at random. But there were phones of course, and a proper room service, and everything had that touch of old-fashioned luxury mentioned three times in the itinerary. Dinner

24

was good too: watercress soup and little roast potatoes with sea bass and kidney beans. She would have loved some of the towering trifle but knew it wouldn't be wise.

She spent ages having a shower and investigating her room. The mini fridge was full of delightful bottles, fruit juices and her favourite tomato juice. The carpet was thick, the tea-making facilities included hot chocolate and coffee, and there were two kinds of biscuits and a mini box of chocolates. She wafted around in her best nightdress with her summer dressing gown slung over her shoulders in case anyone called. Well, you never knew, Nathaniel might decide against the Dove Inn. She sat with a drink and watched the television, switched it off, got into bed and read her book for a while, then, switched off the light and was almost immediately asleep.

She woke very suddenly knowing she needed the bathroom, completely forgetting she was no longer at home. She stumbled to the door, turned left and opened the next door, pulled on a light and immediately realized she was not at home. It was a bathroom but not hers. Better than hers. She grinned at herself and hastily used the facilities. The toilet seat was warm; the hot tap in the basin produced hot water; the pristine hand towel was thick and gorgeous. She returned, still grinning, and only then realized that her door had closed and locked behind her. She couldn't get in; her dressing gown was at the bottom of her bed and the room key was on the dressing table.

She leaned her head on the door — her door — and closed her eyes and whispered several serious curses. Oaths. Good old-fashioned oaths to match the good old-fashioned castle. She lifted her wrist and looked at her watch. Three o'clock. Ack emma. Three ack bloody emma.

Of course she was going to laugh about this later; perhaps share it with Sybil or even Nathaniel. The thing was, what could she do now; at this moment? She had no idea where anyone else's rooms were, and they had been the only group at dinner. My God, it was like a murder novel. Someone had been murdered, and she was the only one wandering around outside her room. She forced a giggle at such absurdities. She must pass it on to Jack. He could do a comic strip and save her at the end — perhaps she could have neglected to flush the toilet? A perfect alibi?

If only Jack were here, he would go to such extremes, and they would laugh just like they used to. If only Naomi were here . . . they would sit on the top step of the beautiful curving staircase and Naomi would mock herself, going through the alternative choices they must make, "We are responsible for our actions, and therefore must be responsible for their solutions . . ." She had had a deep-throated laugh, and she would close her eyes and tilt her head up as if to let the laugh soar up to the ceiling like soap bubbles . . . And she was dead.

Judith took a very deep breath and noticed how it caught in her throat. She mustn't be found out here in tears; that wouldn't do at all. She began to move along

26

the landing, listening at each door, then tapping lightly, then hitting the door with the side of her clenched fist. There were four doors on the left of hers and another four on the right of the bathroom. All eight rooms were empty. So was hers. This was not funny any more.

She ignored the lift; if that got stuck she might lose what little self-control she had. She flicked every light switch she could find, and then started down the stairs. Dammit, she hadn't even stopped to put on her slippers; the polished wood was distinctly chilly under the soles of her bare feet. Opposite the landing an enormous curved stained-glass window that had seemed benign in the setting sun was now black and ominous. She was glad when the stairs turned and the view was of another landing. Nine bedrooms and a bathroom. All apparently empty; not even the gentlest snore. She gave up hitting the doors with her fist and went to the stairs again; the window went with her.

She ended up in the entrance hall; to her right was the dining room and the sitting room, to her left was the reception area and the lift. The lights she had switched on above revealed a telephone on the highly polished counter. She ran to it with a little cry of sheer relief.

It didn't click or tinkle as she lifted the receiver, and behind it was some sort of switchboard; it looked old-fashioned, each switch was numbered. She replaced the receiver and counted the rows: four. Twenty-four rooms and only eight of them occupied. She searched for another key to switch the whole thing on and could find nothing. She leaned on the counter, suddenly exhausted. This was not good. And she was cold. For goodness' sake, why was she here? She felt the ridiculous Gothic pile like a weight around her, cold and probably damp. She dropped her head on to her arms and let something wash through her, thinking it might be a philosophical moment during which she would come to terms with living on her own and perhaps decide to join the gardening club that winter. But it turned out to be a wave of misery, and she wept into the inside of her elbow and felt useless.

How long she was engulfed in self-pity she did not know; the sound of a key in the enormous oak door brought her quickly into the present. She glanced wildly around the big square hall, then up at the enormous stairwell lit by all the switches she had flicked on her way down, then at the nightie Jack had described as diaphanous but that was, in fact, just plain see-through.

The heavy oak door groaned a protest and gave way to the key, and she dropped like a stone behind the counter, eyes so wide they hurt, breath held in suffocatingly over-full lungs.

A draught blew across the floor and skittered behind the counter. A voice muttered resentfully, "Good God, all this talk of bloody economy and they've got every light in the place switched on!" Already Judith could smell whisky, and her heart sank further still. But at least it sounded as if the owner of the voice had a right to be here, whoever he was. She breathed shallow quick breaths while he struggled to close and lock the door.

Then she heard him start towards the lift, his tread uneven, grunting, but unmistakeably leaving.

She made up her mind quickly and stood up.

"Excuse me. Can you tell me whether there is a master key to the rooms?"

The man — a very dishevelled looking man — yelped and almost fell backwards. He grabbed the far edge of the counter and stared in disbelief.

She took another breath and went on, "I've locked myself out, you see. Went to the bathroom and the door closed behind me." He went on staring. "I really am a guest here. I've come to see the Hausmann retrospective."

He peered over the counter and she held her arms in front of her nightie.

He said, "I can see you are sleeping here . . . or should be. You're not Lorna Doone or similar . . . they often pop into my head. But you can't be real. You're like a forties pin-up. I've never painted you." He gestured a gigantic dismissal. "No . . . you're not real."

He turned to go, and she whipped round the counter and held on to him physically.

"Listen. Are you Robert Hausmann? All right, don't talk. I am Judith Freeman and I am real, and I need to get back into my room and make some coffee and get over this. Do you understand?"

He said, "Bowl. Shelf under counter. Get."

She released him and shot back, saw the bowl immediately and grabbed it. He took it from her, turned his back and was gushingly sick. There was a pile of clean tea towels next to where the bowl had been. She snatched two of them and exchanged them for the bowl.

He gasped, "Cloakroom. Be back. Shortly."

She watched him weave towards a door next to the sitting room. She was still holding the bowl. She put it back on the shelf with great care, then covered it with another of the tea towels.

He emerged. Stood still and looked at her with the same disbelief, then gestured with his arm.

"Sit down."

He swivelled on his left foot and went through into the sitting room. She heard the click of an electric fire. She frowned and nibbled her thumb. There seemed no alternatives, and any kind of heating was attractive. She tried to gather her nightie into thicker folds around her body, and went across to the sitting room.

He was standing with his back to the fire; it was a big one with imitation flames, but he was still blocking any heat that might be coming from it. At least he didn't smell. As she stood holding the back of a small sofa she saw that he too was frowning.

He said, "My God, you're still here. And I'm fairly sober now. You must be real. Why are you dressed like that?"

She began her explanation over again and he held up one hand. "I remember all that. What I mean is — the day of the gauzy nightie has gone. It's pyjamas now. And you need them for other reasons besides fashion. This place is always cold. Even in a heatwave. You look like one of Andy Warhol's paintings."

He moved suddenly and the heat from the fire leapt across to her. She closed her eyes blissfully and did not bother to reply to him; he was by no means sober.

The next thing she knew she was being wrapped up. She opened her eyes. He had whipped off one of the throws from an armchair and was, apparently, mummifying her. She freed her arms and took over. It was wonderful. He led her to the front of the sofa and lowered her into it. She sank into its depths. He sank into the opposite corner and watched her.

"Thank you so much, Mr Hausmann. I was becoming just slightly frantic."

"You hid it well. The first person, apart from myself, to position the bowl in time."

"This is a regular thing?"

"Pretty much. Where have you hidden it?"

"The bowl? Where I found it, under the counter."

"I'll see to it."

He stood up and she held out a restraining hand. "Could you also find some kind of master key so that I can go back to bed?"

"You asked me before. I'll look. Can't promise. They hide it, you know. Bart and Irena. I went into their room when I lost my key and they were rather annoyed."

"Oh dear."

"No need for sarcasm. He is my brother." He was in the doorway and he turned for his final excuse. "We were pretty close at one time. Then he got married. I don't think Irena likes me."

Judith twisted to look at him over the back of the sofa. He no longer resembled something the cat had brought in. His hair had dried and was a mass of grey curls, and his face fell in leathery folds like a schnauzer's. His eyes were buried deep and seemed to burn for a moment.

He appeared to be waiting for her to comment on his last remark. Brothers. She knew about brothers because of Toby and Matt. She had met Jack's brother, Len, on only a few occasions but had liked him instantly. She was thankful that he was nothing like Robert Hausmann.

She said starkly, "No."

He shrugged and disappeared towards the counter, and she put her feet up and lay on her side looking at the pretend flames and feeling warm at last. She heard him in the cloakroom; he used a lot of water. Then he came out and was at the counter again, so he had to be looking for that precious key. Then a door closed and there was total silence. She glanced at the clock on the mantelpiece. Four thirty. And it had been three o'clock when she had emerged from the bathroom.

She thought disgustedly that he wasn't coming back. She snuggled down and went to sleep.

When she woke it was fully light and the first thing she saw was a tray on the floor just beneath her. It contained a mug of brown liquid with skin on the top and an enormous roll, cheese protruding from it, a dab of some kind of pickle sitting on top. Lying between the mug and the cheese roll was a key.

32

Beyond the tray the fire still flickered, and looking around and into the foyer she could see the lights were still on. Worse, somewhere above her, the lift clicked into use.

She had not moved so quickly for a long time. The throw dropped off her as she leapt from the sofa. She picked it up and flung it over the armchair, snatched up the tray and ran across the foyer to put it beneath the counter — the bowl was there, pristine. She clutched the key, darted round to the stairs and began to take them, two, three at a time. Her legs might be short but they were strong, and she passed the lift at the first floor. The key slid into her lock without difficulty. She was inside, panting, her back to the door. She dived into bed, put the key under her pillow and closed her eyes.

Half an hour later, when her paper and tea arrived, she opened the door wearing her dressing gown and smiling.

"Good morning!" The woman lifted a tray off the top of the trolley. She was not the housekeeper from yesterday. "I'm Irena Mann and I welcome you to Castle Dove! I hope you have had a good night?"

"I've slept like a top!" Judith took the tray and put it on the bedside table, then held out her hand. "I understand you are Robert Hausmann's sister-in-law?"

The woman was taken aback. "I am, but we never mention it. In fact, I persuaded my husband to chop off the front of our name so that we could not be associated with him." She shook her head. "Sorry. It is one of those family things. We do our best — this exhibition, for instance." Her smile widened painfully. "We do hope you will enjoy it. And the beautiful countryside around. Breakfast will be a little late this morning as we were disturbed in the night. Eight thirty."

"That's absolutely fine." Judith had been moving towards her pillow and the precious master key, but stopped in her tracks. She had intended to tell the tale as humorously as possible and apologize profusely, but it was obvious that Robert Hausmann had said nothing about her. She swallowed her words, feeling bound to support him. She picked up the teapot. "This is real luxury. Thank you. I'll see you later, I hope."

Irena Mann's smile relaxed. She made her exit and Judith sipped her cup of tea and scrabbled the key into her handbag at the same time. She suddenly felt . . . different. She could not identify this feeling. But it was not an unhappy one. She was certain about that.

CHAPTER
THREE

The dining room commanded a spectacular view of the coastline. Sybil Jessup was already standing in the window embrasure and looked round as Judith entered.

"I had no idea we were cut off by the tide like this! It's simply amazing — come and see!"

It was the second long sentence she had said in Judith's presence, and with such enthusiasm, too. Judith joined her, giving up on counting the words, staring in disbelief as she watched the water surge right across the causeway they had taken yesterday afternoon.

"My God. Where's the minibus? Has it gone?"

Sybil actually laughed. "That was my first thought, too. The causeway is a sort of ramp — can you see? The castle end of it is quite clear of the water. I think the bus must be under cover somehow. And look . . . is that a cave? Wait till the wave recedes . . . yes, it is!" She sounded like a schoolgirl.

"Are we marooned?" Judith asked fearfully.

"Only until the tide drops, dear lady!" Nathaniel Jones came in from the foyer, grinning from ear to ear and obviously as excited as Sybil Jessup. "The itinerary says it lasts about half an hour; not even that when the tides aren't strong." He joined them at the window. "Something in our blood, don't you think? We love islands. Well . . . we're an island race, after all!" He guffawed then pointed out where their "coach" and the owners' cars were stabled. "Heard all about it last night — straight from the horse's mouth, as it were!" Another awful guffaw as he pulled out three chairs from the table closest to the window. "Sven and Margaret accompanied me to the Dove Inn, and Robert Hausmann was there! We had a proper reunion — his memory isn't as good as mine, too much drink I imagine, so I refreshed it thoroughly!" Judith took the proffered chair reluctantly and allowed herself to be bounced right into the table. Sybil remained stubbornly standing, watching the sea with evident fascination.

Nathaniel seated himself, shook out his starched napkin and spread it over his knees. "There was another Jewish family in our street. They had a daughter our age — plain little thing, she was. Esmée. Esmée Gould. Robert couldn't even remember her! We used to play together when we were kids. Street games, you know. Hoops and whips and tops and marbles in the gutter. That sort of play was on the way out then, but Esmée's dad was our local postie — 'Gould the Post' we called him — some called him 'Goalposts' — how we laughed! He was around after school and he taught us all these games, and we loved 'em!"

Sybil joined them. Nathaniel shook his head. "Robert couldn't remember any of it. And we are our memories, aren't we?"

Sybil looked at him for a moment, surprised out of her excitement with the sea, then her eyes went past him to the doorway where the other four were entering and exclaiming at the view. Judith had a feeling she did not see them. But she was seeing something, somebody. Her eyes were big and grey and profoundly sad, like a widow's.

Jennifer Markham broke through Sven Olsen's exclamations.

"D'you see the broken bit of cliff, Margaret? That's a cave. When Stan and I came to look at the castle last month the tide was low and we could walk right in — Irena told us that smugglers used to keep stuff there! It reminds me of that cave in Cornwall —"

"I was just going to say that!" Margaret went with her to the window and they stood there reminiscing, almost oblivious of husbands and the other three guests. Judith felt sorry for Sven, who tried manfully to engage Stanley Markham in some conversation. She wondered how on earth this trans-North-Sea relationship had survived for so long when one of the foursome was so obviously unresponsive. Stanley stood there holding a newspaper to his chest until Sven gave up and joined his wife.

Judith leaned back as Irena arrived with milk for the cereal and everyone at their table ordered a Continental breakfast. Nathaniel tried to tell Stanley Markham what a good evening he had missed last night at the Dove

Inn. Stanley gave the tiniest of smiles. Irena told him that he would have an opportunity to meet Robert Hausmann in the Long Gallery, but not until after lunch. Nathaniel guffawed.

"Sleeping it off?"

"I wouldn't be surprised," Irena said with a frosty smile.

Judith poured milk over one of the cereal bars and tried not to look complicit as Stanley moved to another table and sat down. Stolid Stanley, she thought, watching him open his newspaper and turn to the sports section. Fleetingly she remembered doing the same last Sunday . . . had he and Jennifer got sons who would be interested in football results? She felt a physical pang of longing for Matt and Toby.

"Penny for them, Judith!"

It was Nathaniel, of course, full of bonhomie which, suddenly, she could not resist.

"As a matter of fact, I was thinking of the football results!" She laughed. "Both my sons used to play — just locally, you know — so I always let them know how their teams are doing."

He said, "They live away?"

She made a face. "Australia. For the last nine years — nearly ten. I think they will stay there — they've been back several times but they have never wanted to stay. They're with family out there. My brother-in-law."

Len had never married. Jack had hinted at an unhappy romance as the reason for Len's emigration, but there had never been any details. "He's a close one, is our Len," he had said.

Nathaniel said, "There's a country I'd like to see. Do you get out there often?"

"Not often, no." She dabbed her mouth with a corner of the napkin and poured more tea. "They come over twice a year."

She had started well, going out once a year, gritting her teeth for the first two hours of the flight. Then she had stopped going altogether. She could have done it; other mothers with children abroad did it often. But it was such a long flight and she felt physically ill for days afterwards. Jack had suggested finding a professional nurse to live in and look after Eunice so that they could go together, but he'd understood why she wouldn't do that. After all, his parents had died when he was six years old and, only half-jokingly, he had asked Eunice if she would adopt him. They had been close, too. So Jack stopped inviting Judith to come with him and he took reels of film, kept a diary, did lightning sketches for her. She kept one of them on the fridge door; it was of the boys peering into the engine of one of Len's helicopters, both scratching their heads à la Laurel and Hardy.

But after Eunice had died, Jack had not suggested that a holiday would do Judith good. He had cancelled his own visit. He had stopped talking about the boys. Or anything much. She frowned, coming upon the realization unexpectedly.

Nathaniel was chuntering on about opportunities being missed. Sven was shepherding "the girls", as he called them, into their seats as Irena arrived with a trolley holding four full English breakfasts, two racks of toast, a dish of butter curls and marmalade. Judith felt her mouth water. Irena was followed by a man, presumably her husband, bearing coffee and teapots. What had Hausmann called him? Bart. Bart Mann. Sounded strange. Perhaps he was Bartholomew. Or just Mister. Mr Mann. She caught Sybil's eye and saw amusement there, too, then realized with a shock that Nathaniel was proposing himself as a "fellow voyager". What on earth did he mean?

"Look on me as a courier, if you like," he said portentously, spreading a great deal of butter on a slice of toast. "I know the ropes — we could stay over in Singapore if you find the journey too much. It would save travelling alone, after all."

Judith summoned a smile. "The trouble with being short and fair is that everyone thinks I need to be looked after. Actually, I am surprisingly capable."

Naomi had told her that; it was after Judith had cleaned the filter in Naomi's washing machine. Naomi had concertinaed her long legs and body to peer behind the machine, where Judith wanted to show her how to replace the filter. It was obviously a painful manoeuvre, and she had hit her head as she twisted it around the machine. She had given a loud, "Ouch!" then gasped, "Jack thanked me the other day for helping you, and I told him that the shoe was on the other foot!"

Before Nathaniel could decide how to react to her rather assertive remark, Sybil actually laughed.

40

"It's a case of having to when you live alone, Mr Jones." She picked up her cup and held it in both hands, elbows on the table, creating a private intimacy separate from the couples at the next table. "Man, woman, tall, short, once they find themselves on their own, they need a certain self-sufficiency. I am still finding it — Judith obviously has it. You have found it — probably it is more difficult for a man in many ways."

She sipped, giving him a chance to tell them just how difficult it was to reassure a great many female neighbours that he could in fact bake his own cakes and polish furniture. That left Judith remembering last night, and how absolutely hopeless she had been. And then to marvel at Sybil Jessup, who should be a diplomat in the Foreign Office.

The driver of the minibus arrived and was offering a tour of the moor, or in fact anywhere they fancied. "I am at your service, ladies and gents! The tide has dropped and we have twelve hours before it returns — let's make the most of it!" He had a way of making his words sound like a rallying call.

Sven looked at Margaret and held up his hands. "It is just as at home: our lives ruled by the turn of the tides!" He declaimed the words dramatically, so that they were bound to laugh. They laughed.

Martin Morris — Judith remembered the bus driver's name with relief — forced a grin. "Not really. The tide covers the causeway for such a short time. But I am guessing that most of you would like to meet our resident artist this afternoon so that a short drive would suit you best."

Judith said nothing. She had no wish to attend the "opening" and meet Robert Hausmann again. The master key was in her handbag, so some contact had to be made, but the shorter and less public it could be, the better. She could imagine already how the others would react if they got wind of last night's misadventure. Sven Olsen would make it sound like a jolly escapade; Nathaniel Jones would just about manage to hide his disapproval. And she did not want Sybil to relegate her to the rank of dumb blonde. She had a feeling that Sybil could well be a potential friend. Besides which, she needed to catch up on her sleep.

In the end just three of them went off with Martin Morris. Nathaniel was keen to see Tarr Steps, and Sven had probably had enough of Stanley. Margaret tried to persuade Jennifer to come with them, but Jennifer made a little moue at her and took her husband's arm. "We want to explore the castle," she said for him. "Stan is so romantic, when we came to look it over he promised me an experience I would never forget!"

Surprisingly, Margaret laughed. "Oh, you two — you — you're — incorrigible!"

Even more surprisingly, Stanley smiled and nodded. Judith glanced at Sybil, but she was explaining to Martin Morris that she wanted to do some sketching while the weather was so good. That idea was attractive; Judith remembered packing her sketchbook and some of the HBs she liked. But not before she had caught up on her sleep.

She sidled past the others and took to the stairs. Robert Hausmann was waiting for her on the second landing.

"You took your time! Full English, I suppose? You should avoid those sorts of foods — you could balloon right out!"

She was outraged. "I had Continental, thank you very much! I was going to thank you for leaving me this . . ." She was already fumbling in her bag for the key, ". . . also for not mentioning it to the others. But after that remark —"

"Did it sound rude? I meant it to be — well — concerned." He took the key and kissed it. "They almost caught me pinching it from Bart's trouser pocket last night!" He grinned at her, sharing the joke. "I gather they lost quite a bit of sleep trying to investigate what the noise was."

"Might it have been better to rouse him gently and ask if you could borrow the key?"

"No. Definitely not. And I don't want them to see me replace it, either."

She couldn't help joining in with the joke. "You're going to have difficulty there, as he is actually wearing the trousers."

"I'm all right until after breakfast. Didn't you notice he was wearing his blue-check cotton kitchen trousers? She's very fussy about that. Poor old Bart has to change roles half a dozen times a day: different role, different costume." He shrugged. "He always wanted to be an actor." He wasn't smiling any more.

She turned her mouth down. "You'd better hurry. Everyone's leaving the dining room."

He nodded and was gone. The lift doors sighed as they closed on him. She wondered what he would do if the others were waiting for the lift when the doors opened on the ground floor. Then she shook her head; there was a lot going on there. She might find it interesting and quite funny, but she definitely did not want to get involved.

She slept for an hour and woke luxuriously, lying there, stretching, letting her thoughts stay within the walls of this peculiar building, thinking of the tide washing it every twelve hours. She lifted a languid wrist and looked at her watch. Ten thirty. On the unit at the bottom of the bed, the kettle and its surrounding bowls of sugar, longlife milk, tea and coffee bags awaited. She would drink a cup of coffee, and then perhaps look out her sketch pad and sit at the base of the walls and sketch the coastline with the cave in the foreground and maybe a smudge on the horizon that could be Lundy Island. She'd have to find a cushion or something because it would be muddy. What about if she whipped through the Long Gallery before Hausmann appeared? That way, she could look at his paintings properly, without any other comments impinging on her thoughts. Besides which, if she viewed with the others it might be difficult to keep up a pretence that this was her first meeting with Hausmann. He'd be sure to let something out of the bag. He was such a . . . maverick . . . a loose cannon.

She got out of bed and made coffee. That was what she would do. She hated viewing work with other people around anyway, it ruined her concentration.

Downstairs, the lobby was empty and she had no idea where the Long Gallery was. She felt a moment of frustration; what a way to run a hotel! Obviously ridiculously under-staffed. Then reason prevailed; it was ten forty-five and as far as Irena knew nearly all the guests were fully occupied. As for last night, Judith conceded with a slight smile that she could not expect all posts to be manned at 3a.m. Besides which, she rather liked the idea of exploring on her own.

There were three doors on the other side of the lift. She pushed gently on the first and discovered the kitchen; trolleys were lined up, several of them already laid for a meal, probably lunch. Beyond, the kitchen was empty and pristine, with saucepans hanging from hooks on a sort of railway, and plates in wooden racks above steel worktops. Judith let the door swing shut; it gave a sigh. She opened the next door and discovered a big boot cupboard. And the final one gave on to a wide corridor obviously running beneath the two landings above. She shouldered her bag and walked its length; eight doors. She tried two of them and discovered bedrooms either hung with dust sheets or empty. Opposite them, on the wall that also held the enormous stained-glass window which lit the staircase, were diamond-paned windows looking crookedly towards the coast road which had brought them here just yesterday. She found a tissue and cleaned one of the diamonds and peered through. The sea had receded and beneath were the enormous rocks on which Castle Dove was built, spilling on to a shingle beach. Tramping the beach was Sybil Jessup. Judith watched as she set up a stool, sat down and took a sketchbook from her bag. Then she leaned back against one of the rock outcrops and tilted her head back. Judith straightened quickly. Sybil could not possibly see her, of course, but she was under the impression she was alone. And, Judith was almost certain, she was weeping.

It sobered her. She saw now why the disembodied voice on the divorce helpline had told her that anger was a good reaction. In small doses. That was what the voice had said. In small doses. But it had also said that grief was good too, and also in small doses. Judith pushed at another door and discovered an ancient bathroom. The voice had said nothing about despair.

She hurried on around a corner and through another door. The corridor now looked out on to the west side; she scrubbed at another of the diamond panes and looked down the coastline to where the Devon hills dipped and reared. Ilfracombe, Woolacombe, Croyde were all along this north coast. Probably Martin Morris would drive them that way either tomorrow or Sunday. She had brought her swimsuit, but the sea looked unwelcoming.

She opened a door in the panelling and was amazed. The long room stretched before her, slightly curved, no more bedrooms, the enormous space lined with bookcases full of books. There were two library ladders. She pushed them experimentally; they both worked. One was holding a hammer on one tread, a

46

box of rawplugs on another. In the middle of the library was a spiral staircase. She smiled; she had got the hang of the place now and was almost certain that the staircase was a private entry to the Long Gallery and once there she could access her own corridor and bedroom.

So it proved. She caught a glimpse of an orangery from a window above the bookshelves, then the spiral staircase went through a storage space bare and dusty, and emerged into an enormous area that, in spite of being gloomily shuttered against last night's sunset, was obviously the gallery. She could see clearly that the doors at one end must be on the same level as her room. She grinned, running her hand up the spiral rails that encircled the stairs and then leaning against them to look around her.

Even in the half-light she could see that the exhibition had been mounted expertly. Display stands were grouped so that four or five paintings could be viewed in groups, and the alcoves offered a certain privacy for doing that. Running the length of the gallery were the same squashy sofas which were in the sitting room, inviting people to sit and look to their heart's content and in wonderful comfort.

Judith opened several shutters, looking over her shoulder now and then, sometimes closing one and opening another. When she had the light to her complete satisfaction, she began to move from one alcove to the next.

They were all 'scapes: land, sea and sky. Her sort of painting. She began to feel a sense of coming home; it was not a home she recognized, but she knew that's what it was. There were no dissatisfactions, and no lack of confidence, no fears. It was not a physical, nor a spiritual home. It was light and colour fastened to the earth by some magical force called gravity.

  She moved very slowly, incredulous that the man who had vomited before her last night had actually seen these things, let them creep under his skin and become part of him, then painted them and given them back again to whoever needed them. There were traditional English scenes: urban landscapes, a furrowed field, a hill dominated by an electricity pylon. She recognized Selworthy, the Tyne Bridge, the Angel of the North, the hill ranges under dark skies and then sunshine. Boats in a harbour, crates of fish . . . and other settings she was not familiar with. She needed a catalogue . . . not that a catalogue would explain this sense of belonging . . . grounded and centred on this planet. But it might help her with the enormous well of tears starting in her chest . . . the mysticism would be explained away: "Number thirty-five, Guardian of Northumbria"; "Number six, The Pier at Sunset". She would have to come this afternoon when they were being handed out. She got to the end and turned to move slowly down the other side. He was there. In the middle of the space, he was holding a pile of papers — must be catalogues. She stood motionless. He was still a shambles of a man.

  He said, "Oh, Christ. Why are you crying? If you tell me I'm a modern-day Constable, I'll have to kill you."

  She gasped, "It's so beautiful. Thank you."

48

She dashed past him and through the big double doors at the end, now open. She turned the corner on to her own landing and was deeply thankful she had not locked her door. She lay face down on the bed and wept.

CHAPTER
FOUR

Judith lunched on biscuits and cups of tea, drying her eyes in between each mouthful and then taking a gigantic bite of a Rich Tea biscuit and spluttering crumbs everywhere as a racking sob came from somewhere in her chest and exploded in her throat and nose. Stubbornly she kept going until the biscuit supply ran out, then she pocketed her key and went to the bathroom and showered and washed her hair. When she emerged she crept around the corner of the corridor and listened at the big double doors of the Long Gallery. The noise of chatter was unmistakeable. She identified everyone except Stanley and Sybil, but he would doubtless be there even if he hated every minute of it, and Sybil would be totally absorbed. As she herself had been.

Tears threatened again, and she bustled back to her room and pulled on jeans and a sweatshirt, thrust her sketchbook and pencils into a canvas shoulder bag, and locked her door before she left.

Irena was actually at the desk in the lobby and looked up.

"Mrs Freeman! I knocked on your door just now. Are you all right? I can make you a sandwich or there are sausage rolls. Mrs Jessup and Mr Jones were worried about you."

Judith smiled reassuringly. "I fell asleep, I'm afraid. I'm going to get some fresh air before joining the others."

Irena smiled back. "It's wonderful that you feel so relaxed here — just what Bart and I had in mind. Do your own thing — that's how Bart puts it! Anyway, to be honest, once you've seen one Hausmann landscape you've seen them all, haven't you?" She came from behind the counter and walked over to open the door for Judith. "Take your time. That's what it's all about. I'm making tea and taking it upstairs in about an hour. Then I'm having an hour off myself — join me in the kitchen if you miss the upstairs show." Irena rolled her eyes on the last two words and Judith could have hit her. She went through the door and started on the enormous flight of steps which led down to the shingle beach, muttering under her breath. She was at one with the battered Hausmann: his sister-in-law was — as Jack had said once — "Straight from Crufts, a prize bitch."

By the time Judith had found a spot in the sun and out of the breeze coming off the sea it was past three o'clock. She wedged herself between two rocks and fixed her eyes on the cliffs while she fumbled her sketchbook and a pencil on to her knees. Still staring at that rank of small headlands thrusting towards the incoming tide, she made lines on the square of paper she could feel beneath her hand; perpendicular lines falling from the top of the page to the bottom; sky to sea, a small army defending a land. She paused and squinted as the sun silhouetted them blackly. They were not straight, they were concave. The grassy tops were thrust out aggressively, the base stood firm. The cliffs were rampant, just as on an heraldic device; they curved towards the enemy, snarling defiance. The pencil moved swiftly . . . one line better than two . . . look again and again. Rocks like fallen soldiers at the base of the curves, seaweed dripping from scars beneath the maw of the clifftop, bleeding from a long-ago battle.

Time passed. She noticed that the light was changing and the sun disintegrating into exquisitely careless streaks. She made horizontal lines and told herself she must remember they offered some kind of reassurance for the aggression of those clifftops. But the cliffs themselves became tired as the sun left them; how much longer could the battle go on? She drew a deep breath. That was all out of her hands, and all she could do was to record what she saw.

When she thought she had enough to work with, she looked at her watch. It was just before six o'clock. She must go and change for dinner. The tide was already at the base of the castle's rock. She pushed herself out of her friendly cleft, stiff now, put her sketchbook and pencil into the canvas bag, and trudged around to the steps. She was tired and the steps were endless and uneven. She wrestled with the big door just as Hausmann had done last night, and staggered in as he had, too. Irena was still at the counter, though common sense told Judith she must have moved from there at some point.

"My dear! You have been working — we were getting a bit anxious, and then Mrs Jessup spotted you from the Long Gallery and told us you were all right, and poor Mr Jones thankfully stopped demanding that we should phone the coastguards . . ." So Sybil had seen her, just as she had seen Sybil. There was a link somewhere, she was sure of it. Neither of them liked to be the centre of attention. Judith smiled wryly; Sybil was so much better than she had been at keeping out of the limelight.

But Irena was talking about the dinner menu now. There were copies of it in the lounge. Why didn't Mrs Freeman sit by the fire for half an hour, and Bart would bring her a tray of tea? Dinner would be at seven thirty. A little late, because they had all lingered in the Long Gallery far too long.

Judith discovered she could not face her bedroom just yet. She smiled and moved into the sitting room. Her sofa from last night was pulled close to the electric flames, and she sank into it gratefully, easing off her trainers and keeping a protective hand on the canvas of her bag. She thought of the sketchbook inside and the half-a-dozen pages of lines and squiggles she had made, and wondered whether the feeling of satisfaction would last until she could find an art shop and buy some basic watercolours. Or acrylics? She had worked once or twice with acrylics, and Jack had much preferred them. But Jack always went for the unconventional. And there was a subtlety to mixing watercolours that was missing with other media. Unless it was egg tempura. She liked the idea of that.

She held a menu in her hand but barely saw it. She was considering colours now: the soft orange of the September sun as it touched the mottled surface of the invading water and became another colour completely. The plain fact was that water held no colour that man could identify, and yet changed and amplified everything that shone through and into it. It was a mixture of two gases, yet was full of its own enormous and terrifying properties. Its weight as it had surged around the castle that morning — how on earth did anyone paint water's weight?

She grinned slightly and glanced at her watch; time, which had dragged unbearably since Jack's . . . departure — she could not continue to call it desertion — was now completely out of hand. It was seven o'clock. An hour since she had sat in this chair and picked up the menu. And anyway, someone was coming in behind her and coughing politely. Probably Nathaniel Jones. Or Bart Mann with her tea.

She half-turned. It was Hausmann.

He coughed again. "Look. Tell me to sod off if you like. It's just — are you all right? I thought I'd better not chase after you. You sort of exploded. I didn't know what to do. Especially when you didn't turn up with the others this afternoon."

She stared at him. "Are you fishing for compliments or something?"

"Don't be stupid. I realize that the artwork triggered a memory that was unbearable —"

54

"Not at all. If a work of art symbolizes a work of God, then it is probably God who has to take responsibility for my . . . my explosion, as you put it!"

He held on to the back of the sofa as if she had slapped him.

"I don't believe in God."

"You probably do. Otherwise you would have said that you did not believe in his existence. You mean your faith has taken a knock." She half-turned away, not wanting to hear about his background or enter into a discussion, then turned back suddenly.

"Tell me, why have you used oil for some of your stuff, watercolour for others? And what do you think about acrylic? Have you ever used egg tempura?"

He still hung on to the back of the sofa. His heavily lidded eyes opened wider and then narrowed again, concentrating.

"A hammer. You are like a hammer with your assumptions about my faith. And now you hammer questions at me." He walked around the sofa and sat down. "Yes, I have used egg whites and acrylics. And I have made colours from the earth. Tempura clings, but is as delicate as watercolours. More easily controlled. Acrylic is not so subtle, but on occasion there is nothing like it. Bold. It can make statements. Some of my earth pigments are good, some not so good. Does that help?"

"You are saying everyone has differing opinions?"

"Am I?" He opened his eyes, bewildered. "Yes. Perhaps. It is what I say to my students all the time. But

55

you are not a student. And you are not young. Why haven't you tried this stuff for yourself?"

She was taken aback. "I don't know. I suppose . . . there were higher priorities. The boys. My mother. I've sketched at times. But I've never taken it further."

"Yes. Nat was telling me about your sons in Australia. I have to warn you he is very keen to accompany you there."

"Nat? Oh yes. Mr Jones. I had forgotten you were neighbours long ago."

His heavy eyelids drooped gloomily. "The past is always with us."

She smiled. "Surely that is why you paint your wonderful memories? So that after humankind has destroyed the world as we know it, your paintings will emerge from a lead-lined chamber and tell them what it was like." In spite of her ironic tone, she felt her eyes filling again, and blurted quickly, "What a beautiful place it was."

He waited, and she mumbled "Sorry," and fished for a tissue.

He said, "Not many people see my stuff like that. Thank you."

"That's all right. And I will experiment with tempura. I'd better go and swill my hands . . . change into a skirt, perhaps . . ."

"I have to tell you something —"

"Not now."

"Come to the Dove tonight with Nat —"

"I don't think so. The tide is all wrong."

"Oh bugger, so it is."

She was at the door to the lobby. She looked back, suddenly grinning.

"We're all prisoners, Hausmann!"

He looked up. She thought afterwards that she had never seen such raw terror in a man's face before. She ran for the lift.

When Judith came down again she realized they were all in the dining room, the conversation led by Sven Olsen but including Nathaniel, who was expounding on the "accessibility" of "Bob's stuff".

"A kid of seven could appreciate most of those landscapes. They have a feeling of Constable, every detail there, historical, factual . . ."

She veered sideways so that she could look into the sitting room and see how Hausmann was taking this opinion. He was not there. Bart was picking up a tea tray. He looked at her and made a face.

"This was for you. I take it he drove you away."

She shook her head. "Not at all. He answered a lot of questions. I'm glad he had the tea and cakes." She tried not to look defiant. "I like him."

Bart looked genuinely surprised. "Do you? That's good. His manner — he can often seem offensive." He bent to pick up a saucer from the floor; it had been used as an ashtray. He put it on the tray. "We are brothers, you know."

"Yes. He did mention it. You must be proud. His work is very special."

Bart nodded. "Robert went back. To Germany. To see the camps. He tried to paint what he had seen, but because he knew ... our great-uncle survived and spoke of it to him ... it wasn't what he saw, but what he knew ... can you understand?"

She nodded; the tears were waiting just behind her eyes again.

"He paints everything in this country. As if he is trying to block out the rest of the world."

She nodded again, then squeezed her eyes tightly shut and opened them wide.

"I am glad that *you* understand," she said.

"There seems to be nothing anyone can do. We hoped — Irena and I — that he would take an interest in this place. Help us to get it together. But ... well, he dashed off tonight — wanted to beat the tide to the causeway. It means he won't be back till midnight." He shrugged.

Judith went on into the dining room and was confronted by a barrage of questions all about her painting.

"We did not know that we had another painter in our midst!" Sven beamed at her.

Nathaniel actually came forward, took her arm and led her to the table by the window where Sybil sat, smiling sympathetically. She said to Sven, "Actually, Judith did mention it when we were first introduced." She widened her smile as she turned to Judith. "Did you enjoy it?"

"I think so." Judith settled herself. The questions from the other table had already died. "I think it was your example that gave me the idea. Actually I haven't done anything for years and years." She thought of the

58

spare bedroom that Jack had insisted on calling "Jude's stude" and added, "Not really."

"My example?"

"I saw you down there. When I was exploring the castle this morning. I suppose that was what got me going." Judith remembered the agonizing poignancy of the Hausmann exhibition, the desperation to do something herself. A kind of therapy?

Sybil gave a rueful smile. "When I saw the exhibition this afternoon, I realized how absolutely pitiful my work is." The trolley was approaching, and Nathaniel, who had been talking to Sven, came back to their table. Sybil finished hurriedly, "I think I'll stick to greetings cards. Makes me a living."

Judith opened her eyes, surprised. Years ago Jack had asked her whether she intended to paint postcards. It had been a valid option in the commercial art world and he had done it himself on occasion. She wondered whether Sybil knew Jack. She shrank back as Irena offered her soup. She had almost imagined herself a respectable widow like Sybil. She had seen similarities that had somehow comforted her.

Irena said, "Did you enjoy your afternoon?"

There it was; not quite respect, but a darned sight better than the scorn Irena reserved for her brother-in-law. If she knew that Judith was not a widow . . .

"I did. Thank you."

Nathaniel tasted his soup cautiously, then smiled. "I did not think I would like fish soup. Never had it before." He savoured another spoonful. "I slightly preferred the watercress last night, but this is delicious in quite a different way." Both his companions murmured agreement. He turned to Judith. "So my old neighbour inspired you to try your hand at a seascape?"

Judith smiled widely. "I suppose he did."

She would have chuckled if she had not been enjoying the soup so much. It really was that simple, after all. One of her mother's favourite adages had been "Never stew in your own juice", closely followed by, "Keep those fingers busy, Jude!" And she had been right, of course. Everything seemed to have stopped dead after that morning when Jack had told her he was leaving. For two long months her fingers had so often been idle, and she had stewed her own juice into a bitter brew. And now, this afternoon, she had tried her hand at a seascape. Her smile widened.

And then Sybil pushed her soup away and said quietly, "But Robert is painting for the end of the world. Surely that is what his work is about?"

Judith stopped smiling. This woman had seen exactly what she had seen. The agonizing poignancy of Hausmann's work. Nothing was simple after all. She kept silent, head down, intent on her soup. Nathaniel laughed.

From the other table, Margaret Olsen called across, "We're trying to agree on an outing tomorrow. Sven wants to stride across the moor — the sort of thing we do back home in Sweden. Jennifer and I want to go to Exeter and see the shops. Stanley — of course — will do what Jennifer does!" She gave him an unbearably arch smile.

Nathaniel said, "I don't mind. I have friends in Exeter. But I would like to see the moor. The weather forecast was good."

Judith did not look up. She would drop out of any of the arrangements and go back to the Long Gallery. Unexpectedly Sybil spoke up.

"I would like to be dropped at Lynton, whichever route you choose. I want to go down to Lynmouth on the rack railway and walk up the combe." She paused. "I am hoping Judith will come with me. The views are breathtaking."

Judith lifted her head, almost shocked. This bond with Sybil Jessup took a leap. She spoke without thinking, "Yes. I would like that." She held her breath. Now Nathaniel would offer his escort service and the whole thing would be ruined.

But he didn't, and Sven asked him to give the deciding vote, and after a lot of laughter from the two women, he opted for a trip to the city. Jennifer kissed Stanley lightly. "There will be time to see the old orangery before we leave," she promised. Margaret caught Judith's uncomprehending gaze and rolled her eyes.

After dinner they broke up quickly. Stanley and Jennifer disappeared, and Sven roped in Nathaniel and Martin Morris to make a foursome for bridge. Sybil asked whether they would mind if she watched the ten o'clock news later on, and Nathaniel plumped up the sofa cushions and moved a coffee table within reach. Judith would have liked to have gone to her room and looked at the sketches she had made, in case there was something she could work on back home; already she was doubting the value of those three hours she had spent trying to absorb the ancient coastline and those pathetically defensive cliff-heads.

Sybil said, "Come and sit. Let the afternoon drain away a little. Don't feel you have to do the Lynmouth trip with me, but I really do recommend it. I was hoping to take my sketchbook and get down a few impressions."

Judith hovered in the lobby. Irena was coming and going and might want to talk if she went towards the stairs. She smiled at Sybil. "I doubt whether I can stay awake for the news, but it would be good to . . . be with people for a while."

Irena brought in coffee and a baize-topped card table. Martin Morris, who obviously knew the room's layout well, opened a drawer in an ornate chiffonier and produced playing cards. The four of them settled themselves around the table. Bart came in with two boxes of dark chocolate peppermints; he went to the chiffonier and brought a large album to the sofa.

"We found it here. Pictures of Castle Dove when it was built. It's not that old, actually — there's a steam-driven crane on one of the pages." He smiled and left them to it.

Judith ran her hand through her short hair and grinned. "I haven't had any chocolate since last Christmas! And I shouldn't now — but — shall we?"

Sybil said, "Why not?" She opened the box and took out two of the small envelopes. "I find one is hopeless.

It has to be closely followed by another one in order to be savoured — even tasted!"

"Ye-e-es." Judith removed three envelopes. "You are right, of course. The second one is to be tasted. A third one, however, is necessary for the savouring."

They smiled at each other; Judith felt herself melting with the chocolate. The calves of both legs were aching from those fifty-five stone steps, her head still throbbed from the total concentration of the afternoon. She said through her second chocolate, "I'm obviously out of condition — feel a wreck."

Sybil said, "You don't look it. Your hair just . . . sort of . . . goes. Is it naturally curly?"

"Yes." She was surprised again; she had not expected salon talk from Sybil Jessup. "And you're right, it does just go. I've had it styled so that it sweeps around my head, but within an hour of leaving the hairdresser, it's back like this again. They can straighten hair now, I might try that."

"Please don't!" Sybil looked almost stricken. "You'll regret it. You'll end up with a blonde ponytail."

"I would do what you have done and pile it up with a comb — it looks distinguished."

"It falls about. It's a bloody nuisance. Don't even consider it."

They smiled, each taking another chocolate. Sybil said, "Why is it that women always talk about hair?"

"You started it." Judith pushed the box away. "Were you testing the water?"

"Not really. I thought we should talk about ordinary things, and I couldn't think of anything else!" Sybil fastened the lid of the box and put it on the table, then picked up her coffee. "Apparently my reaction to Robert's work this afternoon was the same as yours this morning. Luckily I was lurking in one of the alcoves, and Nathaniel was trying to tell Jennifer that Robert's work has been likened to Constable's . . . I apologized to him later and he told me that you had been similarly . . ." She smiled ruefully, ". . . afflicted."

"Oh dear."

"Don't apologize. The more of us who can see what he is really doing, the more he will be appreciated. He is seen as a nostalgic artist. Yet he is painting contemporary 'scapes."

"You have followed his career?"

"Always."

There was a silence, during which Sybil ate another two mints and Judith wondered why Jack had never spoken of Hausmann's work. And then continued to wonder why Jack had never gone further with his own work. And whether he had been an artist or a cartoonist or a political commentator or a newspaper journalist . . . she felt her head thump again and closed her eyes. She was nearly fifty. Was this the menopause? Never mind that, where was Jack?

Sybil's voice was very quiet; Judith opened her eyes in an effort to listen.

"Moss promised that when he was well again we would look him up. Go to galleries. Make enquiries. Start a Hausmann revival!" She smiled. "Moss was a publicist, he could have done it. But then . . . he died."

She looked at Judith's face. "Moss Jessup was my husband. Have you heard of him?"

Judith swallowed. "Yes."

Jack had lampooned Moss Jessup so many times: the square, jowled face had been easy to draw, and the eyebrows had been all that was necessary to identify the man.

Sybil gave an inverted grin. "I miss him," she said.

Judith swallowed again and her head thumped a warning.

"Yes."

"I wondered whether I could do anything for Hausmann. But . . . he is his own worst enemy. The gallery owners I have contacted . . . they say he is too difficult."

"He can be difficult. Yes."

Sven's laugh filled a sudden gap. It seemed he and his partner had won. It was nearly ten; they moved armchairs around the television. Judith got up and made her excuses. She did not want to listen to the news; since Jack had left she had barely watched the television. Naomi would have said she was deliberately burying herself in grief; it was one of the reasons Judith had been glad of the anger that had swept over her occasionally when she had labelled Jack's disappearance as desertion. It was different now. She climbed the stairs slowly, thankful that no one was manning the desk in the lobby. She had literally moved away from the grief and the anger; put herself into this strange Gothic place and rediscovered . . . what? Exactly what had she rediscovered in the thirty-six hours since leaving home? She fitted her precious key into the lock and went into her room, flicking on lights, moving to the window, where, below, the dark sea had surrounded the castle and was massaging its walls insidiously. She watched the water for a while, wondering how long it would take to fall away from the causeway and let Hausmann back in. Whatever her rediscovery was, Hausmann was part of it. Perhaps Sybil was, too.

Somehow she managed to undress and slide into her ridiculous nightie. She was wonderfully tired and the bed was wonderfully comfortable.

She woke at two o'clock. Ack emma again. The clock was highlighted by the table lamp next to the kettle; she had forgotten to switch it off.

She would have to go to the bathroom. She put on her dressing gown this time, and pocketed the key. The landing was very dark, no wonder she had been so disoriented last night. On the way back she switched on all the lights and hung over the banister looking down into the lobby; it was of course empty.

The kettle took ages to boil and then she couldn't find her thermos; it was still in her bag on the luggage rack just inside the bedroom door. She rinsed it, dropped in some of the instant coffee, put it into a supermarket plastic bag with a tiny tub of milk and a long stick of sugar, and took it down the stairs. She stood it on the counter, then reached behind and took out the bowl and two of the tea towels and put them next to the thermos. Then she went back to bed.

She might have heard the heavy door open and close; she might have dreamed it. But it was full daylight when she woke up, and Irena was knocking on her door with fresh tea and two unpacketed digestive biscuits.

"Another lovely day," she greeted Judith with professional cheerfulness. "I hope you slept well." She barely waited for Judith's reply. "The tide is a little later today, so Mr Morris has suggested a departure time of ten thirty."

"Fine." Judith beamed at her; she was, after all, part of the rediscovery.

She said, "Your husband mentioned last night how supportive you are of his brother. It is so good of you. And so worthwhile. He is a genius."

Irena was already on the landing, moving towards the lift doors. She stopped and looked round; her expression was one of complete astonishment.

"Do you think so? I am — was — a great admirer of your husband's work, Mrs Freeman. Your opinion means a great deal . . . Thank you."

Judith closed the door, put down the tray and nibbled at one of the biscuits. She had never actually said she was widowed, had she? Surely Jack's daily comic strip was still in the *Magnet?* He had always called it their bread and butter. If Irena was such an admirer, would she read it and know that he was still alive?

The papers had arrived pre-high-tide and she scooped the *Magnet* from the pile in the lobby and took it into the lounge. There it was, one of Jack's less caustic comments on life in the twenty-first century: "Fish-Frobisher and Family". She smiled slightly; it had always been her favourite, and she had not taken the *Magnet* since Jack had left her simply because the way he dealt with the Fish-Frobishers was . . . loving. And she wanted to hate him.

She stood there, looking at the familiar cartoons, wondering where he had been when he did this latest one, unable to stop that last terrible memory of his departure. She heard her own voice, breaking up, bewildered, incredulous . . . "Is there someone else?" She had tried to laugh and mimic her own words. "I mean . . . another woman?"

She waited to hear him tell her not to be such an idiot. And he had said, "Yes, I suppose that's what it was."

She looked and looked at the Fish-Frobishers as if there might be an answer to all the questions she did not ask that day in a very hot July. Eight — no — nine weeks ago. It did not sound very long, but every day, every hour had been measured into a foretaste of the rest of her life.

She read the tiny byline and did not immediately take it in. "Reprinted from 1990." She read it again, frowned and thought it was a mistake. Then she moved along the six boxes of the cartoon story. Magnus Fish-Frobisher was grabbing his bowler hat and umbrella and making for the front door. Edith was telling him she was going to the hairdresser's. He pecked her cheek and told her to have a lovely relaxing day. She was turning to the daughter and saying that he must think she was off to the beach, and did he not realize the sheer humiliation of sitting beneath a dryer? The daughter was saying how boring they both were, then Magnus was returning that night with a bunch of flowers, pretending he did not recognize the glamour puss who was his wife.

She remembered it because it was the very first of the series. Jack had called it totally bland, and guessed it would not run longer than a month or two at the most. But it had taken off. It was still going strong. A day-to-day diary of a strangely pretentious yet loving family.

Except that they were reprinting it. As if — as if — Jack was dead.

She pushed the paper into her canvas bag next to the sketchbook. Her heart was pounding. She knew he wasn't dead, she knew it. If he was no longer on this earth she would know that, too. They were connected, they had been connected since that day at art college. Jack was alive.

Someone came into the sitting room; she stood as if looking at the sea. There was an explanation; she must not panic.

Hausmann's unmistakeable voice said, "I want to thank you. The coffee was good and the sick bowl was not necessary."

She did not turn. She managed one word. "Good."

There was a pause, then he said, "You are not all right. Are you coming to the Long Gallery this morning?"

"No."

"Ah."

Through her terror she caught a nuance of something. Diffidence. It did not go with the little she knew of Hausmann.

He said, "I was hoping we could talk."

"Not now."

From the dining room she heard Sybil's voice and felt an enormous relief.

"Sybil and I are going to Lynmouth this morning." She turned. "I have to get organized. Excuse me."

She brushed past him, screwing up the paper and forcing it into her bag. This was how it must be for Sybil. All the time.

CHAPTER
FIVE

During breakfast, Judith began to feel as if her head might be about to burst. She would dearly have liked to plead some kind of malaise and shut herself in her room to make phone calls. But somehow there was no opportunity; and anyway what would she say to William Whortley other than, "Is Jack dead?" And if he was in Perth with the boys, why on earth hadn't they phoned her? The obvious answer to that question was that he was with someone else. The other woman. She did not want to know that, either.

So she clambered into the minibus and sat next to Sybil on the front seat. Martin had organized the seating so that they could "nip out quickly and avoid the traffic" at Lynton. Luckily Sybil had nothing to say as they drove along the toll road, and the exclamations of delight from the others as views unrolled themselves made attempts at conversation useless. Judith concentrated so hard on not thinking about Jack that after half an hour she began to feel sick.

Sybil's voice was in her left ear. "Is it the bumpy road, Judith? Not very far now. You need the fresh air."

Judith nodded and put her hand over her mouth so that no speech was possible. Suddenly she could block Jack out no longer. He had said, "Death makes it so much worse — you can do nothing about death."

She could hear his voice speaking those words. And of course they were out of context, whatever that context had been. It need not mean he was contemplating suicide — in fact, obviously, it *could* not have meant any such thing. She half stood up and Sybil joined her. Martin Morris steered into a lay-by and pulled on the handbrake. Lynton might well be a bottleneck for traffic, but at that moment there was not another vehicle in sight.

"Is this close enough for you, ladies?"

"Fine," Sybil said. The doors folded themselves back and everyone said goodbye and promised to be in this same place at five pip emma. That got through to Judith, and she removed her hand from her mouth and gripped the handrail. Nathaniel was demanding reassurance from Sybil that they would manage all right on their own, and she was nodding and hanging on to the collar of Judith's fleece. They stood on the sandy road, and Sybil waved the minibus on its way, then turned, suddenly anxious.

"Something's really wrong, Judith. Would you prefer to go into Lynton and sit in a cafe for a while?"

"No. But thanks for stopping me falling out of the bus just then!" Judith actually managed a laugh. "I did feel a bit odd."

"You did not have any breakfast."

"No. I sort of . . . forgot."

"Let's sit on this bench for a few minutes. Get our bearings."

There was a bench just beneath the railway's timetable. Judith managed a shadow of a smile. "Martin seemed worried about where we were."

"I think he was being ironic." Sybil smiled. "Any further and the bus would have been on the rails!"

"Oh, I see." Judith felt foolish. She looked around her and drew some deep breaths. Her body settled itself, and she was conscious of the steady beat of her heart. She said, "This is marvellous. We're so high up. It's a sheer drop."

"Not quite. The railcars work on the weight of the water — they use the seawater, of course." Sybil tilted her head back, closed her eyes, took a deep breath. "I used to love going down the side of the cliff — we probably only came here twice — maybe three times — before we left Cardiff, but I've never forgotten it."

Judith felt suddenly better. She stood up and stared out to sea. "Strange you should say that — about the weight of water. I was wondering how on earth a painter can paint the sheer weight of water."

"Quite. Even more difficult is the fact that what works for one, doesn't for another. I mean for the viewer. Yesterday I could see quite clearly that Robert had got all the properties of water in his seascapes. But I heard Sven say to Margaret that the one thing missing in the whole exhibition was a depiction of the sea."

"How pompous!"

"It's his slightly foreign English. He was genuinely regretful, I think."

The railcar appeared, roof first and then very slowly its full length, each seat making a flight of giant steps to match the sharp descent. The guard, green flag at the ready, ushered them in, and they moved to the front on Sybil's advice. "Easier to get out at the other end," she said knowledgeably.

They were the only passengers. The guard took their money and issued tickets, telling them that once the school holidays were over, passengers were few and far between. "We'll stay open until half-term, but then close until the Christmas holidays. We do a lovely Santa Claus trip."

At the bottom, the jetty was to their left. At its end was a lighthouse crowned with an open fire basket instead of a lamp. To their right was the Lantern Inn, and then the land rose abruptly, funnelling the River Lyn as it ran down the combe and gurgled over rocks and stones before lining up rebelliously alongside the jetty and flowing into the sea.

Judith stood looking at it. "It's spectacular! So unexpected . . . so grand for such a small place . . . my God . . . it's beautiful . . . thank you, Sybil . . . this is just right. Just absolutely right!"

Sybil was laughing. "I knew you'd appreciate it. Now . . . let's have elevenses — coffee and a bun or sandwich or something. It's a pull up to that hotel on the top, but so well worth it. We can work there till lunchtime. What do you say?"

"I don't need coffee."

"Yes, you do. Come on."

Judith fell in behind her willy-nilly, wondering at the unexpected change in this woman, and only too glad that she had taken charge. They drank coffee, sitting outside on one of the two benches, chatting to the girl who served them. They were very end-of-season and therefore special. It was all somehow heart-warming. She thought suddenly: Of course he's not dead, what a ridiculous idea!

The pull up the side of the combe was unbelievably steep. The path had been cut into a zigzag in an effort to lessen the incline, but they had to stop frequently, clutch at a bush or a rock, and look back and concentrate on breathing.

"You see? We're already halfway!" Sybil encouraged.

"It's getting steeper!"

"Just a bit. Nothing to worry about." Sybil leaned back against a copper beech. "Looking down like this, do you feel the sheer weight of grief — which after all is composed of a great deal of water — do you feel it left behind for a little while?"

Judith looked at her; she seemed to be projecting something. Some emotion, some force. As if, by the very strength of her will, she could lose her grief, let it fall like a stone into the water. Judith felt a fraud; a cheat. Sybil was a genuine widow, mourning her husband. But she understood exactly how Sybil felt.

She said quietly, "Yes. I feel it too."

Sybil turned and smiled wryly. "I knew you would. That's why I wanted you to come with me today." She patted her shoulder bag. "Come on, we have to get this recorded somehow!"

Judith fell in behind her.

The hotel, which had looked so isolated and ethereal from below, proved to be fronting the road into Lynton, with a very modern sign indicating the way to Croyde, Woolacombe and Ilfracombe. The car park was full. They booked a table for lunch and hurried back to the terrace and the riverbank. There were picnic tables beneath a grove of willows; the sound of the water masked the traffic noise. "I had completely forgotten all that!" Sybil was disappointed.

Judith said, "That's part of its charm, surely? The wildness of nature and man side by side?" She grinned. "Martin did warn us, after all. And this is perfect — enhanced by all that . . ." She jerked her head at the hotel, then leaned back in the old-fashioned steamer chair. "Let's have an hour before we eat, shall we?" She gazed down the way they had come. "I've got a perfect frame here. The focus is the inn at the base of the jetty. It's pillowed in the trees." She pulled her canvas bag on to her lap and began to unfasten it, never taking her eyes from the view below. "It's the absolute opposite of the cliffs around the castle. Almost homely."

Sybil watched her as she fumbled at the pages of her sketchbook and chose a pencil. She followed suit. They fell silent, both absorbed, almost unconscious of the other. Judith chose her defining lines carefully. In spite of the enormous view this was a domestic scene; no fiercely aggressive pencil strokes could capture the intimacy of the inn. It was made tiny by its surroundings, but still offered a homely sanctuary to a traveller. She thought of the wild sea and the snarling cliffs so near to that open beacon at the end of the jetty; she thought of her mother, Eunice, wooed with a dozen red roses day after day and then so cruelly struck down; she thought of Jack, who had whispered, "I can't cope with all the housework any more, Eunice, you'll have to come and live with us." Exactly the right thing to say to her mother. She thought of Jack trying to keep the family thing going: trips to Perth, meeting the boys when they came home, yet never ever trying to persuade them to return permanently, setting them free. She thought of Jack, without anger.

Tears blinded the view. What had happened? How had it happened, whatever it was? There had been no time for him to conduct some sort of clandestine affair; anyway, that wasn't Jack. Yet . . . yet . . . even through the grief of her mother's death, hadn't she noted a change between them? How long since their gazes had locked, since they had reached for each other's hands and then, once joined, had laughed at themselves? Had it started before Eunice's death? Jack had wanted her to socialize. She did remember him saying, "Live life again, my love." When she had taken his advice and asked Naomi for that cup of tea, had he imagined that she was moving away from him?

She was no longer seeing the view, no longer visualizing Jack with his straw hair and blue eyes, so like her own, yet not one bit like hers. She was seeing Naomi. Naomi Parsons, who had been the best friend she had had. And might — could have — become a tiny wedge between Jack and herself.

Beneath her hand the pencil head snapped against her sketchbook.

Sybil looked up. "I wondered what that was!" She saw Judith's face and said quickly, "Have you had enough? Let's pack up and go for lunch. It's almost two o'clock. We must start back in good time. Can't imagine Martin being a minute late, can you?"

She began to tidy away her things, giving Judith plenty of time to recover. And Judith looked at her sketchbook where, already, she could see the gently shaded pillow shapes of the trees, the tiny inn standing steadfastly beneath the crazy lighthouse with its empty brazier raised to the sky. She began to close the book page by page. Four pages of the sketches she had made yesterday. Four pages of the harsh cliffs of Dove. The force of nature and — not far behind — the absurd efforts of man to tame, to subdue. She drew a trembling breath. Denman and Freeman.

They struggled back up to the terrace, and a waiter took them to their table. They were both out of breath; Judith's silence was not obvious. They ate mussels and Sybil turned the discarded shells so that the light caught their iridescent blue. "What does that remind you of?" she asked, placing a shell against the plate, then dabbling her hands in the finger bowl. "I suppose it's some sort of camouflage?"

Judith made an effort and blinked at the mass of shells. "Just the opposite — they seem to be signalling their presence."

"How do you mean?"

"Well — a mass of blue police cars all flashing like mad."

Sybil threw back her head and laughed unrestrainedly. Her neck was like Naomi's: long, terribly vulnerable.

She said, "You certainly know how to bring things down to earth! You remind me of my husband."

Judith was startled. "I thought . . . he was an ideas man, surely?" She saw the instant change in Sybil's face and added quickly, "Sorry. Newspaper knowledge — always unreliable."

"No. It's all right. And — in a way — the newspapers were right. But that was what he fed them." She turned the shells again. "He made sure they saw the blue flashing lights, never the blackness beneath them."

Judith looked; the sun had gone behind a cloud, the mussel shell was indeed black. She felt a tide of sadness creeping from her feet upwards. No anger, bitterness, recriminations, excuses. Just sadness.

Sybil said slowly, "He was a spin doctor. He could spin a yarn. Make not very good facts into splendid ones. Or . . . vice versa."

Jack had called him a manipulative liar, a wheeler-dealer, a smiling hypocrite. It was Jack's job to unmask hypocrites.

Sybil said, "I was so attracted to him, I cannot tell you . . ." Her voice died, and Judith reached out and covered her still-damp hand. It lay quiescent beneath hers for a moment, and then turned convulsively and gripped Judith's fingers.

"Sorry . . . sorry, Judith. I really did leave it all behind at the bottom of the combe — that's why I can talk about it. But I know it will be there when we get down."

Judith nodded. She wondered whether Sybil had ever seen any of Jack's scathing series in the *Magnet*. It had never been disguised. "Moss Mockup alias Cockup" had run for six months four or five years ago.

Almost telepathically, Sybil said, "I know lots of people saw through him — of course they did. I forced him time and time again to face up to the fact that his spin was often a form of deception. But in the end he would convince me." The grip on Judith's fingers became painful. "I miss him so much . . . I didn't know what to do. I can't do anything without him. Anything."

"You came to see the Hausmann exhibition," Judith reminded her.

"Yes. I did. And I came to see Robert. And I got Nattie as well. And neither of them seem to recognize me. So how much have I changed? Did Moss change me, or did I change myself? I came back to my roots — to the two people who mattered to me — and they don't know me. So am I not me?" Sybil's eyes were wide and panic-stricken. "You feel the same, don't you? I can tell. So who are we? Are we shades of our husbands? So does that mean we are dead, too?"

Judith looked into the dark eyes and said honestly, "I think perhaps I am not Judith Freeman any more; probably have not been for the last eight years. I think I have reverted to being Judith Denman."

She held Sybil's gaze and watched as the panic died, as Sybil thought about her words, turned them over, then nodded slowly.

"Perhaps that is what I want. Perhaps that is why I came on this trip. To become Esmée Gould again."

"Esmée Gould?"

"I lived in the same street as Nattie and Robert. I was ten when we left Cardiff and went to live in London. And I was sixteen when I discarded Esmée and chose to use my middle name and leave behind all the bitterness of my parents' memories. Moss said I reinvented myself. That's one of those buzz phrases, isn't it? Lots of people reinvent themselves. I suppose I was already half of a spin doctor. Even then. At sixteen."

Judith stared, astounded. She said, "How — how absolutely marvellous! Don't you see — you have taken control of your life again. You have seen a way forward — by going back! I mean, it makes such perfect sense —"

Sybil released her hand and laughed again. "Oh, Judith. How can I go forward by going backwards — where's the sense in that?"

"I don't know. But it's there. It's as plain as a pikestaff to me." Judith clasped her hands. The sadness that had reached her knees subsided completely. She thought of Hausmann, caught in the net of inherited terror, and this woman who knew him and could help him and could help herself, too. She rested her chin on her clasped hands and sat back.

"For goodness' sake, Sybil. Don't fight it. It's happening — just go along with it!"

Sybil shook her head. "You don't understand. They called my father 'Goalposts' because he was always in goal when we played football in the street. He didn't mind, but I did. Stupid. My great-grandfather was in Auschwitz and he told me once that the Holocaust began with name-calling. It went on to bullying, then torture. Did you know that you can go on a tour of Auschwitz? Moss took me not long ago. There were no birds. I didn't see a spider. No life at all. Moss thought it would help me. And it did because I realized I could never ever get rid of it. How many generations before some kind of redemption, Judith?"

"I don't know. But by going back to Cardiff . . . might there be acceptance somewhere there?" She thought of the Hausmann 'scapes and said in a low voice, "Perhaps he has found it."

"Robert? I thought that. But no. He paints dreams of the past — yes, they are there before him, but they are already in the past simply because he puts them there for the future!" She spread her hands. "You know what I mean."

Judith nodded. "But I see that as a gift for the future. Not all horror and despair, but beauty. Everywhere." She was suddenly invigorated. She saw a solution for Robert and Sybil. They must be together. It was so obvious. So entirely destined.

She brought her hands together as if closing a book. "Would you like a pudding? No? Then we had better start back. We can have coffee down at the inn if there's time." She was already planning a talk with Robert Hausmann. He would leave the castle before high tide. When was that, exactly? Probably the shock of knowing that Esmée Gould was back would decide him to give up his nightly carousals down at the Dove Inn.

She asked for the bill and insisted on paying it. Some of her energy spread to Sybil, who leaned forward, backtracking on the last half an hour of high emotion.

"Listen, Judith, I should not have let my hair down quite so far!" She smiled wryly. "All that business about my background — you will keep it under your hat, won't you?"

"Well . . . all right." Judith was sure there was a way of telling Hausmann without actually telling him. She bit her lip, already wondering how to go about it. She said lightly, "But why are you embarrassed by it? It's rather marvellous, surely? Especially your decision to come here and meet your childhood friends."

"Well, I must have thought so, but now . . . I don't want them to know, Judith. I must have changed amazingly and . . . it's digging up bad memories. For them as well as me. I'm pleased I came, of course. It made me face up to certain . . . things. I shall go back to Surrey and perhaps keep in touch with you now and then. And — well, make a new life, I suppose."

Judith hesitated. "Yes. All right. If that's what you want. Of course."

"Thank you."

They started back down the combe.

CHAPTER
SIX

The bus was late. The traffic in Exeter had been appalling. The Markhams had dallied in the shopping centre, and the others had gone on to the minibus and had to wait almost an hour until Jennifer and Stanley arrived, dishevelled, hot and bothered, and without the interesting bags of lingerie Jennifer and Margaret had bought between them.

"We just had to see the cathedral!" Jennifer explained. "We must have left the bags in that little chapel — was it the Lady Chapel?"

"Almost three hundred of our precious pounds!" Sven said, his benevolence deserting him. "Just so that you two idiots can clock up another venue!"

Margaret held his arm and said warningly, "You know very well Stanley is interested in churches, and he trailed with us through the shops long enough! We can go back via the cathedral — the bags will be there."

Amazingly, they had been. But the detour added another twenty minutes to the delay, and even Nathaniel's patience was thinning by the time they pulled into the lay-by.

Judith and Sybil settled into their front seat. Sybil whispered, "Stanley looks like a cat who is very well pleased with himself!" Judith glanced back and saw the tiny grin on Stanley's normally expressionless face. The two women started to giggle.

It was good to trundle over the causeway and take the much shorter flight of steps up to the big front door. Nathaniel said loudly, "It's like coming home. Imagine that. Coming home to a castle."

"An Englishman's home is his castle," Sybil put in unexpectedly, smiling at him without irony. "A castle for the master and a nest for the mistress."

"Wonderful, dear lady!" He took her arm and piloted her towards the sitting room. "And how did your day go?"

She began to tell him. She was unbuttoning. Before Judith's very eyes, she was doing exactly what she should be doing. Nathaniel would pick something up, surely . . . and he would pass it on to Robert. Judith climbed the stairs slowly, the muscles in her legs protesting vigorously. The sheer rightness of Robert Hausmann and Sybil Jessup was incredible. For once, the right time, the right place and, above all, the right people. The others were still in the lobby, milling around ordering trays of tea to be sent upstairs. She would make her own and lie down. Behind all the thoughts that had possessed her today, she knew that the ache was still there, between her eyes. But it had been so worth it.

She saw from the first landing that Hausmann was waiting for her outside her room, and her heart sank a little. It would be best if she did not see him until Sybil had been unmasked, as it were. She did not quite trust herself to keep Sybil's secret. She trudged on, smiled as she came to the top step, spoke as normally as she could.

"Lynmouth was wonderful. You should go and look at it."

"I painted Lynmouth some years ago."

She tried to gauge his mood from his face, but it was difficult. Unless he actually smiled he looked perpetually grim. Something else was added now; was it nervousness?

"It is a gem. Your sort of gem."

"I want to talk to you. This morning I told you."

She knew already that his tone was not meant to be peremptory, but she was tired and some of the afternoon's euphoria was wearing off. And perhaps he was already suspicious about Sybil and wanted to sound her out. Besides all that, she was emotionally drained and exhausted.

"Not now, Hausmann. I must lie down."

He nodded once, turned round, opened her door, went through and held it open for her. She was astonished.

"Hang on. I locked that door this morning!"

"I borrowed the master key once more."

She went into the room and looked around. Her thermos was on the table. The bed had been beautifully made, but it was evident someone had since been lying on it. He followed her outraged gaze.

"I, too, was tired. I was out all morning and a coachload of people were here to see my work when I returned. They tried my patience, and eventually I turned them out. Your room is just the other side of the gallery doors. I am sorry, Mrs Jack. I can see you are annoyed. I did not go through your things."

She stood by the bed, her back to him. What was this Mrs Jack stuff? It side-tracked her fury slightly.

She said, "So. There has been a row? More ammunition against you, Hausmann?" She turned round. "When are you going to get it together? Bart would let you use this venue permanently, you know that. Irena's OK really. She just doesn't want you to drag your brother down too far — natural, surely?"

He said nothing; stood in front of her, arms hanging helplessly, his dark face darker still, with what she took to be a hangdog expression.

She sighed theatrically. "Listen. Make some tea, will you? I have got to lie on this bed even if you had dirty boots when you did so."

Before she had scuffed off her trainers, he was at the kettle. She lay down, adjusted the pillow, sniffed suspiciously, closed her eyes.

"There is a smell of paint, yes?"

"That's what it is. I don't mind that. Two sugars. A dash of milk."

"A biscuit?"

"No. You can have both packets. I had mussels at the hotel and a cake with my cup of tea at the Lantern Inn." She relaxed. "Oh, Hausmann, it was beautiful. You should have been there."

"If you had asked me, I would have come. And then there would have been more trouble still. Apparently I had promised to do the exhibition and be nice to everyone." He mimicked Irena's voice and Judith laughed.

She heard him put two teacups on the bedside table, and opened her eyes a slit. He drew up a chair and sat down.

She said, "Well?"

"Drink your tea first. It is difficult."

She pushed herself further on to the pillows and reached round for her cup. The tea was as she liked it: fairly strong and very sweet. She held it between both hands and let the steam soothe her eyes. The knot between them began to relax very slightly. If only he would leave quickly she knew she would sleep until their evening meal. The silence stretched out.

He said abruptly, "That idiot driver, Martin Morris, he told me you were Jack Freeman's widow. I did not know he was dead."

It was as if he had hit her in the stomach. She leaned over, holding the cup so tightly she thought it might break.

He said, "Don't speak. I knew Jack for a time. I went to Australia two months ago. Got lost in the bush. Jack's brother came and found me. Jack was visiting. I saw his stuff, he saw mine. I loved him and I thought he loved me. He did in a way. He kept calling me a 'poor bugger'. If anyone else had called me that I'd have done them an injury. But not Jack. Whatever he thought of me, I still loved him. I had some kind of fever, and he sat with me all one night and talked about you."

She straightened her back slowly; her eyes were wide.

He said, "When I saw you first I didn't realize . . . He didn't describe you very well at all. But he told me — when he said goodbye — that he had been talking about his wife." He looked up from his own cup. His eyes were full of tears.

"He was a marvellous man. I'll always love him. I knew him for just over a week and saw that he too was as sick as I was. We helped each other. If there is anything — anything at all — I would be honoured to help you, Mrs Jack." He stood up, put down his cup, walked to the door, and left.

She watched him go. He was slightly crouched and looked like a bear. When the door closed she watched that too, and in her mind she saw him shamble down the landing and into the gallery. Jack had sat with him all one night, and because he was a stranger and probably delirious, Jack had talked to him. About a woman.

At last she put her cup next to Hausmann's, turned carefully, and lay on her side. After a time she began to weep.

Everyone was very quiet that evening. Nathaniel expounded on the cathedral and its golden colour and Sybil mentioned a train journey from London to Penzance when the red sandstone became very obvious along the Dawlish coast. Martin Morris joined them and told them about the Dorset coast and its plethora of fossils. Judith noticed that when he said that word — plethora — his top denture fell slightly. She would have glanced at Sybil except that she was no longer certain how she could help her. When the trolley came round Judith was conscious that Sybil glanced at her, and she wondered why. Then she realized. The starters were mussels in white wine. She gave a brief upward smile.

At the other table almost total silence prevailed. Jennifer and Margaret did their best discussing the relative merits of shops in Bristol and Exeter but this came to an end when Margaret said very definitely that Stockholm beat both places for shopping.

"I just wish you two would come and stay with us for once," she said. "Especially at Christmas. It's magical. And of course the people are wonderful."

"We couldn't possibly Christmas anywhere except home!" Jennifer looked at Stanley and he smiled. Yes, that was how the Cheshire cat did it — a disembodied smile. She smiled back. Intimately. Margaret looked annoyed and Sven put his arm across her shoulders. Judith wondered fleetingly and without much interest what on earth was going on there.

After the meal they congregated in the sitting room at Bart Mann's request. Judith almost excused herself on the grounds of her headache, but then the thought of her room and its solitariness on that second landing made the sitting room full of disparate people seem attractive.

She sat in a corner of the sofa and Sybil joined her. For a few minutes they were alone while the others found seats and Bart set up a sort of screen next to the television. Under cover of the general settling-down, Sybil said, "I don't know what has happened, Judith.

You were so different this afternoon. Now you are not. Are you sure you're not ill?"

"I've got a nasty nagging pain between my eyes. I get it when I am tired and, lately, I seem always to be tired." She smiled as she spoke. She wondered whether Sybil had guessed at Judith's wild and stupid plans to act like some old-fashioned matchmaker — she despised herself. Oh God, who was the woman Jack had described to Hausmann? If it had been her he would have started off with, "She doesn't like being called a blonde bombshell but . . ." Her heart started to pound; was this the beginning of madness?

Nathaniel came and sat next to Sybil, and Martin Morris squashed in beside him. Sybil whispered, "Just stay for this, there's a dear. It's the talk that Robert was meant to do this afternoon in the Long Gallery, and apparently he made a mess of it. Give him a chance now. Can you manage half an hour?"

So Sybil had definitely come to see Robert Hausmann. Perhaps to pick up on their shared memories of the past? With a view to a relationship? Judith nodded but closed her eyes as she pushed herself against the arm of the sofa.

When she opened them the screen was lit, the other lights dimmed and Hausmann was skulking behind the television, using it as a surface for some notes. He clicked a switch and the screen was filled with a view of Lundy Island.

"Historically, this was a vital defence site for the West Country, and indeed for Wales." His voice took on a certain drone. He ran through a list of events obviously taken from a guidebook, but included exciting stories of pirates and sieges and royal edicts. Unfortunately, without any expression in his voice, it remained just a list of events. After a full ten minutes of this, he paused, switched again and they were confronted with a scene of a Welsh castle. He started droning once more.

The slide lecture lasted an hour. There were no personal reminiscences of the work behind each painting. When he paused for questions, Sven said, "Was it raining when you painted the Devon seascape? I could see no horizon."

"I can't remember. But if there had been a horizon I would have painted it."

"Then I will assume it was raining." Spoken in Sven's very precise English, the words sounded heavily sarcastic. Sybil's hand, which was suddenly covering Judith's, tightened convulsively.

Hausmann clicked back to the painting, looked at it and droned, "A realistic assumption." Then clicked off.

Nathaniel said, "What makes these paintings so amazing is their attention to every detail. I wish you had talked us through some of that, Robert."

Hausmann said, "Good old Nattie! You should have been in the diplomatic service. Isn't it enough that they are there — every bloody detail — for you to see for yourselves?"

Nathaniel stuck to his guns. "I want to know how you go about these things — is it just me? Am I being too inquisitive? Is that something entirely private to the painter?"

Hausmann looked across the television. "To be honest, Nat, I don't know. Perhaps I am unable to make myself so vulnerable — honesty is vulnerability, is it not?"

Stanley Markham cleared his throat and everyone looked at him. He said, "I think it is more basic than that. Mr Hausmann can paint. He can find ways of showing us exactly what we are missing when we look at things. But . . . perhaps he cannot find the words to tell us. Perhaps someone else might do that. A poet?"

The silence was one of sheer astonishment. Stanley had spoken at last.

Hausmann said nothing. The silence was broken by Sven. "A poet? Or perhaps a teacher like yourself? What is your so-realistic saying in England? 'If you can't do it, teach it!'"

The silence changed and became apprehensive. Sybil's grip was painful and Judith could see that in the chairs opposite the sofa, Margaret and Jennifer were also holding hands. She looked across at Hausmann. He was bending down unplugging the projector. He straightened slowly and began to wind the cable on to a spool.

"I think you are right, Mr Markham. I have no words. My eyes and hands are what I use." Suddenly and unexpectedly he looked round the room and gave a mighty grin. "I am not known for tact — that was always the area of my good friend Nathaniel." He made a little bow towards the sofa, and for once Nathaniel Jones was silent.

Everything changed. There was much laughter, congratulations for Hausmann, a general discussion about his work, during which he seemed enabled to talk about the process of painting. Irena brought in coffee, cheese and biscuits. Bart produced chocolate mints again.

Judith said, "I'm going to slip away. Thank you for today, Sybil."

"Shall we do it again tomorrow? Perhaps Porlock?"

"I . . . I don't know."

"I could persuade Robert to come with us. I might tell him who I am."

"Oh . . . oh. I really don't know. Honestly."

"Sorry . . . don't mean to pressure you. See you at breakfast. Yes?"

"Yes. Yes of course."

She escaped and made for the stairs. Once in her room she locked the door carefully and leaned back against it, steeling herself physically not to cry.

Then she emptied her bag on to the bed and found her address book. She skipped through it and found the private number of the *Magnet's* editor. William Whortley. She propped the book against the two teacups, which were still on her bedside table, and sat on the edge of the bed.

Almost automatically she looked to see what the last call to her mobile had been. She started to write it down and then stopped in mid-flow. It was her home number. She held the receiver away from her, staring at it. Then rang it back. She counted eight rings and then her own voice said, "Can you leave us a message, please? We'll ring you back as soon as we can." Jack had wanted her to do it — friendly but firm, he had said. Short and to the point. Keep it short, Jude, don't use two words when one will do.

Nobody left a message and the phone sang emptily into her ear.

She sat still for some time, wondering whether she should ring enquiries. One of Jack's golfing companions lived on the same road and was a policeman. She could tell him where she kept the spare key. It took an age to get the number, but eventually she was able to tap it out. There was no answer, not even a machine. She remembered him saying to Jack that his private phone was his private phone. Jack had kissed her later and told her never to be as precious about the English language. "It's not only that he was stating the obvious — it's because if he really wanted privacy he'd go ex-directory!"

And then she suddenly had a wonderful thought. Jack was the only one who had a key, and even if he'd lost it he knew that she kept a spare one underneath the third rock in the rockery. It must have been Jack. Jack must be alive.

She sat on the edge of the bed, eyes closed, so deeply thankful she almost forgot that he had left her for another woman. Even when she did, the thankfulness did not go away. She didn't care — for the moment — that he might love someone else. The fact that he was still on this earth was enough.

After some time, she stood up, collected her things and went to the bathroom, showered, and returned to her room. And then, and only then, did she ring William Whortley.

The phone in the Surrey house — genuine Elizabethan with stables at the back — rang a lot of times before the answering machine kicked in. She left a brief message asking whether William had any idea of Jack's whereabouts. No mention of the rerun of his cartoon strip. Just a bare question with her phone number. And then she went to bed.

She slept fitfully. She thought at one stage that someone tried her door, but she had locked it and left the key in. She slept again. This time she dreamed of Matt. He was asking someone where Toby had gone. And then he was running along a road, absolutely straight with no beginning and no end. He was wearing shorts, and she watched his beautiful legs pumping rhythmically and his arms punching the air with each stride. He looked round and saw her and shouted, "I'll find him for you, Mum. He'll be with Dad!"

She woke up sweating and lay straight, telling herself over and over again that it was a dream, absurd, ridiculous, like all dreams. It was no good, she could not sleep. She got out of bed intending to make some tea. The phone rang.

It was William Whortley.

"Judith. My dear. We've just come in from the theatre and I listened to the messages. I hoped you knew where Jack was. I have no idea, and I am worried about him because he hasn't been himself, has he? I've emailed him, sent him texts."

She said blearily, "I think he's with Toby — one of our sons — not sure. If he is he won't be able to text. Poor signal."

He laughed; a gust of relief that filled her ear. "Thank God. Judith, I can tell you now. I thought he might be on his deathbed! I expected something to come through from him: a skull — alas, poor Yorick — you know the sort of thing. Your message sounded desperate, somehow."

"Bad hair day." It was one of Jack's sayings, and convinced him more than anything. He became bluff and avuncular.

"Don't worry, my dear. You know what he's like. First one to hear from him gets in touch, all right?"

"Sounds good." She was responding like Jack again. He said goodnight, and she said, "Sleep tight", and they rang off. She sat on the edge of the bed. It was just past midnight. The Whortleys had come in from the theatre and would be having nightcaps and going to bed. And she had done with sleeping, yet was still tired.

She made the inevitable tea and drank it slowly, remembering her dream and the rattle of her bedroom door before that. Hausmann had got away from all the sudden interest in the sitting room and followed her to make sure she was all right. She pictured him cradled in Jack's arms, ill and haunted by ghosts. He had probably run to Australia in search of solace, and had found it with Jack. Jack was good at solace. Jack had always been good at solace.

She refused to weep; weeping could become a habit. And she refused to stew in her own juice. She put on her dressing gown and then wrapped herself in the duvet, suddenly realizing how cold it was. Then she pocketed her key and went along the landing towards the Long Gallery. The heavy old double doors were unlocked. She pushed them open clumsily, duvet slipping down, another rush of cold air finding her shoulders. She got through somehow and closed the doors carefully, then hoisted the duvet almost over her head. She looked down the length of the gallery; it was flooded with moonlight. It was breathtaking.

She waited for some time, not even looking, simply waiting for her perceptions to settle into this new dimension. Nothing was defined. Because she already knew that the display units were set at angles and that every flat surface held the Hausmann paintings, she could start from there. But the silver-grey light showed few details; the Long Gallery itself was what she was seeing, the zigzag of the units was its artery system, the unseen paintings its nerve-ends.

She held the duvet tight to her shoulders, and the corner that had shielded her head fell back. She could hear. She listened.

There were myriad sounds and she was alarmed, wondering whether someone else was in the gallery; Hausmann himself, perhaps. But he — anyone — would have made themselves known when she had opened the doors. These sounds belonged to the castle itself. The wind pressed against the windows and the walls breathed it in. Timbers expanded and contracted as if the gallery were the prow of a ship; an old sailing ship, rising and falling in a swell. And the tiny sounds . . . were they mice who had lived behind the wainscoting for years and rightly considered the gallery to be theirs? She smiled, thinking of the stories she would have made from these sounds when the boys were small. Easier to think of mice dressed in Beatrix Potter ginghams than rats seeking refuge from the full tide. She began to move away from the door.

The sofas were placed back to back for easy viewing; there were three pairs, one commanding each alcove of paintings. She sat in every one of them, looking through the moonlight, identifying the pictures, feeling again the ineffable sadness of something that was perhaps as relatively ephemeral as a moth's wing. Yet at the same time seeing the amazing and glorious hope that Hausmann was offering — perhaps unknowingly. Humankind . . . nesting . . . in the face of chaos? She remembered her sketches; yesterday's, today's. The battling cliffs and insidious seas. Then the tiny haven of the Lantern Inn set among pillows of trees.

She came to the last of the squashy sofas and sat very still, no longer looking, sensing the moonlight bathing her, incorporating her into the gallery. She saw that her terrors were now separate from herself. Toby was looking for Jack, and Matt was close behind. Everything was out of her hands: the human plight and the domestic one. She surrendered, curled herself into the back of the sofa, tucked her head against the arm and went to sleep.

CHAPTER
SEVEN

When she woke the moonlight had gone and the sun
was sparking the diamond-paned windows and glowing
lovingly on the pictures in the final alcove. Judith
turned on to her back and stretched, bracing her feet
and shoulders against the arms of the sofa. The
wonderful sense of freedom that had released her into
sleep last night was still present, though she
acknowledged with a little self-mocking smile that it
could not last.

She hoisted herself up to look over at the paintings
behind her. They were the ones that had earned
Hausmann the name of the "Constable of Somerset".
No wonder he was bitter. They were so much his own,
so very much his own.

She leaned her head back against . . . a pillow? She
wriggled and pulled it out. It matched her duvet.
Staring down at her feet she saw a blanket.

She propped herself up again; so Hausmann had
sought her out and done what he could to make her
comfortable. She had become a sort of homage to Jack.
Yesterday that might have made her weep; today it
made her smile. It would make Jack smile too. She
closed her eyes and imagined them reaching for each

other, caught — first of all — in a level of emotion neither could sustain. And so bursting into laughter. She opened her eyes quickly before the threat of unwanted tears could overcome her . . . and the door at the end of the Long Gallery opened.

Hausmann entered back-first because he was holding a tray. As he came nearer she saw it was beautifully laid even to a slender glass holding a cornflower. She began to laugh when he was half way along the gallery, and by the time he set it carefully on the floor within her reach, she was almost unable to speak.

He sat on the floor. "What is funny?" he demanded.

She controlled herself. "Nothing really. Just . . . the situation. Did you fetch my pillow and this blanket? You did, didn't you? Thank you, Mr Hausmann. Thank you very much. I have had a wonderful sleep. And now — this."

"I do it for Jack."

"I know." Her voice became very gentle. "So I have to tell you. Jack is not dead. He is doing what you did. He is walking in the deserts of Australia. Perhaps wanting to die — as I think you did — but his rescuers are close."

"How do you know this?"

"I had a dream. And then I came in here and your paintings told me."

He said nothing, just looked down at his feet, then leaned forward and poured tea, then added a full spoon of sugar, then a dash of milk.

"You remembered!" she marvelled.

"It is my curse. I remember everything. Even when they are not my memories, I still remember."

She stared at the top of his head. His hair was like a bush, but it was soon going to turn from grey to completely white.

She said, "Somebody has to."

He looked up. "Why should it be me, Mrs Jack? Why should I carry the burden for others — others who are dead — why can't they take their memories with them?"

She wondered whether he had looked at Jack the way he was looking at her. If he had, what had Jack said?

She leaned down and took the mug of tea from his hands. She inhaled appreciatively as she always did, and then she said matter-of-factly, "Because you can put down the burden whenever you will."

He looked at her incredulously. "Because I can paint? You think I could paint those memories? I would be sectioned — put into a secure unit where I would be watched in case I found a weapon —"

She put a hand down and over his lips and made shushing noises, as she had to the twins years ago.

"No. That would never happen. But you could do a Manley Hopkins. You should read his poetry — beauty in the midst of death or Nature's cruelty. None of his work was seen until he had died."

She took her fingers from his face, and he grabbed them, opened her hand, and put it over his eyes for just a moment, then released it. She put it back on her mug of tea and sipped again.

He said in a low voice, "I thought that perhaps the hand that stopped my speech could also stop my eyes from seeing what they see."

She was aghast. "Robert! You must never wish for blindness of any kind! Don't ever talk like that again! Your sight and your insight are precious — gifts — never to be thrown away because you do not like what they see!"

He looked at her, startled, then a little smile lifted his mouth.

She was further incensed. "Don't laugh at me, Robert Hausmann! I am serious!" She turned her head from shoulder to shoulder, taking in the whole of the gallery. "What you have done gives us hope — can't you see that? What you can leave for the future is the realization that one has to remember — has to — so that the hope will always be there. Valid. Possible!"

She was breathing quickly and made herself subside against the pillow, made herself sip the tea. He was silent, looking down again. After a while he buttered a slice of toast on a plate, opened a tiny carton of marmalade and spread it carefully, cut the toast into fingers and placed it on top of the duvet.

Then he said, "It was the fifteenth of July when Leonard Freeman airlifted me from the desert of Western Australia and took me to hospital in Perth. It was that night that Jack Freeman sat with me and recognized my despair." He leaned forward so that his face was in front of hers. "Was that because he was despairing, too?"

She thought back. Jack had left at the beginning of July.

She said, "It's the right timescale. And the despair was . . . yes, he was desperate. But he wasn't going to Australia. Not then. He was going to the . . . the . . . dammit . . . the other woman!" She sat up straight. "D'you know, Hausmann, that was what hurt so much. The other woman. But now — since I thought he was dead — that doesn't seem so . . . I'm not sure about it. What I *am* so sure of is the wonder of him still being alive. And out there with his family instead of . . . instead of —"

"I understand." Hausmann had removed the plate and now gripped her hands. "Nothing can be done about death."

She stared at him. "You don't believe me, do you?"

"I believe the dream —"

"But you still think he is dead?"

"Mrs Jack, I do not know what I believe. That is why I am a mess. It seems logical that he is alive, otherwise his brother would have contacted you. That is enough for now." He released her hands and produced the toast again. "Now, eat. And today I will take you and Esmée to see my project."

She was already munching the toast, and spoke through it. "Esmée?"

"Yes. You are finding her an interesting companion?"

"You mean Sybil Jessup?"

He stood up with difficulty. "Hasn't she told you? She lived next door to me on one side and next door to Nattie on the other. Many years ago. She was Esmée

104

Gould then. Her father was a marvellous man and taught us how to play games he had played, and his father had played before him . . . Nattie, Esmée and Robbie. We were inseparable."

"But she thinks that neither of you recognize her!"

"Ah, so you do know. Nattie wouldn't have a clue, of course. He showed me a tiny snap he has of her at ten years old. He thinks she would never have changed. But she is far more beautiful now than she was then." He took the empty plate from her and stacked everything on the tray. "Come on. Irena will be up with morning tea at any moment. Let us appear to be very conventional. It makes her happy."

She wrapped the duvet around her shoulders and pushed her feet into slippers as she tried to thank him. He would have none of it. The lift was whining a warning as they passed its doors and he hurried past her and began down the stairs. Then he paused on the first landing and looked up.

"I have lied to you, Mrs Jack. I did go through your things. Your sketches — work on them when you are home, try different media. And for now . . . start drawing Jack Freeman. Please. You might keep him alive, and understand what is happening." He went on down very fast; she watched, terrified he would slip and fall. Wanting to ask more questions.

The lift-whine stopped and she just got inside her room before the discreet tap heralded Irena. Her head was buzzing but not aching any more. She reopened her door.

"I was just off to the bathroom." She took the tray; Irena's eyes were on the duvet and she was not her recent obsequious self.

Judith smiled. "I brought the wrong nightclothes, didn't I? Did you find it chilly in the night?" Strange how the word "chilly" was soft, whereas "cold" was not.

"I tend to sleep very deeply unless Robert wakes us up. He often needs help with his pink elephants, as you probably know."

Judith was angry on Hausmann's behalf — how could this woman not see through to his good intentions? She did her best, rolling her eyes and saying gushingly, "This is the trouble with geniuses, isn't it? Jack used to get terrible nightmares. I had to sit with him and calm him down often."

"Did you? Really? Yet his work was so humorous — never ever *nasty*, was it?"

Judith improvised gladly. "He loved people, of course. Even the ones he disapproved of — politics, power mad — *you* understand; he still drew them with kindness."

Irena melted. "Oh my dear, how can you be so brave? You are trying to be like him, aren't you? Kind to people like Mrs Jessup and Bart's brother. That sweet smile you have sometimes — it is heartbreaking!" She drew in a breath and let it go in a small sob. "I read an article about him once. How close he was to his wife and children. I can see why."

Judith took the tray and the duvet fell to the floor. She exaggerated a small shiver into a violent tremor. "I think I'll go back to bed with this, Mrs Mann. Thank you so much. I feel ... I feel ... I feel you understand."

The door was closing. Irena said, "Oh I do, I do. But I have to warn you about my brother-in-law. Sometimes he can be a little mad. Will you let me know if —"

"Of course I will. Naturally. And thank you. Thank you again." The door clicked shut. Judith put the tray down and hurled the duvet on to the bed. She knew it would not help Robert if she fought his corner — quite the opposite — but she still felt she had betrayed him.

Breakfast was almost jolly that morning. It was Sunday, and the Olsens and the Markhams had been to early Communion at St Beuno's, the smallest church in the west. Martin Morris had driven them, but was glad when there proved to be no room for him inside the church. It was raining — a sea-fret Martin called it — and the priest had offered a cycling cape as the rain blew into the porch. He had assured Martin that he would be able to hear the service through the door, and the cape was windproof. Martin had opted to sit in the minibus and promised he would find a service on the radio. He had not been successful, but he had opened the window and heard the small congregation singing "We plough the fields and scatter".

"Took me back," he said.

Sybil asked Nathaniel whether he had been tempted to join the others.

"Not really. I'm Chapel."

Sven called across, "We also. But this was inter — inter — what was it, Margaret?"

"Inter-denominational. It's a tourist thing, really. They hold a service occasionally, and it just happened that today it was an early one. Which meant we would be back for breakfast and then for our day in Ilfracombe. Who knows? We might be lucky and be able to go across to Lundy. I have never been, have you?"

Judith shook her head, but Sybil and Nathaniel both spoke at once and then laughed. Sybil said, "So you, too, did a school trip there?"

"I did indeed! And you?"

"Only once." She glanced at Judith. "Very easy to imagine all the pirates — and other worse criminals — who spent time there."

Margaret said eagerly, "Come with us, why don't you? Even if we can't get a boat across to Lundy, Ilfracombe is a delightful and rather Victorian seaside town. There is a tunnel through the rocks leading to the beach —"

Jennifer said eagerly, "Yes, why don't you all go? Stanley and I found yesterday rather tiring, and we thought we would rest today."

This was obviously news to Sven and Margaret. Margaret said, "But last night — we had such a good time in the lounge with the slides and Robert being so — so different."

Jennifer said, "Oh dear, have I put my foot in it again? Of course we will come — it was just a thought — if Mr Jones and Sybil and Judith were interested —"

Sven said smoothly, "We understand of course —"

Margaret snapped, "Shut up, Sven!" She turned accusingly to her friend. "There is plenty of room in the bus for all of us — you know that!"

Unexpectedly, Nathaniel leaned over, holding out a propitiating hand. "I'm sorry, it seems as if we are spoiling your outing, but Robert and I have planned to take the girls walking today." He looked wryly at Stanley and Jennifer. "It seems you are committed. Perhaps you can rest this evening before dinner?"

His efforts at diplomacy were so obvious they were almost pathetic, and no one felt able to spoil them. Sybil opened her eyes wide at Judith. It was Stanley who actually spoke again.

"I think we can just about cope with that, can't we, darling?"

Jennifer nodded and held out a hand towards Margaret, and after a moment's hesitation Margaret took it and shook it gently. Sven produced a guidebook and began to tell Jennifer about Ilfracombe as if he had invented it.

Nathaniel said, "I am going to wrap my toast and take it with me. Robert has no interest in food, and whatever this project is, I am willing to bet we will be nowhere near any of the local hostelries. I advise you to do the same."

Sybil said, "What project? When was this planned?"

"He said he had told Judith."

Judith frowned; she did remember something vague about a project. She said, "There were so many of us in the sitting room all talking at once. Did he mention it then? My head was aching — I didn't hear him."

"We are to meet him at the Dove Inn. Eleven o'clock. I asked about walking boots but he said trainers would do. I'm going to ask Mrs Mann for some cheese. Excuse me, ladies."

He left them and Sybil said, "Do you mind, Judith? I don't want to go if you don't. It could be awkward."

Judith did not know whether she minded or not, but she did not want to spend the day with the two married couples. And neither did she want Sybil to get too close to Hausmann. She couldn't tell Sybil that Hausmann knew she was Esmée without explaining how she, Judith, hadn't betrayed Sybil's confidence — and there wasn't time to do that here and now. Also, after yesterday's talks she realized that her schoolgirl dream of bringing Hausmann and Sybil together after over forty years was out of the question, even without the strong suspicion she now had that Hausmann was gay.

She said, "Yes. Yes, I can see it could be difficult." Heaven knew how she could keep the two of them apart, but at least she could make an effort.

Sybil looked suddenly animated. "This could be fun," she whispered. "When we were kids Robert used to organize what he called 'expeditions'. We explored all the back alleys in the city one summer. And we swam at Barry Island on Guy Fawkes Night. Perhaps he has renamed his expeditions and they have become projects!" She laughed. Even tendrils of her hair were curling around her face. Robert was right: she was beautiful.

Judith laughed too. "Well then . . . bring on the projects!"

110

They began to wrap their breakfast rolls in napkins; Judith pocketed some apples, Sybil scurried into the sitting room and returned with one of the many boxes of dark mint chocolates that Bart obviously kept for evenings. They felt and acted like naughty schoolgirls, and Sven hurried over with his roll and some hard-boiled eggs. "Enjoy!" he said, in imitation of Bart. And then, as Nathaniel returned he shook his hand and said, "Many thanks. You are most kind."

Nathaniel blushed slightly. He waited until Sven was out of earshot and then said to Judith, "I learned to be extra tactful when I was a kid because of Robert!"

It took half an hour to walk to the Dove Inn, and when they arrived Hausmann was at the bar, one hand protectively around a glass of cider, the other tracing a route on an open map.

He frowned at Nathaniel in greeting.

"You're late."

"Five minutes, old man! We're not going to fall out over five minutes!"

"Not easy to fall out with you, Nat." Robert's face split into a grin. Judith was amazed; she had Robert Hausmann classified as a man who did not suffer fools gladly. He turned to Sybil. "Are you up to a hike of perhaps five miles — maybe more?"

"Yes," she said immediately. "And so is Judith. We climbed the face of the Eiger yesterday."

He grinned again; he was obviously used to this reaction. Nathaniel glanced at Judith, slightly surprised, but she nodded confirmation. She wanted to go along with this threesome; she imagined telling Jack about it afterwards: the complicated dynamics of their relationships, and the fact that Robert Hausmann knew that Sybil had come looking for her past, but that she had no inkling that he knew this. And Nathaniel Jones, open as a book, was reacquainting himself with his childhood friend but had no idea that Sybil was Esmée Gould. Judith smiled slightly; it was like a childhood game of hide-and-seek and Jack would appreciate that.

She stopped her thoughts there with a jolt. Jack . . . Jack Freeman . . . had flown the nest and gone. There was still the enormous relief at being certain Jack was alive and in Australia, but after that . . . what? Would he come home to the terrifyingly anonymous other woman? Or was she out there? Had he met her on his last trip to see the boys? She shivered at the thought. Of course, that was it. Jack had had no time to conduct any kind of clandestine affair at home, but when he had gone over to Australia he had had all the time in the world.

Hausmann was talking again, expounding a theory.

"You see, Nat, Esmée always wanted to rewrite the bloody book — don't you remember?"

"What book was that?"

"Oh, for Pete's sake — where are we at the moment — what was Esmée's favourite book of all time? *Lorna Doone*, of course. Her father had a friend with a boat, and they used to come over from Cardiff and explore this area, and Esmée used to come back and say that everyone had got it wrong and she had her own version. Don't you remember any of this?"

Nat was frowning, concentrating. "I do remember her saying that the water slide was somewhere else — she'd found it with her dad — old Goalposts — but then he had an imagination longer than the Blackwall Tunnel —"

"Yes, but his stories and games were always based on something firm. That version of hopscotch, for instance: it was our own hopping and skipping, but his Hungarian chant gave it a special meaning. Anyway, when Bart and Irena leased the castle I was roped in for some hard labour, and when I got time off I explored. Nothing else to do. I had my own project, of course. Mapped all the pubs in the area; look, I've marked each one with a cross. Right over to the west side of the moor — dropping down to the cider orchards — there's a little place right there." He stabbed at the map. "Where they brew their own cider, and you can sit in the front room and sample it. Don't think they've got a licence, but no one's going to let the cat out of the bag unless they're blind drunk, which is, of course, a very real risk."

"Bit like smuggling," Nathaniel put in.

"Suppose so. Anyway, somewhere on one of my expeditions, I came across a river. Usual Exmoor sort of river, wide and shallow and crystal clear. I called it the Gould. After Gould the Post." He did not look at Sybil. "In memory of him, if you like."

"I like," said Nathaniel. "He was a lovely man."

Judith felt a pang; it was as if Hausmann was creating a small world. A world that had gone. She looked along

113

the bar past the map and saw that Sybil was staring at Nathaniel Jones, as if willing him into that world.

"Good. Because this project is called 'the Gould Project', and you are a very important part of it."

Nathaniel looked surprised. "Me?" He snorted a laugh. "I was always odd man out, Robert. And you know it."

"You were the third man, yes. But you were never on the outside. You were always in the middle."

"That's rubbish." Nathaniel laughed again, without regret. "I was the hanger-on. Once Esmée left — you and me — we drifted apart. You went to art college, then on to London. And I did business studies at Cardiff Tech and opened a print workshop."

"You came to my first exhibition. You sent Christmas cards."

"You never returned them."

"No point. I was the outsider." Hausmann grinned, delighted to have come full circle in their verbal volley. "Now, drink up, everybody. The mysterious Esmée Gould always said that she and her dad had discovered the original water slide. I am almost certain that the two of them were talking about my river. The Gould river. The river of gold. Call it what you will. I've plotted it on this map, and we are off to find it this very day, this very hour." He had folded the map as he spoke, and now waved it above his head like a flag. "And we are going to climb it, maybe to its source. The top of Exmoor! The watershed for all the moor rivers, some draining past us now and into the sea of Lundy,

114

some the other side, where they fill the valley with cider!"

Judith started to laugh, remembering the glowering silent man of two nights ago as he had struggled with the heavy front door and been confronted by a crazy woman in the thinnest of nightdresses, who could have been the result of a steady night's drinking at the Dove Inn.

They looked at her as she tried to control the unstoppable giggles which were threatening to escalate into hysteria. Then Hausmann pocketed the map and put a bracing arm around her shoulders.

"Come on, old girl! It's only a game. What's that old saying —?"

"Play the game!" she spluttered.

"That's it. Just like you did when you were a kid — yes?"

"Yes, I know." Suddenly it was as if the whole world tilted slightly; she thought she was going to fall flat on her face. She pulled away from Hausmann and took a huge breath. "But since then my dad has died, and Mum and I — we had to manage — and then my sons went away, and Mum was ill, and she died, and I had a friend, Naomi, and she was killed in a car accident . . . and then two months ago, Jack —" Hausmann grabbed her before she fell.

He said quietly, "Play the game, Judith. Just play the game."

Sybil was on her other side with a handful of tissues. She took them, mopped vigorously and pulled herself upright and away from Hausmann.

Nathaniel was in front of her, looking horrified. "I had no idea — no idea, Judith — so sorry —"

She shook her head. "Why would you? I'm all right. Honestly."

Nathaniel flapped his hands. "Let's go somewhere we can get a nice meal — sit down and talk things through —"

Sybil took the wodge of tissues and dabbed at Judith's chin. "Wouldn't it be better if —"

Hausmann interrupted brusquely. "She needs her mind taken up. We should go on as planned."

Nathaniel snapped at him. "Perhaps Judith would like to have a say here?"

Hausmann stared at him, shocked. Judith said quickly, "It just came up and sort of hit me . . . out of the blue. I'm OK. Honestly. I'm glad we're doing this. And I'd like to be part of the expedition. The fourth man. Woman. Person, I should say." She tried to produce a viable smile.

Hausmann said, "I vote you in."

And Sybil suddenly hugged her arm. "Me, too."

Hausmann took over again. It was as if there had been no outburst from Judith. He picked up the map, pointed it at the door and said, "Here's to the river of gold. And all who sail in her!"

He held the door wide and they went through it, Sybil, then Judith, then Nathaniel. Hausmann followed and muttered something, and Nathaniel said aggressively, "What was that?"

"I simply said we were a motley crew."

"Oh. Right. Yes. I suppose we are." Nathaniel caught up with the two women and took Judith's arm protectively.

Hausmann closed the door behind him and muttered something else. It was "Bloody fool!" But Nathaniel did not hear him.

CHAPTER
EIGHT

When Judith crawled into bed that night, she was so tired she hardly knew whether the project had been successful or not. She could not decide what had been its goal. Even if it had been multi-goaled she doubted whether it had achieved anything at all. Except that they had all actually got back alive. Yes, that was something to achieve in the circumstances. There had been a couple of times on their journey to nowhere — which was how Nathaniel had scathingly described it — when she had wondered whether they should call in an air ambulance, or whatever was sent out to rescue people who were lost on Exmoor in the fog.

It was the fog that had made the map and its red arrows directing them to the river of gold so completely useless. It made no mention of any landmarks, though when they came upon the lichen-covered milestone standing in one of the angles of cross tracks in the heather, Hausmann swore he had seen it before and it meant they took the right side of the cross as a fingerpost. So far as Judith's directional instincts could tell, the track wound in enormous S shapes through heather that turned into furze; and two miles of track probably covered one mile as the crows flew.

She smiled into the pillow as she ran the day's events through her head like a film. As it had happened, yes, it had been a muddle from start to finish. But then, in retrospect it began to make sense. It began to be . . . reassuring. Somehow. She curled herself into a foetal position: she was clean at last, she was warm, she was well-fed. And, most importantly, she had friends. The kind of friends you persevered with even when you didn't like them much. Her smile turned into a slight frown. What on earth did that mean, exactly?

She rewound her memories and started again: on that footpath that was already muddy in the wet fog that pressed down on the moor and turned to rain soon after midday.

Sybil was the first casualty. The furze was not just thorny, it was lethally thorny, and one of the most lethal of the thorns pierced the canvas of her upmarket trainer and the cashmere sock beneath, and went into her second toe. She let out a gasp of pain before she could stop herself, and Nathaniel was on to it immediately.

He removed the thorn and produced a tin of Vaseline.

"I thought it might help with blisters," he said, rubbing it into Sybil's toe. He frowned, stopped rubbing, then started again. "It's all we've got, and it might ease the pain." He looked up at Hausmann. "Perhaps we should turn back, old man. We weren't reckoning on this weather — we've still got tomorrow, after all."

Hausmann said resignedly, "Up to you, Sybil."

"Well, we might as well go on, surely? We must be nearly there."

"OK." He spoke as if it were her decision, her responsibility, and immediately tramped on and was out of sight. Nathaniel replaced Sybil's shoe and tied the lace.

She stood up, laughing. "You're very neat-fingered, Nathaniel. Anyone would think you've done that sort of thing before."

Nathaniel laughed too, but uncomfortably. Judith wondered whether Hausmann and Sybil had always teased — almost baited — Nathaniel like this. But Hausmann was presumably some way ahead of them by now, and he actually had the map. She strode her way through the shoulder-high furze and almost crashed into him.

"Eavesdropping, Mr Hausmann?" she asked in a saccharine voice.

"Absolutely, Mrs Jack," he came back. "Interesting. Nat was always slow, but he got there in the end."

"In that case, he should go first. You've just got us lost, haven't you?"

"Could be." He began to walk ahead of her, until he judged they were well out of earshot of the other two. "Yes, could be that is one of the objects of the exercise."

She stopped dead in her tracks. "Oh no. Oh my God, Hausmann. We must have done over three miles from the pub, so now we have to go three miles back — and Sybil has a bad foot. What's the *matter* with you?"

"It's an experiment. That's all. Breaking points. That sort of thing."

"Mine was first?"

"I wasn't including you in the agenda. I'm sorry about that. Probably did you good, however. You and Jack coming through all that stuff."

"Except that Jack didn't, did he?"

He sounded impatient suddenly. "For God's sake, Jude — I told you he kept talking about you. All bloody night."

"So you did." She did not remind him that the description Jack had given had not sounded very like her.

"So . . ." The path widened and she caught up with him. "Who's next in this great experiment? Sybil has passed the test of pain rather well, hasn't she?"

"I didn't have her on my list, either. No, it's Nathaniel Jones who needs to show his true colours."

She stopped dead again. "What? Nathaniel? What has he done to upset you, Hausmann? Called Mr Gould names when he was a child? Made money from something as boring as a print shop when you can barely survive with your wonderful gift? Oh — or did he manage to grab a kiss from Esmée back in the seventies?"

He was astonished again. "Do you think I'm on some kind of revenge thing? Good God, Jude! I'm trying to put things right; punishment does not enter into it! Now if it was my sister-in-law you might be on the right track. But why should I punish Nattie Jones for kissing little Esmée Gould behind the school? And how did you know about that, anyway?"

She gave up. The others were close behind, she could hear Sybil reassuring Nathaniel that she was quite all right, and there was nothing to worry about. And he was saying, "D'you know I'm having a déjà vu moment — it's as if all this has happened before. Do you ever feel like that, Sybil? It is OK to call you Sybil, isn't it?"

"Of course it is. And yes, I do. Often. That's why I came on this weekend to Castle Dove."

"I thought it was to see Robert's work."

"Well, yes, of course. But I've never lost touch with Robert's work. I wanted more than that."

"Everyone wants to meet him, of course. Are you disappointed?"

"No, not a bit. I love him."

"Ah."

"It's all right. I'm not about to make a fool of myself."

Hausmann turned and, walking backwards, called out, "What would be so wrong about that? To make a fool of oneself is to become completely vulnerable — to surrender to humility —"

He had got that far when his heel caught in a root, his other foot slipped in the mud, and he fell heavily on to his back. The air was knocked out of him with a sound like the trumpeting of an elephant, and then he delivered himself of a string of oaths, some of which might have been in Hebrew.

They gathered around him. Nathaniel got behind him and lifted his shoulders and propped him against

122

his own knees. He panted, "I don't know whether I should do this, old man. If you've injured your back —"

"Of course I haven't injured my bloody back, the ground is like a bloody sponge! Just let me get my breath!"

"For God's sake . . ." Sybil was kneeling in front of him and could see his face. "It's obvious you're in pain. Has anyone brought a mobile phone?"

Nobody had. Nathaniel said, "An air ambulance couldn't do a thing in this weather, and if Robert really is all right we can follow our own tracks back to the Dove Inn."

"What? And give up on the project? Are you insane? We've got this far, and I'm damned if I'll let you give up now!" Hausmann struggled away from Nathaniel's support, rolled on to his knees and, gasping, got to his feet. He straightened, cursing loudly now and then, and lifted his arms high. Mud dripped from his shoulders. "See?" None of them said a word. "Listen. I know what I'm doing. We're in that triangle of land between Dulverton . . ." He jabbed a mud-covered hand ahead of them, ". . . the Ridds' farm, and the Devon border. We're still going uphill, so we're this side of the watershed. We should hear the rushing of the Gould river fairly soon."

There was a silence; this was his project, no one wanted to resist him.

Judith said, "Let's give ourselves another half an hour. How does that sound? If we haven't come upon a stream — any stream — by then, we should turn back." She pushed up the sleeve of her jacket and peered at her watch. "It's just before one o'clock. We've been walking for nearly two hours. We're all covered in mud. And the weather is getting worse." She looked round.

Nathaniel said, "Well done, Judith — a generous suggestion." He made a rueful face at Hausmann. "Sorry, old man. I'd go along with that if you hadn't had that fall. But let's face it, John Ridd's water slide has been mapped and explored ever since *Lorna Doone* was in the top ten reading lists in the mid eighteen hundreds. We're on a wild goose chase —"

Hausmann said, suddenly angry, "Isn't that another name for a project, Nattie? I seem to remember you calling all my expeditions wild goose chases!"

He turned to Sybil. "Come on. You've got the deciding vote here, Esmée. You always had the deciding vote. Go along with Jude's suggestion, or turn back now?"

There was another silence, very tense. Nathaniel stared through the fog at Sybil and she stared at Hausmann. Judith discovered she was holding her breath.

Nathaniel croaked. "Esmée? What are you talking about, Robert? For God's sake, man! Are you saying Sybil Jessup is Esmée Gould? Our Esmée Gould?"

Sybil turned and faced him. "I was, Nattie. I'm not any more. I'm Sybil Jessup, and I came on this trip to see the retrospective. That's all. To find you and Robert here — it was a shock. But you didn't recognize me, and if Robert guessed who I was all along, then he did not *want* to know me, so I left it at that."

Hausmann barked a laugh and she glanced at him and shrugged.

"All right. I have the casting vote. I think we need to go on for half an hour, just as Judith has suggested. It depends on you, Robert. Let's see how it goes, shall we?"

Nathaniel said nothing. He stood where he was and made no attempt to help Hausmann. Sybil took one of Hausmann's arms and Judith took the other. Hausmann made an enormous effort to stride ahead of them, but after the first few steps it was obvious that was not going to happen. Judith held the elbow of his right arm, and after the first stagger he cursed impatiently and put his arm across her shoulders, using her as a crutch. She was exactly the right height. They went on together. Hausmann's breathing was laboured and loud, but behind that Judith realized that Sybil had dropped back to Nathaniel. She heard him say something about keeping him in the dark, then Sybil replied in an apologetic voice and Nathaniel answered vigorously that it was, after all, a deception. Sybil said crisply, "I had no intention of deceiving you. I was here on an errand of self-preservation, new beginnings, whatever you like to call it."

He said quietly, "Nothing has changed then, has it?" She was silent.

Hausmann said in a low voice, "He's right there. She was always a selfish, spoiled brat."

Judith closed her eyes as he levered himself over another intrusive furze branch; he was no mean weight.

The picture she had had of the three children in Cardiff was being torn to pieces.

She gasped, "Hausmann, can we pause a moment?" He stopped abruptly and she nearly fell. "If you could shorten your steps — match them to mine — I think we would do better."

"No need. I can hear water, Mrs Jack. Listen."

She heard the water. Then above that came Sybil's furious voice. "I *know* Robert is domineering and totally unreasonable! I have always known that! But Moss was domineering, too! Haven't you heard that there are some women who actually fall in love with those sorts of men?"

"Then they are fools. Judith is grieving for a husband who was a partner, who looked after her —"

"And who stalked my husband through a series of lampoons. D'you know, he cried over that! Yes, actually cried, Nattie! Rather like you did when Robert and I ganged up on you! You didn't like being called names — Moss didn't like it. It's ironic that Jack Freeman and Moss Jessup must have died at the same time! And Judith is no saint, either. She told Robert I was Esmée when she'd promised not to."

"No, I didn't," Judith called out. "He recognized you."

Hausmann bellowed back, "Shut up, you lot! We're there! Come here, Esmée — tell me if this is the river you and your old Goalpost found. And just why you always insisted it was John Ridd's river! Come on, stop that stupid bickering — the past is the past. Let's see if it was as important as we imagine! OK?"

126

There was another silence and they all heard the stream, running downhill, sliding over pebbles, pulling at the weeds on the banks.

Sybil said quietly, "How can I tell? Every stream and river has its own voice, but I need to see it to be sure, and in this fog —"

"Did you climb it? Of course you did! We'll have to climb it."

Nathaniel said flatly, "Well, I am going back. Now."

Judith exploded, "Don't be ridiculous, Hausmann! It's dangerous — remember how hard it was for John Ridd, and he was the biggest man on Exmoor. And younger than any of us!"

"He was a child when he did it first —"

Sybil said in a tired voice, "I think we've had enough, don't you, Robert?"

He said, "I'll do it alone, then. I know what to look for. The little grotto at the top where Lorna had her secret room . . ." He was already on the move, edging carefully over the tufts of heather. They followed him, Nathaniel telling him not to act like a romantic idiot, and Judith grimly silent, angry with herself for being here in the first place.

Sybil said warningly, "It's very shallow, Robert. Hardly any banks."

Hausmann discovered how right she was. He stood ankle-deep in the typical Exmoor stream, turning his face towards them — white in the grey fog — grinning happily. "Come on, you laggards! We're wet and muddy enough already to make poor old Irena foam at the mouth! Let's give her the full works! Forget all that has happened, this is a bonding exercise of the highest order. Come on in, the water's fine!"

Nobody moved. Judith said in a low voice, "Sybil, he's doing all this for you; you'll have to go. Nathaniel and I will wait here."

Nathaniel moved down the shallow bank. "I'll go with him. You two had better do some exercises — running on the spot — something. To keep warm."

But Sybil was moving too. "According to Judith I have to go." She splashed noisily into the water, bumping into Nathaniel as she passed him. He flung up his hands and gave a despairing shout, and would have landed face-first in the stream if Hausmann had not grabbed his arm and swung him round. They clung together, finding their balance, and then, unexpectedly, they began to laugh.

Judith watched them from the shore. Though they were less than two yards from her they were blurred and indistinct in the wet fog, and when Sybil joined them and was scooped into their embrace, they became one mass. And they all stood there, the clear water washing their calves, and the sound of their laughter was muffled yet loud at the same time. And in that moment, she understood them. It was so like the sudden laughter she and Jack had shared. It was a gift. A recognition that they themselves were absurd, and there was nothing to do about it except laugh. The moment became so poignant she thought Jack might materialize at her side, and she looked upstream at the wall of fog; willing him to be there, willing him to send a sign that he was still around.

Hausmann shouted, "Come on, Mrs Jack! You can't stand there all day!"

She splashed into the water. And they began to climb.

Luckily, Nathaniel had tied his scarf to a bending alder before they had left, otherwise they would never have found their old route when they returned. The project — now most definitely an expedition — took them over as they scrambled through the water, often on all fours. Luckily it had been a dry summer and the water never came higher than their knees, but there were two miniature waterfalls where Hausmann — already soaked — hauled himself up with the help of protruding rocks and convenient branches, and then leaned down to haul Nathaniel beside him, and then the two of them swung Sybil and Judith over the lip. Judith had to admit that once she had given herself over to the stream, the sheer hard work drove everything else from her mind; and when they reached some kind of platform and found they were coming out of the fog, she shared the triumph of the other three.

Nathaniel panted, "We should do this again — when there's no fog and we can see the view." He was unwrapping their improvised picnic and handing around the rolls and hard-boiled eggs.

"It must be stupendous!" Sybil agreed, wiping the moisture from her face with a bundle of soggy tissues. "We could probably sketch from here, Judith. Like we did at the top of the Lyn."

Hausmann laughed. "Your sketchbooks might get a bit damp." He accepted a cold sausage and bit into it with relish.

"There's bound to be a footpath, Robert."

Nathaniel passed around the cheese, then bent over, squeezing water from the bottom of his jeans. "Don't think so. Let's face it, there are loads of these streams draining off the top of the moor. This is nothing like John Ridd's. I think we've got to admit that the official water slide is the right one."

Sybil said stubbornly, "You can't be sure, Nattie."

He spread his hands. "Look, we're above the fog and there's no sign of a waterfall or a grotto. Remember Lorna had her secret room in the rock face? Also, I hate to tell you this, but only John Ridd, the strongest teenager on Exmoor, could climb that particular water slide. We're all hovering around middle age, we're out of condition, yet we managed this one."

Hausmann said, "That's not the point. Is this the Gould river? Is this the river you and your father adopted, Esmée?"

Sybil's face was alight. "I think it is! I'm coming back here tomorrow if the weather is fine. I'm sure this is the one!"

Judith said, "We go home tomorrow. The weekend is over."

"Not till five o'clock! We can do it. Say you will! We can bring our sketchbooks."

Hausmann said, "Judith has another engagement tomorrow, Esmée. You'll have to make do with Nathaniel." He stepped gingerly into the water. "Come

130

on. We've got a couple of hours' walking ahead of us, and it's almost three o'clock. We don't need any search parties!"

It was more difficult going down than coming up. By the time they spotted Nathaniel's scarf they were soaked not only by their many falls but by the rain which developed from the fog.

The landlord of the Dove Inn eyed them suspiciously. "Been trying to re-enact some of the witch trials, 'ave 'ee? You know Judge Jeffreys was round these parts not all that long ago!"

"Nearly four hundred years back," Hausmann growled. "And what has happened to the lights in here?"

"Dun't need 'em yet, my dear. Clocks dun't go back for another month. Which is just as well 'cos there's been one of they dratted power cuts most of the day — we 'ad to get wood for the range and keep the kettles and saucepans going on the hob. Dry your daps in the ovens, if you like."

Hausmann groaned. "That will please Irena — dinner will be late. Better get a move on; she'll want me to light the fires."

"Bart's got Calor gas stored in the orangery," Nathaniel put in. "He was always one for providing for the future."

Hausmann groaned again, louder this time. For some reason Judith giggled. They tramped the mile back to the coast and crossed the causeway without difficulty. The door was as stubborn as ever, the foyer lit by the colours of the window and some oil lamps placed here and there. It was bitterly cold, and no one was about.

They hesitated, suddenly at a loose end. "What now?" asked Sybil.

Hausmann leaned on the counter. "They've gone to bed — Irena and Bart — I bet you they've gone to bed!"

Nathaniel grinned. "Can't imagine it, somehow. What about the others?"

"They won't be back yet. Probably eating at Ilfracombe or something." Sybil looked around. "I don't want to go to my room. It's pretty bleak down here, but better than being alone. Where did you say the calor gas was, Nattie? Can we get it and fix it up somehow?"

"Why not? I don't quite know where the orangery is —"

Hausmann said, "I do. There's a walkway around the base of the castle. The orangery was built later — it faces southwest, so catches all the sun. It will be a devil trundling gas cylinders along there in the dark."

"I think we might be able to get at it from inside." Judith was warming her hands at one of the oil lamps. "I did a lot of exploring on our first morning — d'you want to have a look? I can show you."

Strangely, she felt like Sybil; she did not relish her own company, especially if there might be no hot water in the bathroom. She picked up the lantern and made her way confidently to the third door on the other side of the lift and the others followed her very willingly. If it had been bonding Hausmann was aiming for, he had succeeded; they were definitely a group by this time. Judith no longer felt outside it.

The passageway past the rooms beneath her own was lit only by the windows, and by this time seemed very dark indeed, but it was straightforward enough and she reached the corner and found the door in the panelling which led into the library — if that was what it was. Nathaniel was at her elbow, the other two close behind. Hausmann was nagging Sybil to admit this was the best expedition yet, and she was laughing reluctantly and eventually admitted he was right.

The cavernous depths of the library silenced them all. The light from the lanterns did not penetrate very far, and reflected back from the windows, screening any sense of the outdoors beyond.

Judith stopped by the spiral staircase. "This is where I climbed up to the Long Gallery, and halfway up I could see the roof of the orangery — so it must be built on a lower level. If we go to the end of the library there should be a door into the next angle of the castle and . . . another staircase leading down."

Hausmann, already ahead, confirmed there was a door. "I think the damned thing is locked . . . hang on . . . let's put the lantern down . . . no, it's OK . . . there's a whacking great key here, but it's not locked. God, it's heavy! Sorry, I'm pushing instead of pulling!" They joined him and watched as the door swung majestically inwards without a sound. "Well oiled, thank goodness. It's as heavy as the entry door. I must remember to oil those hinges."

He picked up his lantern and held it high. Another passage turned to the right, following the angle of the castle, but to the left a much narrower opening framed a staircase. A glimmer of light from below illuminated a layer of dust.

Hausmann said, "Well, obviously Bart brought the gas bottles this way — footprints all over the place. But we've still got to lug them back up —"

Sybil made a hushing sound. "There's someone down there. Now."

They all paused; the sound of the sea clawing on the pebbles as it came towards the land, and the usual creaking from the very fabric of the castle, mingled with the silence rather than interrupted it.

Sybil spoke again, a thread of a voice. "The light, that's lantern light. See how it flickers."

They waited for Hausmann to state the obvious: that Bart and Irena were ahead of them and were already sorting out the bottles. But Hausmann said nothing.

Nathaniel whispered, "Is it one of the cleaning staff?"

They formed themselves into a huddle at the top of the narrow staircase, the better to hear each other. Hausmann said, "No voices. So just one person?"

Nathaniel shook his head. "Bart wouldn't send someone off along these corridors, unless he came himself."

Sybil said, suddenly relaxed, "Of course. It must be Bart. He's come to suss out the gas bottles, just as we are!" She started down the stairs; her lantern illuminated a half-landing, and she turned to go on down. And then stopped abruptly.

134

Suddenly Judith knew. She crept past the others, finger to lips, and joined Sybil. There was no need for their lanterns, no need to be silent. The orangery was lit by about thirty candles, none of them flickering in errant draughts: the two doors — one leading to a railed walkway outside, the other to the staircase — were obviously well-sealed. The couple inside the glass bubble could see and hear nothing outside it. They were dancing.

The orangery contained no orange trees; it was furnished like most modern conservatories with cane furniture well-upholstered with squashy cushions. Bamboo tables and large pot plants were here and there, and on one of the tables was an old-fashioned gramophone, obviously wound and playing a slow waltz. The couple were joined as one; their feet in perfect unison. He was dressed in tails and a white tie, his suit a pale grey, his hair slicked back in imitation of Fred Astaire. And the woman wore a satin dress cut on the cross and wrapping her like a glove. They held their elbows at a perfect level, her head tilted sideways so that they were cheek to cheek. They both wore gloves.

Nathaniel and Hausmann crowded behind on the stairs. They were all silently amazed, gazing fascinated at the scene below them. The record came to an end and the man kissed the woman and then turned and went to the gramophone, removed the playing arm, and lifted a switch. She wandered dreamily to a pile of records on another table, chose one and took it to him. He wound vigorously.

This time it seemed to be a slow foxtrot; they took long steps, her body arched to fit his, he kissing the length of her neck, his lips wandering down to the deep V-neck of the dress. Judith felt her eyes fill with tears. The couple straightened and stood together, still in their dance position, then the man dropped his partner's hands, and with his gloved hands he slipped her dress from her shoulders and let it slide to the mosaic-tiled floor. She was wearing nothing beneath the dress.

Judith turned and went back up the stairs, picked up her lantern and pushed at the gallery door until it silently opened. She had reached the spiral staircase when the others came through; she thought she might scream at them if anyone so much as tittered, but no one did. They made their way down the stairs to the library, through the door in the opposite wall, and turned left past the rank of bedroom doors. No one spoke a word.

The foyer was still empty, still cold and unfriendly.

Sybil placed her lantern carefully and said, "Oh dear. What are we going to do?"

Hausmann said, "I'm going to raid the drinks and go to my room. There will be quite enough hot water in the tanks to provide baths for all the rooms. I suggest we have hot baths, stiff drinks and hope to God the power comes on in time for Irena to rustle up some food. Otherwise it will be sandwiches and long faces. Unless the Markhams decide to join us."

It was the first time they had mentioned the dancers in the orangery and Sybil drew an audible breath of relief.

"It was them, wasn't it?"

Nathaniel nodded and Hausmann said vigorously, "Of course it was them — I overheard the Swedish chap saying something cringe-making about them doing something in every room in the castle!"

Sybil said, "It was so amazing . . . so . . . so . . . bizarre."

Judith risked blubbing all over the place; anyway it was too dark for anyone to see. "It was wonderful. It was . . . rather like our expedition. Recreating something very special. Hallowed. In some way actually hallowed."

Nathaniel said slowly, "Yes, you're right. They had put time and trouble into creating . . . recreating . . . something."

Hausmann barked his laugh. "Except that they are not soaking wet and muddy!"

Judith refused to laugh with the others. She said, "That was wonderful, too."

At that moment all the lights came on in the foyer and in the two rooms beyond. The kitchen behind them was staggeringly bright with its fluorescent strips flickering into life. The radiators began to crackle.

Sybil spread her hands. "Resurrection!" she cried.

They all made for the sitting room. Hausmann switched on the fire and drew the sofa close, Sybil went round checking the radiators and finding sherry glasses. Then she gathered their outdoor things and took them into the downstairs cloakroom. In spite of Hausmann's disgusted face, Judith poured four sherries and took hers close to the fire. They raised their glasses and then hesitated. It was Sybil who said, "To this weekend, which has been pretty amazing. On the whole."

They all repeated the words obediently, drank and then laughed together.

"What about that green stuff Nattie hung on to? It gave way almost immediately!" Sybil remembered through her helpless laughter. "That was the first full immersion baptism! Dad would have loved that!"

"I managed to baptize myself in mud," Hausmann reminded her. "Look, it's still under my fingernails!"

"The green stuff was cress. Don't you remember how John Ridd loved to pick the watercress?"

"All that iron. No wonder he was so strong."

"Do we know where the farm was, actually was?"

"Plovers' Barrow? No. Not far from Porlock; remember John rode there to buy lead shot."

"He was a lovely man." Judith was curled very small into a corner of the sofa. "He loved people; most of them, anyway. His mother and sisters and cousins as well as Lorna Doone." She knew that was how Jack was; he always said he had to understand his caricatures before he could draw them. Understanding was surely a way of loving?

There was a rattle from the foyer, and Irena wheeled a trolley into the sitting room. She beamed at them with untypical approval. "My goodness, you sorted yourselves out quickly! I've brought some hot toddies. Thought you would be perished out on the moor in that fog and then rain." She took the sherry glasses and replaced them with glass tankards, steaming, packed with lemon and orange slices. "Plenty more in the jug."

138

She went to the windows. "The rain has at last got rid of the fog. You can see the tide coming in. Look at the phosphorescence; isn't that wonderful?"

Hausmann joined her and actually gave her a bear hug. "Everything is pretty wonderful if you've got the right specs on, Sis. How are you going to manage supper tonight? We don't mind sandwiches. In fact, I'll help you make them!"

She looked at him, astonished. "We've got the Calor gas, Robert, have you forgotten? I've had an enormous casserole in the oven all afternoon, and there's bread and butter pudding for the last course." She almost smiled at his lip-smacking approval but then said, bewildered, "You've never called me 'Sis' before."

"No, I haven't, have I? I must do so in future. I know you're a marvellous cook and a marvellous manager, and Jude tells me you've got a kind heart. What more do I need in a sister?"

"Someone to keep you on the straight and narrow!" she came back. But she was smiling. "Dinner in an hour. The Olsens should be back by then. The Markhams are having theirs in their room."

Sybil said innocently, "Are they not well?"

Irena looked at her significantly. "Hopefully they are very well." She lowered herself over the two women on the sofa and spoke confidentially. "It's her fertile weekend. They want a baby. They came to look at the castle five or six weeks ago. Thought it would be ideal: make it romantic instead of . . . well, medical." She smiled widely. "If it happens, they're going to call the baby 'Dove'."

Sybil almost choked on her toddy. "Oh my God!"

Nathaniel said, "What was that? I didn't hear."

All three women seized cushions and threw them, not very accurately.

In the cocoon of her bed, Judith heard something and tried to rouse herself sufficiently to identify it. But she had gone too far into sleep. She knew that the promised casserole had been delicious. She knew that she had somehow acquired three rather odd — and definitely flawed — friends. She recalled with great pleasure the sight of Stanley and Jennifer Markham dancing in the orangery by candlelight. And now she knew the reason for that, and it warmed her heart.

A key rattled in the lock, but her own key blocked it from inside. She slept.

CHAPTER
NINE

Judith woke to a crash of thunder that seemed to start in one of the towers and rush down to the causeway. She lay still, enjoying the contrast between the weather and the sort of languor that often followed a long night's sleep. Rain was hurling itself at her window, and a draught was moving the heavy velvet curtain. She drew herself up on to the pillows and stretched her arms. A flash of lightning heralded a response of thunder. She turned down her mouth; it seemed as if they were meant to be housebound until the five o'clock departure. What a pity the weekend had to end like that. The castle was big enough, heaven knew, but she had been curious about Hausmann's plans for her; he had been most insistent that Sybil and Nathaniel should go off by themselves while he took Judith somewhere else. He called her "Jude" regularly now, but he had been a little more formal then, and she had detected a slight hesitation as he spoke the second syllable. It was later that she realized he lisped when he said "Esmée" and "Sybil". He was a man of many contradictions, but she had also noticed that his honesty — sometimes brutal — encouraged her to be just as honest and almost as brutal.

She grinned at the thought, and the lightning flashed again; she drew the duvet to her chin before the thunder followed. She had always loved thunderstorms. They brought out character traits, just as Hausmann did. She was at ease with the weather, and she was at ease with him. She grinned and eyed the tea-making facilities, then decided she was too happily relaxed to make the effort. She wriggled down a little and closed her eyes and wondered whether she would ever see any of these people again. Perhaps Sybil might get in touch? Judith decided she would make the first move; she could suggest that they have another go at climbing the river of gold. If it was a good spring it could happen next April. Seven months away; winter months, too. She shivered. What on earth was going to happen about Jack? How could she bear to let him go to someone else? It was unimaginable, and she spent a few hectic minutes going over, yet again, exactly what he had said about another woman. Of course those two words were enough. Another woman.

She felt her body begin to bunch, and tried to force it back into that complete relaxation. If only he hadn't said those two words it would have been so much easier. She need not have seen his departure as desertion; it might have been some kind of breakdown. He had never looked at anyone else, and they still had what he called "magic moments"; not so many, true, but they happened. Just like that first time in the lecture room when they had been physically drawn together. She tried to remember the last time that had happened. Was it before or after Naomi's death? It was

142

after. When Judith was still stunned and disbelieving that life could be so suddenly and easily snuffed out, and Jack had said, "It was an accident — the wrong place at the wrong time — there's no way anyone can avoid such a cruel trick as that."

She had looked at him and seen his hands reach out, and automatically she had moved to him and put her hands in his. But there had been no laughter. She had hung on to his hands, put her head on his shoulder and wept uncontrollably.

She realized now that already, at that time, he had been planning to leave her. He stayed until she appeared to have accepted the loss of her friend, and then . . . at the beginning of July . . . he had gone to Perth. He had met Robert Hausmann. And then what? Had he gone to someone else?

There was a knock on the door and she scrambled out of bed, clutched her dressing gown and unlocked.

"Come on in, Mrs Mann." She got back into the bed; it was reassuringly warm, like a nest. Like a den.

"It's me."

Sybil came in tentatively; she was wearing an enormous dressing gown and looked rather aristocratic.

"No electricity again; the lightning is to blame this time." She stood at the end of the bed. "Irena is using the gas. I met her as I came away from the bathroom. She's in a bit of a state."

Judith was surprised. "I thought she took it all so well yesterday."

"Not about the power failure. About our chaps. They left a note. They've gone to Lundy."

"Nathaniel and Hausmann — our chaps?"

"Well, we seem to be pretty divided down the middle. Even Martin Morris is with the famous four!" Sybil tugged at the tie belt on her dressing gown. "This damned thing won't stay across. I should use my own but . . . oh God, I'm so sentimental about Moss's clothes. I wear his sweaters all the time."

Judith thought she might do the same. Or perhaps not. Probably Jack would eventually take all his clothes. Was that why he — or someone else — had phoned through on Friday night? Was she going to go home and find the house empty of all Jack's things?

She swallowed fiercely. "Why have they gone to Lundy?"

"Well, naturally Robert has not *explained* anything!" Sybil rolled her eyes. "But it's bad enough trying to land there in good weather; they're going to be dashed to pieces in this storm."

"No one will take them if it's that bad."

"Robert's got his own boat and a mooring at Porlock."

Judith was finally startled out of her cosiness, which anyway had been fast disappearing since Sybil's arrival. "Surely they won't even try it in this weather?"

"That's the thing. They hung on last night chatting, and before I actually went to bed I heard Robert ask Nattie to go with him to Lundy. I imagine they listened to the weather forecast, and these storms weren't supposed to start till mid-morning. So they left at midnight. The note just says, "Midnight, leaving for Lundy." She cinched the dressing gown again with sheer frustration, and sat on the end of the bed. "I just cannot understand Robert. He is totally selfish. Nattie will do anything for him, but he doesn't like boats; and he'd had enough of Robert's projects after today. Robert must have had some kind of lever to get Nattie to agree."

Judith said slowly, "I think he was going to ask me. And the weather forecast must have made him change his mind."

"My God! I bet you he used that — told Nattie he'd come and wake you up — something ridiculous!" She sighed sharply. "You have no idea about Robert. He's twisted you around his finger. I can tell that."

"Not at all. But he is a great manipulator. I've watched you and Nathaniel being manipulated, but I would have been quite up to saying no to him. Especially on such a harebrained idea as this; it's worse than the river of gold, for goodness' sake! Has someone tried to phone either of them?"

"According to Irena Mann Robert refuses to get a mobile phone, and nobody took down Nattie's number. They haven't phoned here. Perhaps there's no signal."

Judith swung her legs to the floor. "I'll get dressed and see if Bart has got hold of the police yet. And then, well, we've just got to get on as best we can until we get some news." Lightning flashed again, then came the thunder. Sybil gave a little scream.

Judith said, "Take it easy."

"Sorry. I've always been terrified of thunder. When we were kids Nattie used to tell me it was the clouds bumping into each other." Sybil looked small inside the oversized dressing gown. Easy to imagine the slightly older Nathaniel acting as a brother.

"Oh." Judith looked at her. "You're a chameleon, Sybil. Very changeable."

"Oh Lord. You're starting to *sound* like Robert!"

"Am I? You mean straight-talking? Perhaps I should have done that earlier. It makes things much simpler." She shrugged out of her dressing gown. "For instance, I'd be much happier — and quicker — if you went back to your room and got dressed. We'll meet in the dining room."

"Well . . . OK. Sorry. After yesterday . . . we were all so close . . . and now —"

Judith said loudly, "Go!"

She turned the key in the lock again, threw on a clean sweatshirt and jeans and picked up the phone. It was dead. She rummaged in her bag and found her mobile. Nathaniel had insisted on giving his number to everyone last night, and she had been the only one to write it down. She tapped it out and waited, and the voicemail message came through. She said curtly, "Ring me back as soon as possible. We are all very worried about you. Especially Sybil."

She returned the phone to her bag and found clean trainers on the floor of the wardrobe. Irena had taken all their muddy wet clothing away last night and promised it would be ready for packing in plenty of time. It struck Judith, not for the first time, that between them — and in spite of Hausmann — Bart and Irena ran things very well. Rough seas and power cuts had hardly made any difference to the comfort and

146

service they provided. Judith made up her mind she would have a very straight talk indeed with Robert Hausmann, and point out one or two ways he might make life easier for them. That is, if he ever reappeared after this latest escapade.

She ran down the stairs, almost enjoying the way the lightning sent blazes of purple and gold through the stained-glass window and on to the carpeted foyer. Irena was wheeling one of the trolleys to the dining room and stopped automatically, almost cringing, as the thunder elbowed in a few seconds later.

She glanced up. "Oh, Mrs Freeman, I'm so worried about that nice Mr Jones. If anything has happened it will be Robert's responsibility. Everyone knows that Lundy is always cut off in these Atlantic storms!"

Judith hurried to her side. "Mr Jones knows your brother-in-law very well; they are probably in the Dove Inn having breakfast as we speak."

"I wouldn't be surprised. After he left us that note, too. You'd think he'd have the courtesy to phone us, wouldn't you? His idea of a joke, no doubt! I don't know how Bart puts up with him, I really don't."

Bart appeared from the kitchen door with another trolley. "I put up with him very well, my dear. As should you. He rescued us from boring jobs in Portmeirion and set us up here doing what we do best." He smiled at Judith. "Don't you agree it's a good idea, Mrs Freeman? Space for his work — he can see now how very important it is to have a permanent hanging space — and time to develop some of his family portraits."

Judith was surprised again. She said, "I had no idea that your brother was a man of means. He seems . . ." She stopped, at a loss for words. Bart laughed.

"Down and out?" he supplied. "Far from it. He just likes to give that impression, of course, but there have always been buyers for his work. It looks good, it's traditional, and it has a delicacy and sweetness; not quite nostalgia but bordering on it."

Irena said, "You should be his PR, Bart."

"I would be, if he would let me." Bart smiled and continued into the dining room, speaking over his shoulder. "I've made coffee and toast for you and Mrs Jessup. Would you like poached eggs to go with that?"

"Not for me, thank you." She trailed Irena to the Olsens' table. It had been slightly embarrassing to listen to Irena getting what amounted to a dressing-down from her husband, but she herself was amazed at this latest revelation. Castle Dove's incarnation as an hotel was financed by Hausmann? Nobody — but nobody — was what they seemed! She noticed that the Markhams were missing; surely they weren't still in the orangery?

She caught her swirling thoughts. "Isn't there anything we can do, Mrs Mann? Shouldn't we try to get hold of the police or the coastguards?"

Irena said stiffly, "Bart has done all that. They are in touch with the Lundy people, but the signal is very weak."

Sven Olsen said jovially, "Martin — our good driver, you know — has taken the little coach and is driving to Porlock to see if the boat of Mr Hausmann has gone, or if it is still moored safely."

Margaret added quietly, "Stanley has gone with him. And Jennifer discovered she could get a signal on their phone if she sits in the west tower, so she is having her breakfast there." She looked directly at her husband. "And I will join her after we have eaten. Just she and I. Sven is going to walk to the Dove Inn to meet the others."

Sybil, coming up behind the trolley, said, "But the storm . . . the lightning is so dangerous . . . surely it is better to wait here?"

Sven Olsen smiled reassuringly. "I am physically unable to sit and do nothing in the face of danger, my dear. Already I love Mr Hausmann like a brother. And Nathaniel is one of Nature's gentlemen. I appreciate, very much, both of these Englishmen."

Judith said, "That's . . . that's absolutely marvellous, Mr Olsen!" She turned to Sybil. "Did you want eggs on your toast? I said not."

"No. Just toast will do." Sybil smiled briefly at Judith. "Difficult to eat breakfast in the face of all this . . ." She waved her hand at the windows, where the rain was lashing and running like waterfalls.

"Why don't you come with me to the inn?" Sven Olsen beamed.

"I'll see. I might. If only Nattie would phone."

As if on cue, Judith's phone began its peculiar chant in her bag. She fished it out and pressed a button. It was Nathaniel. She looked up and nodded at the others. They crowded closer. She pressed the tiny phone to her ear and said slowly and clearly,

"Nathaniel, your voice is breaking up. Just tell us: are you safe?"

The roaring sound could be heard by everyone, and Judith caught a single word in the midst of it. It could have been "yes". Another word surfaced above the interference. And then he was gone.

She terminated the call, still frowning with concentration. The others waited.

"I'm really sorry, everyone." Judith looked round. "Did everyone hear him say 'yes'? That's what matters. There was another word. I think it was 'must'. But with another syllable after. Almost like 'mustard'." She smiled wryly. "At least we know they're safe."

Tension was released; they babbled wild guesses at various interpretations of that second word, but nobody could make much of it.

Judith and Sybil drifted to their table and Judith poured the coffee.

Sybil said, "At least we had that wonderful day at the top of the Lyn."

"And yesterday." Judith grinned. "All right, pretty hairy at the time, but retrospectively such . . . *fun*."

"I was thinking of the weather, actually. And I can't go all the way with the fun idea." Sybil smiled ruefully. "Nattie gave me several lectures en route. And of course Robert always disapproved of me!" She sighed. "But that last part in the orangery . . . oh, Jude, that was so romantic." She tightened her mouth against tears, and then said gaspingly, "Sorry. But it was the sort of thing Moss would have done: you know, the candles and the music."

150

Judith put down her coffee cup and reached across the table to touch Sybil's hand. It was impossible to relate the hard-nosed Moss Jessup lampooned by Jack to Sybil's picture of him. There was just nothing she could say.

Sybil nodded and fished for a tissue, and managed a smile at Irena as she brought the toast and marmalade.

Irena noticed nothing amiss. "Bart and I were just talking in the kitchen. If none of you have urgent appointments for tomorrow, we would like to offer another day here. Martin has just returned from the inn, and he is able to fall in with that. The Olsens are rather doubtful; they will talk it over with Mr and Mrs Markham."

Judith felt another small lift of spirit. The relief of knowing that Hausmann and Nathaniel were safe was now compounded by a possible delay in returning home.

Sybil said, "We'll have to see. When the boys get back."

Irena obviously had no idea who "the boys" could be, but she murmured something and turned to welcome Stanley Markham, who was followed by Martin Morris. Margaret actually leapt up and kissed Stanley. Bart arrived, accompanying Jennifer, who burst into tears at the sight of Stanley. They hugged, rocking back and forth.

Martin held up his hands. "All we know is that Hausmann knocked them up at the inn just after midnight, and wanted the key to the garage where he keeps his motorbike. The weather was windy, but it was

151

coming from upcountry, which means the landing beach at Lundy would have been usable. The landlord said it did not become really rough until around four in the morning, when one of the shutters came loose and woke him. So they had almost four hours to get to Porlock, drive the boat to Lundy, then back again." He lifted his shoulders. "We went on to Porlock. The boat — *Goalpost* — is there. So we have no idea whether they actually did it or not."

They all stared at him. Stanley Markham cradled his wife.

Sybil quavered, "But one way or another, surely that means they are safe?"

Martin Morris lifted his shoulders again. Stanley said, "I overheard Hausmann talking to Nathaniel last evening. The ladies had all gone to bed. He said it was a rescue operation." Everyone looked at him. He, too, shrugged helplessly. "That's all I heard. Sorry."

Sybil said bitterly, "That's how he talked Nattie into going! Rescue operation, indeed!"

Margaret turned to her husband. "Sven, we must stay until we have some news of Nathaniel. He is, after all, one of our party."

Sven said nothing. Judith said, "Of course we will all stay. It is so fortunate that Bart and Irena have our rooms until next weekend."

Bart murmured reassurances. And then the telephone in the foyer began to ring and one or two lights came on. Lightning crackled ominously; the lights flickered but were still there as thunder crashed around the castle. Both Irena and Sybil jumped in unison. Bart ran

152

to answer the phone. The others waited in uneasy silence.

Judith said, "Perhaps we should eat something. Everything will be back to normal soon —"

"Bart seems a long time on that phone," Irena said tremulously.

"Two minutes so far." Judith looked at Stanley who was still cradling his wife. "I think our two intrepids could manage some bacon? And coffee?"

Margaret Olsen took over and loaded two plates with food; Sven poured coffee. Judith spread marmalade on a triangle of toast and put it on Sybil's plate.

"Come on, have something to eat. This whole thing is getting out of hand. They're both safe, just as we were yesterday after our adventure —"

"Nothing like this, Judith." Sybil took a bite of toast nevertheless.

"No," Judith agreed soberly, wondering what on earth Hausmann had up his sleeve this time; wondering if it would have persuaded her to get out of bed and go with him to Lundy.

Martin Morris was regaling the others with descriptions of the rainfall.

"If it goes on much longer the Lyn will flood again at high tide," he forecast with a kind of doom-laden satisfaction.

Stanley shook his head. "They've put in flood protection. I've worked all my life in maritime engineering. Schemes to divert rivers. Barricades that turn the sea back in on itself."

Judith leaned across the table. "Like the coastal cliffs. The sea itself has eaten them into concave shapes."

Sybil smiled and nodded. "Perhaps, if we have to stay another night, we could sit in the Long Gallery — by the windows — and have another session. What do you say?"

"Yes!"

Martin Morris was talking to Sven Olsen.

"When the tide begins to ebb, probably midday, the weather could change. In which case I could take you back to Bristol, if you prefer."

Sven looked across at Stanley and Jennifer. "I think our friends will want to stay until this mystery is cleared up. I cannot expect you to make the journey twice."

"I would ask you for petrol money only."

Margaret said evenly, "I shall stay with Jennifer, of course."

"But we have to make our way to Newcastle for the ferry —"

"Which does not sail until Saturday. If you remember, we planned to stay with Stanley and Jennifer. They have theatre tickets for Thursday evening. And Jennifer has invited another school friend for lunch on Wednesday." She spoke very clearly, emphasizing that English was his second language.

Sven flushed, but before he could reply Bart came back into the dining room. They all fell silent and stopped eating, looking across at him. Irena stood by his side.

Bart smiled. "It's all right folks, relax, it's not bad news; at least not as bad as we feared. Robert had a couple of artist friends staying over on Lundy, was going to visit them today, anyway. Then he heard last evening that one of them was ill, seriously ill, I gather. When the forecast was so ominous he decided to go over himself. He rang Lundy again, and was told that an air ambulance was on its way. Minutes later another call arrived: the wind was already too high for a take-off and landing. He recruited Nathaniel, and they left immediately. They landed on the east — the only safe landing beach on the island — and were met by three of the workers, who had stretchered the sick man to the beach. They returned immediately but had a long trip of it — blown off course — and eventually landed at Minehead, where they were met by an ambulance and taken to Taunton. Musgrove Park Hospital."

Judith said, "Of course. I thought Nathaniel had said 'mustard'!"

Stanley sat back, relieved. Sven said, "You see? All is well, just as I said."

Margaret snapped, "Of course it's not well! For goodness' sake, Sven . . . the man is seriously ill . . . you heard —"

"But he is in hospital and will be well cared for. Nothing to stop us going home later on."

Stanley looked at Jennifer, who was now sitting sedately next to him and actually smiling. He smiled back at her. "I think we would like to stay another night." Her smile widened and she nodded.

Sybil said, "And I would like to see the boys before we go. Is that all right with you, Judith?"

Margaret said acidly, "I think the vote has gone against you, Sven."

He was very red, but did his best. "I surrender!" He smiled. "It will be interesting to watch the tide come in today. The weather is driving from the Atlantic, I believe."

Jennifer's smile revealed a pair of dimples. "Let's watch it from the orangery. We explored yesterday afternoon, and found loads of candles and a marvellous old gramophone — His Master's Voice — the genuine article!"

Judith did not meet Sybil's knowing glance. She had thought of the orangery as a sort of shrine, and had no intention of trespassing there.

"Sybil and I have already decided to sketch from the Long Gallery. We'll see you at lunch. Perhaps the weather will have changed by then and we can venture out of doors."

Bart started to clear the tables. "You are welcome to borrow stuff from my brother; his studio is in the south tower." He fished in the pocket of his overall. "Here's the master key. Do go and look round. He would be delighted, honestly. He told me if you had longer here he would show you some of his more recent paintings. Apparently you said something about painting the family's war memories. He has in fact tried to do so."

Judith shook her head. "Perhaps he will get back before we leave."

But Sybil leaned forward and took the key. "I would like to borrow some pastels." She smiled at Judith. "We

156

always shared our stuff, Jude, don't look so shocked. I won't be long. Meet you in the Long Gallery."

Judith watched her as she walked towards the lift. She wondered whether she knew that Hausmann was gay. She moved with a natural grace, thoughtlessly, self-confidently. Since yesterday when she had reacquainted herself with both men, she had changed again.

Judith sighed and started to clear their table on to a trolley. Bart said, "Let me, Judith. Believe it or not, you are on holiday!"

She laughed and used one of her mother's truisms to put him at ease. "A change is as good as a rest. Certainly true in my case. I was going quietly crazy at home."

She trundled the trolley to the kitchen. "Are you older or younger than your brother? Did you play hopscotch with him?"

"I'm seven years older than Rob. Quite a big difference when it came to the games we played. I was more interested in Welsh rugby at that time. But I knew immediately that Sybil Jessup was Esmée Gould!"

She smiled as she left him and went up the stairs. Sometimes it all sounded so completely normal. But then again, as her mother might well have said, "It depends what you call normal."

She went into her room and picked up her canvas bag. She felt around for her phone and tapped in the familiar home number. The answering machine clicked in. She left her room and went along the landing to the double doors which led directly into the Long Gallery.

CHAPTER
TEN

The Long Gallery was more like the prow of a ship than ever. Judith walked its length, pausing now and then as a lightning flash spotlit one of Hausmann's paintings, randomly, theatrically. The rural landscapes became, for an instant, a reminder of summer: she tried to find a word that would encapsulate what Hausmann found so heartbreakingly ephemeral, and came up with "tranquillity".

She held on to the back of one of the sofas and waited for the next flash. This time it lit one of the industrial landscapes. It was Avonmouth before legislation had abolished the smoke stacks. One tall funnel emitted a thin, dark red plume of pure poison. Somehow Hausmann had perceptually triggered something else with his paintbrush, and for an instant she thought she could smell the sulphur.

She shook her head and went on, unable to find a word for the anger in that painting.

At the end of the gallery the full-length windows looked straight down the Bristol Channel, Wales to the right, Devon and Cornwall to the left. The spray had mottled any real views, and at ten o'clock in the morning the light was filtered through heavy clouds.

She pushed the final sofa round so that it faced out to sea, and tried to stop making pictures in her head of a tiny white blob in the middle of an enormous sea of slate-grey: Hausmann's boat, *Goalpost* — doubtless as shambolic as its owner — fighting through the wind towards an invisible island somewhere in all that turbulence.

Lightning forked down again, and the doors behind her opened. Sybil backed in just as Hausmann had done that second morning. She was pulling one of Irena's trolleys and carrying a bag on one shoulder. She swung the trolley round with difficulty and as the door closed behind her she was spotlit, like the paintings. She let go of the trolley, covered her face and screamed.

Judith hurried to her. "It's OK, relax, the storm is moving away. Count the seconds before we hear the thunder." She paused and it rumbled over the castle.

Sybil let her hands fall and took a deep breath. "I keep seeing him in one of his own paintings. I bet his bloody boat leaks like a sieve. And what was Nattie thinking about, for goodness' sake? He's the one with common sense; why did he let it happen?"

"They know more than we do. This friend they've rescued, he could have died if they hadn't got him to a hospital."

"I should think his chances of survival were shortened by giving himself over to Robert!" But she laughed as she spoke, and took the handle of the trolley again. "Come on, there's coffee in the thermos and a whole packet of chocolate biscuits. And I've rummaged around Rob's studio and got a selection of watercolours.

That pastoral scene you were sketching from the top of the Lyn, it cries out for watercolours."

In spite of her reservations about invading Hausmann's quarters, Judith found herself thinking about those sketches: the tiny vulnerable inn pillowed in autumnal trees. Ochres and saffrons and deep, deep crimsons.

Sybil pulled another sofa at right angles to the first and poured coffee; the aroma filled the small area, the sofa backs made it theirs.

"I believe in comfort, physical comfort." Sybil closed her eyes and immersed herself in steam from the jug. "When the three of us were kids I was always the one to make the den."

Judith picked up her cup and imitated Sybil, blissfully inhaling the strident scent of the coffee. "I would have thought Nathaniel would have enjoyed playing house."

"He did, of course. But Robert disapproved strongly. And he loved Robert. As I did. As so many people did." She sounded sad. "It's so difficult to explain, Jude." She was musing now, looking into her cup as if for answers. "Robert would hate me for saying this, but I can't think of another way." She looked up suddenly and gave a small wry smile. "He suffers — actually *suffers* — for other people!" The smile turned into a laugh. "He often gets toothache because he's worrying about someone else — just ordinary but painful complaints. I know it's hard to believe when you've seen him 'drunk and disorderly', and even when he's sober and bullying everyone around him. It sounds absurd to talk about him as a supersensitive artist but — honestly — that's what he is!"

Judith said, "I thought it was . . . his dark side. When he spoke of Auschwitz, not being able to paint any of that, oh God, I told him . . . I think I told him that he should paint it as therapy . . ." She put down her coffee cup with a click. "He must have thought . . . how crass!" She looked at Sybil. "I knew you understood him when you said that he was painting for the end of the world, so his 'scapes would stand as a reminder of how beautiful our world had been."

Sybil gave another rueful laugh. "He's not a saint by any means, Jude. Those 'scapes are what sell. He must be a very rich man."

Judith nodded sadly. "He is financing Bart and Irena in this hotel venture."

"Did he tell you that?"

"No. His brother blurted it out, to stop Irena from slagging him off. Just now, when they were both trying to serve breakfast."

"That's interesting . . . much more constructive . . . I didn't give him credit for being so practical."

"He did it basically for Bart and Irena," Judith reminded her.

"Yes. I see that. He's already got a place on Lundy. It's a sort of hermitage he goes to when things are bad. I found that piece of information on the internet!" She grinned. "I bet he doesn't know it's there . . . he'd be livid! It's how he got his name for being a West Country artist. Apparently he lends it to people sometimes. I think that was why he wanted to take you to see it this morning, in case you could make use of it in the future. But someone was obviously already there, that's what the rescue was all about." She finished her coffee and put her cup next to Judith's. "Poor old Robert. At present there are too many of us needing his kind of first aid, and all at the same time! Thank God he didn't kill Nat in his rescue attempt! I would never have forgiven him."

Lightning lit up the far reaches of the gallery; then there was a full five-second interval before the thunder rolled in. Sybil did not flinch. Judith realized she had not even noticed it.

Sybil picked up a digestive biscuit and broke it in half absently. She said, "I think that's what yesterday's project was all about. To make me realize that I was in love with Nat. I think I always knew; he was so kind. Robert was not always kind. I wanted to be in love with Robert, actually — he was good-looking when he was young — I thought he looked like Heathcliff. And he was always taller than me; I fought against loving Nat because he's shorter than I am!" She laughed and looked round at Judith, half-ashamed. "Imagine being so small-minded . . . so vain, I suppose." She bit into one half of the biscuit and laughed again. "Robert is clever: he knows how people work. To confront Nat with me; it was such a shock. I saw his face and knew that he had loved me all the time, and I knew I had loved him, too." She swallowed her biscuit. "It seemed so natural, didn't it? When he called me Esmée instead of Sybil? Almost innocent! Ha! Shock treatment! For Nat, of course, but for me too." She registered Judith's expression and put out a hand. "It's the way Robert works: always making you look at yourself to recognize the truth. Even when we were ten years old."

Judith took the hand. "I think you're right. That is exactly what he was doing yesterday."

"Your outburst . . . did it help, or make things worse?"

"Both." She thought about it, and added with some difficulty, "I saw that my marriage has taken second place for some time. Yes, it helped." She smiled ruefully. "So did the scene in the orangery."

Sybil shook Judith's hand once and released it. She set aside the tray and began to pull out her sketchbooks. The drawings she had done from the top of the River Lyn were far more detailed than Judith's. She set one of them aside. "Nat might like to print that one for a greetings card. But this one is just a series of outlines because I want to paint it." She produced tubes of powder paint: blue, yellow, red and black. She cleared the lower trays of the trolley and started to set out brushes and rags, saucers and a bottle of water.

Judith tidied the coffee things. She did not want to start on her own sketches from Saturday, it brought in a competitive element she shied away from. Eventually she left them in the bag and opened her sketchbook on a clean page. She sat still for a moment, then reached down again for a stick of charcoal and put it in the centre of the page, as she had watched Jack do so often.

She closed her eyes and sat very still, hardly breathing. She had told Sybil that Hausmann had forced her to face some unpalatable facts. Was that true? She recalled her outburst without embarrassment; what had happened afterwards during Hausmann's "project" had wiped away feelings of embarrassment. So it must have been . . . good. But she had not had time to explore it then; attention had been turned on Sybil, then Hausmann himself. Yet he had wanted Nathaniel Jones to be in the spotlight!

She opened her eyes, saw that Sybil was completely engrossed in her work, and smiled slightly. Hausmann's plans for Nathaniel and Sybil appeared to be working, plus he had accomplished his rescue attempt, too. He would doubtless be insufferable. She looked down at her empty page; the charcoal was in exactly the same position. Hausmann had not worked any magic for her. She frowned, concentrating hard. He had forced her to admit to herself that she had not . . . what was the word she wanted? She had not *nurtured* her marriage; she had relied on Jack to keep it going without help from her. She closed her eyes again and saw Jennifer and Stanley Markham dancing by candlelight. She put the charcoal in her lap and tightened her hands into fists.

Had it been her mother? Had she given too much time to Eunice? She racked her memory; once, before her speech finally disappeared, Eunice had found some words and told Judith she must let her go to a nursing home. Judith had told Jack, and he had been genuinely astonished.

"Darling, we can get help here. Mum is our family. She keeps us together."

Judith had wept then. But he had been right. The togetherness had gradually seeped away after Eunice's

164

death. That was the time she should have nurtured it. Then, out of the blue, she found herself remembering last Christmas. The office party hosted by the Whortleys. Jack, grinning, "Get something new, Jude. Go on, spoil yourself."

And her response. "Darling, I simply cannot face an office party. Listen, why don't you take Naomi? She's such a good friend to me but you only see her when she's leaving here. It would allow you to get to know her better and I'm sure she'd just love it."

"Don't worry, love. I don't need to go either. It's just . . . I thought we might start getting back to normal."

"We are back to normal, Jack. It's just that I'm so tired, I can't make that sort of effort. Oh dear, I feel rotten about it but . . . say you don't mind!"

He had rolled his eyes and intoned, "I do not mind."

And in the end, he had agreed to take Naomi.

Had he felt pushed away then? He said he wished he hadn't gone. The awful thing was that Naomi had not enjoyed it either. "It was OK." She had shrugged. "I didn't know anyone, of course."

Judith took a deep breath and came back to the present. She should have gone to that office party. She had known it at the time but suppressed it; now she knew it again. Behind her closed eyes she visualized letters and made them into words. And the words all said the same thing, "I'm sorry . . . I'm sorry . . ." They multiplied, and as they did she picked up the charcoal stick and started to draw. She recalled Jack saying, "I do my best stuff with my eyes closed."

When her hand stopped moving, she opened her eyes and stared down at the page. A single hooked line made a nose, two lines level with the nose's bridge became eyes, a lopsided slash beneath the nose made a mouth; finally a quiff of hair and, of course, protruding ears. More slowly, watching the charcoal as it moved, she circled the collection of features into a head.

"My God, who is that?" Sybil looked over her shoulder. "I had no idea you did caricatures too!"

"I don't. I never have. But this is Fish-Frobisher! I can't believe it . . . he drew himself!" She looked away from the page, eyes wide. "My God. It really is. Magnus Fish-Frobisher himself!"

"Who on earth is Magnus Fish-Frobisher?"

"You don't know the Fish-Frobishers?" Judith grinned suddenly. "You only looked at the Jack Freeman cartoon when he drew your husband! Free publicity, that's what Jack called it. A week — maybe two — and that was that. But the Frobishers have been ongoing for years. They gave everyone a chance to see themselves, for better or worse. They really are awful. Snobs, unconscious racists, but underneath it all they can be kind." She puckered her mouth, considering. "A bit like Nat, I imagine."

Sybil laughed and began to mix some paint. "Go on with it. Let me get to know them. Is there a wife?"

"Certainly there's a wife. Edith. And a daughter called Stargazer. Her school friends call her 'Popeye'." Judith went on looking at "FF", as Jack called him. "This is peculiar."

166

"No. No, it's not. It's true therapy. Representing the happy times?"

"Probably. They were conceived when the twins were still at school and my mother was well. Twenty-three years ago, I suppose." She went on staring. The few lines in front of her which made up the face of Fish-Frobisher, were almost a facsimile of Jack's popular creation. But they reminded her of someone else. The slicked-back hair, the long thin mouth, the considering eyes and — most of all — the protruding ears: they also belonged to Jack Freeman. Had he intended that?

Sybil leaned forward, applying paint from the very tip of a fine brush. "I'm doing the purples first, there were a lot of purples." She swung back and forth, looking then dabbing. "Moss made me promise to take my painting seriously after he died." She paused, brush poised high. "Oh my God, is that yet another reason I came to see Robert? To hang on to his coat-tails?"

"You came to see Nathaniel Jones, remember?"

"I didn't think so. Not until later. Though when he was being so courteous in the coach coming here, I felt a real pang. He never understood Robert, nor me, but he was so loyal. He thought he was an outsider, but I see now he had a big role. He looked after us. Just as he went with Robert last night, to look after him." She leaned forward again and began on the beech trees, adding ochre to the crimson paint.

Judith turned a page and started to draw again. "It's as if Jack has his hand over mine. This is Edith Fish-Frobisher. She was a good woman, actually." She gave her a perfect hairdo. "In between perms she did good works." She held the sketchbook away from her and looked hard. "Yes, that's Edith. I must have watched Jack working — watched every line he made — it is exactly Edith Fish-Frobisher." And it was modelled on someone; someone real.

Judith stared in disbelief; it was her mother.

Sybil was talking, as if to herself. She was deep into mixing paints; the trolley had half-a-dozen saucers full of wonderful colours. Judith turned to tell her about Edith Fish-Frobisher, alias Eunice Denman, and was completely distracted by the colours. She pushed her pad away and watched Sybil as she applied paint here and there and brought the beech trees to life.

Sybil started to speak again, almost to herself. "I was sixteen. Robert had got a place at the Slade, and he looked me up. It was wonderful to see him. I realized I had been homesick for him. I told him I loved him and would always love him."

She looked up and saw Judith's eyes on her, and said, "You've got the clearest eyes I've ever seen. Be careful. He's fallen for you — because of your eyes, I think — and he could hurt you."

Judith shook her head slowly. "It's not like that. Not at all."

Sybil made a face. "My God. You're falling for him, aren't you?"

"Don't be silly! Jack's been . . . gone . . . two months!"

"Quite. But this is something different. Be honest, I'm right, am I not? He's not only a wonderful painter.

He's a tortured soul. And more than that, too. He's a pirate!" She laughed without humour. "You're doing exactly the same as I did. I did it at ten years old, sixteen years old, and again when I got the invitation to come here for his retrospective exhibition! Don't be such a fool, Jude! My God, you're better than this! You're practical, imaginative, caring. How can you get a crush on Robert? You can see that wherever he goes he takes disaster with him."

Judith said, "Not really. And of course he loves you. That's why he wants you to be happy. I think he probably rigged this exhibition; all right, he knew it would help to get the castle started as a sort of cultural-weekend-away. But then he saw it could also bring you and Nathaniel Jones back together. You say you had an invitation. I didn't, and I'm willing to bet neither did the Olsens nor the Markhams. What about Nathaniel?"

Sybil took a rag and cleaned her brush. "Yes. Yes, you're right. Yesterday out on that dratted moor, Nat did say something."

"There you are! Your husband had only been dead two months, and Hausmann knew you would be trying to make a new life. The Markhams live in Bristol or nearby; they were probably looking for something they could do with their Scandinavian friends! Hausmann is known as a West Country painter, and as far as I know the weekend was advertised in the local press only." She shrugged. "You live in Surrey, and Nathaniel lives in Wales. I doubt Martin Morris's advertisement got that far. There were just seven of us, that's all. I think it was arranged for your sake, Sybil. Surely that is love?"

Sybil's frown disappeared. She laughed and shook her head. "I suppose so. Not the sort I wanted, or thought I wanted. But I still think you should be careful; he certainly is very interested in you!"

"Not really. It's because of Jack. He . . . he admires . . . admired . . . Jack."

Sybil stopped laughing and dried the brush with studied care. "But . . . sorry, Jude . . . but their stuff is so different, and I'm afraid would have come between them. In Robert's eyes, cartoonists are not painters, they are journalists. Sorry, but that's Robert."

"I mean he admires Jack. The man. Not necessarily his work."

"He knew your husband. Personally?"

"Yes."

"So you knew him, too: you came here to see him as well as his work?"

"No. I didn't know him, but I've seen a couple of his exhibitions and enjoyed them, and it seemed a good thing to do. I needed to do something, you see. I was gardening and cleaning and shopping for food I wasn't going to eat, and it was all so pointless. Booking a weekend away was . . . was . . . meaningful."

Sybil loaded the brush carefully with olive-green paint. She said, "Jude, if he engineered this weekend so that Nat and I would meet up again, don't you think it is more than likely you were included in such cunning plans?" She rolled her eyes and vowels on the last two words. But she was not smiling. "He kept his eye on the

170

bookings. If you hadn't booked a place I rather think you, too, would have received an invitation."

"I don't think so." It was getting too difficult. She was going to have to admit that Jack was alive.

Sybil gave a little snort of derision. "Sorry, but I know Robert through and through."

Suddenly Judith was annoyed. She hated this conversation; the assumption that she could possibly be looking for someone else was disgusting. Sybil obviously thought she was a flirtatious widow. Yes, it was all disgusting.

She said tersely, "You need not worry about Robert and me. You must know he is gay."

Sybil's reaction was slow. She held her brush in mid-air while she stared at Judith with astonishment. Then she exploded with genuine mirth, somehow or other replaced the brush in its saucer, and lifted her head to the ceiling. She looked so like Naomi with the long throat exposed that Judith wanted to weep. All the good that she had felt emanating from Castle Dove — and Robert Hausmann's work — was swept away. She looked down at her sketches: the Frobishers, one like Jack, the other like her mother. Now Sybil was reminding her of Naomi Parsons. All of them lost.

Sybil spluttered, "Did he tell you that?"

She said, hopelessly, "Yes. In a manner of speaking." She would have to confess that Jack was alive, and that would finish any kind of friendship she might have had with Sybil.

But Sybil was only interested in Hausmann. She controlled her laughter, fished for a tissue and wiped her eyes.

"Jude. He is not gay. I can vouch for that. What sort of game is he playing now, for God's sake? My dear, be more on your guard than ever. He is most definitely up to something!"

Judith was surprised at her own relief; Sybil was not going to cast her off after all. In that moment she almost told her about Jack and the other woman in Australia. And then she didn't. Instead, after a while she said, "Thank you, Sybil."

They went back to their work. They had no more to say; Judith's feeling of discomfort, of insecurity, of imminent loss, grew steadily stronger. Underneath it all was a basis of guilt. She was living some kind of peculiar lie that was absolutely unnecessary.

At one o'clock Sybil sat back, satisfied. "I've got to a point that I can leave until after lunch. What about you?"

It was obvious that Sybil had not picked up any of Judith's discomfort. "I'm still working on the Fish-Frobisher strip; I can leave it at any time."

Sybil said, "Let's go, then. It's been great, Jude. We've been so honest with each other. I didn't offend you, did I?"

"No. Of course not." Judith put away her things and stood up.

Sybil said, "I'll leave our stuff on the trolley. We can push it out of sight and perhaps go on with this for an hour later."

There was nothing of Judith's on the trolley, and for a moment she wanted to say pettishly that it all belonged to Robert.

Instead she nodded. "Better put the sofas back, I suppose. The others might want to come and look at the paintings again."

"What? You must be joking. The Markhams are only interested in trying to make a baby, and the Olsens are thinking about a divorce."

"Are you serious?"

"Not really. It's much easier not to be serious."

"Yes."

Sybil took her arm as they walked the length of the gallery. "It would be good to keep in touch, Jude. I've got a lot of room at home. You could stay . . . we could go and see what's on at the Hayward or Tate Modern . . . that sort of thing."

Judith closed her eyes for a moment. "Thank you, Sybil," she said. It would not happen, of course. But for the moment she was grateful to have a friend again.

They separated at the lift doors. Judith went into her room, and immediately settled at the table and spread out the sketches she had done. She began to jot down possibilities that could make one of Jack's episodes. The daughter — Stargazer — would have the punchline, as she so often did. She had never aged — none of them had — since the comic strip began. Her aim in life was to shower scorn on her parents. She was the stereotypical teenager. Judith nibbled her lower lip and considered. Jack would say, "Is that a pimple I see before me?" and Eunice would say, "Omigod, and it's the Dalrymples' sherry party this very morn!" and

Stargazer would say, "You would do anything to be the centre of attention!"

Judith nodded to herself; it was so Fish-Frobisher — incredible — the whole thing could have been Jack's. She read her notes and then read them again with one hand across her mouth. She had renamed Magnus and Edith. Stargazer was the only Fish-Frobisher there. She removed her hand and wrote the three parts again. And then she enveloped dialogue and sketches and stuck two first-class stamps on them and addressed the envelope to William Whortley at the *Magnet* offices.

The Olsens were in the sitting room drinking sherry and talking to Bart and Martin Morris. Bart immediately offered to post Judith's envelope for her.

"I'm off in the car to pick up Nat after lunch. Anything you need that Taunton might provide?"

"You provide just about everything here. But thank you, anyway." Judith accepted a glass from Sven Olsen. "Aren't you bringing your brother back home with you?"

"No, not at this point. I don't quite get the whole picture, but Robert will explain when I see him, I expect." He did not look particularly hopeful on that score. "The main thing is, the patient has double pneumonia. He is taking antibiotics intravenously and oxygen intermittently. He would probably have died if Robert hadn't taken him off the island in the small hours of this morning. His companion is young and desperate. He won't leave the bedside, and Robert has taken a room nearby and is hoping he will use it tonight."

"So the crisis has not been instantly resolved," Sven took up. He smiled. "I think Mr Mann will be receiving a great many phone calls this week! We will all need to know exactly what is happening!"

Margaret said sharply, "This is not a television serial, Sven! I hope Mr Mann will let us know the outcome of his brother's courageous rescue attempt." She smiled at Bart. "Hopefully you will be back this evening, when we shall still be here."

"We shall be in the way, Margaret," Olsen said. "We did agree — or so I thought — that it would be better if we left the family in peace."

Martin Morris stepped in. "If we could all wait until the morning I would be much happier. A mud slide has been reported just down the coast. The forecast for tomorrow is overcast but dry."

Sybil arrived on the scene and was delighted to see Bart. She listened as the sparse news was told again.

"Of course we will hang on, Mr Morris! Nat will be able to fill us in with the full details tonight, but I don't imagine he will be in any state to take to the road! Hopefully a good night's sleep will put him right. Tomorrow will be fine. Don't you agree, Jude?"

"Of course." Judith spoke heartily, but her heart was not in it. Her heart was not in anything; she could feel her sporadic good spirits falling rapidly.

Sybil turned to Sven with her wide smile. "We all appreciate your concern for Bart and Irena, dear Mr Olsen. But we can all pull our weight. Judith and I know our way around the kitchen here; if Irena is all right with serving our lunch, we promise to do the clearing up afterwards, and you can help us if you like."

Sven blinked, dazzled by the unaccustomed smile. Margaret took his arm.

"You see, darling? Everything is as it should be."

Judith turned to Sybil and said in a low voice, "Did we leave our coffee stuff in the gallery?"

Sybil rolled her eyes. "I'll go. How long does it take to drive to Taunton and back?"

"Probably an hour to get there. Afterwards, I'm not sure how long to pick up Nathaniel and his stuff; but then another hour to get back here."

"So he should be here in good time for dinner." She smiled. "Lovely. I'm going to spend a long time in a scented bath."

It was Judith's turn to roll her eyes.

"Not only that — have you got a spare nightie like the one you were wearing this morning?"

"As it happens, yes."

"May I borrow it? And I'm going to scoot down to the orangery and pinch some of the candles."

Irena came out of the kitchen wheeling the inevitable trolley.

"Lunch is served!" she called across the foyer.

"Come on for now. I'll see to the coffee things." Judith took Sybil's arm and they walked over to Irena, who looked at them without pleasure and spoke tersely.

"There is a trolley missing, Mrs Jessup. I shall need it for the evening meal."

176

Sybil gave her the special smile. "I couldn't find you to ask if we might borrow it. We're using some of Robert's paints, and it is making a very useful table for them; and for everything else!"

"Perhaps you could return it as soon as possible."

Judith said quickly, "We do apologize. Especially as — if you will accept our offer to clear away this afternoon — we shall need it down here ourselves. I'll see to it right away!"

Irena softened immediately. "Oh, please, my dear! Have your lunch first. This is the first time you have been in for lunch. And I wouldn't dream of allowing you to work in the kitchen. Your holiday has been ruined, and it's down to my stupid brother-in-law!" She cast a dark glance towards the others, who were filing into the dining room. "I suppose they are all thinking he is some kind of hero! If anything had gone wrong it would have been his fault entirely! He took his friend over to Lundy on Saturday; he must have shown symptoms of his illness! The weather forecast was already talking of westerly gales —"

Judith could feel Sybil by her side boiling with anger. She said as smoothly as she could, "Irena, you must not upset yourself like this, all is going to be well now, that is what matters."

Irena calmed down immediately, even managing a smile. "I know you are right. You see through to what matters; like your husband, like your dear husband."

Sybil peeled away from Judith and walked into the dining room.

"What is the matter with Mrs Jessup now?" Irena asked. "Bart has told me about her. What was the word he used? Unpredictable. That was it. Apparently her father blamed the boys for her odd behaviour, and moved to London. But she's found them again, hasn't she?"

She did not wait for an answer, but strode into the dining room, cutlery clattering on the trolley as it jerked over the threshold. Judith took her chance, and went upstairs and down the second landing to the Long Gallery. She pulled a newspaper out of her bag and spread it on the floor, smoothing its crumpled surface and revealing the Fish-Frobishers unable to find their car keys. She put the contents of the trolley on to the newspaper, and set the coffee things in their place. It meant she had to use the lift. She bent down to see the buttons and saw that the vinyl-tiled floor of the lift was damp and muddy. She had not seen any cleaners since she had arrived. Surely Irena didn't do the cleaning as well as the cooking?

The lift arrived on "entry level" and the doors slid open. She wheeled the trolley into the kitchen, unloaded the mugs into the dishwasher and found a tea towel. She rinsed it under a tap and wiped the trolley clean of all paint remnants.

Then she put the wet towel into the laundry bin and joined the others.

It was rather embarrassing when Irena brought in the puddings and was loud with praise of, "Judith's excellent work in the kitchen."

Sybil barely waited until she was out of earshot before she said, only half-jokingly, "You creep!"

Judith responded coolly. "I put the paints on some newspaper and brought the trolley down — at a gallop rather than a creep!"

"So we can go back there after lunch; unless the Markhams need the Long Gallery for any unspecified reason?"

"Oh, Sybil, don't!"

"Sorry. It's difficult for me. Moss and I decided on no children right from the outset." She turned down her mouth at Judith's expression and added, "But I do see how totally committed they are, and it was wonderful . . . magical . . . surreal —"

"Shut up!" Judith said.

Sybil raised her brows. "I reckon we're friends. You wouldn't have told me to shut up yesterday. Probably not even this morning."

"It hasn't worked, has it?"

Sybil grinned, misunderstanding. She pursed her mouth and drew a finger across her lips as if zipping them closed. Judith looked up and thanked Irena for the coffee that had appeared in front of her. Then she bent down to pick up her handkerchief, and for the first time she let herself picture Jack. He seemed to be reaching out to her. Then he was gone. She whispered, "Jack. Don't leave me. Please do not leave me!"

Sybil said, "I didn't hear what you said then."

Judith looked up and smiled. Some part of her suddenly relaxed.

"I didn't say anything. But if it's so hard to stay shut up, then please feel free to start a conversation!"

Sybil laughed. Judith laughed. It cleared the pain in her throat. And it was as if the laughter sealed a bargain.

CHAPTER
ELEVEN

After lunch they agreed to meet in the Long Gallery in an hour. Sybil was making a routine phone call to an elderly cousin in Dundee, and Judith wanted to help out in the kitchen. She found Irena had loaded the dishwasher and was cleaning the surfaces. She took another cloth and started on the hob. Irena was flustered at first, then much too grateful.

"I thought I could get ahead of myself . . . no one else offered . . . why should they, after all? And you've lost that wonderful husband yet you —"

Judith could not let it go on. Even as she reassured Irena, she told herself to come into the open and announce that Jack was still alive but had left her. Admit to the stupid and despicable deception. She did not do it.

She escaped as soon as she decently could, and went to the bathroom to rinse her face and hands. The hand towel was damp, so Sybil must have stopped by on her way to the Long Gallery. She must have gone into the bedroom, too, because the nightie was missing from its place on the pillow. Judith was taken aback; was this how Sybil saw their friendship pact, or was it some kind of joke? She opened a drawer and took out the clean nightie and put it in a bag. Picked up some fresh charcoal, and walked down the landing. At least Sybil had knocked this morning. The door had been locked then, of course; Judith frowned, trying to remember whether she had locked it when she went down for lunch.

She put her shoulder to the gallery door and immediately could hear voices. She paused, taken aback again. Sybil's voice was unmistakeable: beautiful enunciation with just a touch of south London. It was raised now, the consonants emphasized even more than usual, definitely Welsh. The other voice made sounds only; hushing sounds. But she knew whose it was.

She pushed inside and both voices stopped abruptly. Sybil looked round, her expression scornful.

"Here she is now!" She rushed to Judith and took her arm. "Jude, he is denying everything! I thought it was really funny when you told me he was gay, and then I realized it was another of his bloody games! Making you feel secure and relaxed with him!" She shook Judith's arm roughly. "But he's denying it. So, in effect, he's calling you a liar! And if I have to choose between you, I know full well who is the liar!" She pulled Judith forward. "Go on, use his own words if you can remember them! Tell him what he said to you, go on!"

Judith looked at Hausmann and saw the exhaustion in his eyes. She said, "What on earth has brought this on? Of course I can't remember what he said. For goodness' sake, Sybil, does it matter one way or the other?"

"Yes. It matters. Oh yes, it certainly matters! Because when I was sixteen and he was eighteen, he got a scholarship to the Slade. He didn't want it. He wanted to live on Lundy like a gypsy and paint every day and eat fish and mushrooms! And if he could make me pregnant, then we could get married and do exactly that! I was sixteen, Jude! Sixteen years old! And I hated living in London; the thought of living on Lundy sounded like heaven." She stopped and took a big breath. "Jude, he seduced me, and I can assure you he was not gay then! I did not become pregnant, and by the time I knew for sure, he was already settled in at the Slade." She looked at Hausmann. "I didn't see him again until he appeared in this gallery on Friday afternoon. Tell her, Robert! Is that how it was? Or can't you remember all those years ago — thirty-four years?"

Hausmann stared at her; he said nothing.

Judith freed herself. "For Pete's sake, Sybil! Does it matter? Robert is in no state for this sort of thing; he's going to drop at any moment. All right, so he was not gay when he was eighteen. You were the girl from his past already — he had romanticized you from a ten-year-old schoolgirl to a sixteen-year-old on the verge of womanhood — and he fell in love. Simple as that. Don't forget, you didn't exactly wait for him, did you? Whereas he is still unattached!"

Sybil looked wildly at her, covered her face with her hands, collapsed back on to the sofa and wailed.

Judith turned to Hausmann. "Look, I've no idea what has brought this on: sheer fright at the weather and the possibility that you and Nathaniel had drowned at sea!" She rolled her eyes in an endeavour to make it all sound perfectly reasonable, yet absurd at the same time.

Sybil's wails escalated at this, and Judith said quickly to Robert, "My door is open. Can you cope with making a thermos of tea? Bring the biscuits, too . . . just give us a moment to get ourselves together."

Still Hausmann did not speak. She watched him shamble the length of the gallery, wondering quite seriously whether he would be able to manage to open the doors. He did so, and they swung behind him.

Sybil was crying in earnest, as far from her usual composed self as was possible. Judith settled her into a corner of the sofa, found a clean rag and wetted it from the bottle of water Sybil had brought to mix her paints. She smoothed the rag over Sybil's forehead, and murmured, "Let it go, Sybil, it's so long ago."

Sybil controlled herself with difficulty, and started to breathe deeply. "I know." She spoke in her normal voice but jerkily. "I do know. Honestly, I haven't thought about it for years. Moss took up all my time and energy — one of the reasons I adored him. But when he — bloody Robert — tried to sell you the idea that he was gay, it didn't matter at first. I was almost amused at his sheer effrontery. Then I came in here for a quiet hour with you, and there he was! Sitting on the arm of that sofa as if nothing had happened! I could have killed him! I had to . . . to . . . hurt him in some way. Oh, Jude, it means nothing now, and the least I could have done was keep it to myself. After all these years . . . I never told Moss . . ."

184

Judith took one of Sybil's hands in hers and rubbed it reassuringly. "It was the shock of seeing him here. Why on earth does he skulk around like he does? It . . . it's ridiculous."

"He'd only just arrived — came in via the orangery. Would you believe he's got a key to that, too?"

"Nothing would surprise me any more." Judith dabbed again at the tear-streaked face. "I can quite understand your father wanting to get you out of such a close relationship with those two boys." She rinsed the rag and tried to remove some of Sybil's smeared mascara. "Everybody loved your father, didn't they? He sounds a wonderful man."

"He was. He knew about the camps, just like the Hausmanns knew. But he didn't let it ruin our lives. I was spoiled, Jude. I was always his star, and if he'd known about Robert it would have killed him." More tears poured from her eyes. "If only it had been Nat. We would have got married as soon as we could. Everything would have been different." Sybil seized the rag and scrubbed at her own eyes fiercely. "But of course Nat would never have let it happen." She lay back, discarded the rag and closed her eyes. "I'm not going to let this spoil anything I've got now, Jude. I'll drink my tea like a good girl, and then I'll disappear. The bath, the candles, the nightie . . . may I still borrow your nightie? I'm going to work at this scenario like the Markhams are doing. Too late for babies, but as much time as we've got just to be wonderfully happy!"

Judith was taken aback yet again; it was all becoming much too complicated. She said, "I've got it here." She put the bag with the nightie in it next to Sybil, who clutched it to her as if for comfort. "Will you be all right?" she went on. "I've never seen you like this. Should I come with you? What about Hausmann?"

"You deal with him. You know the truth now. Hear what he has to say and pack him off to Irena. Let her look after him. He's paying through the nose for his board and lodging, but that's up to him." Sybil opened her eyes and took a deep breath. "I'll be all right, Jude. But I don't really want Nat knowing about this — is that unreasonable?"

"Of course it's not unreasonable. As I said, let it go. It's the only way."

"You're right." Sybil struggled into a sitting position. "Listen, I'll go now. The sight of Robert might start me off again, and I need to compose myself before Nat arrives."

"But if Robert is here, then surely Nathaniel is, too?"

"No. Apparently, Robert's got his motorbike. He and Nat used it last night to get to Porlock, and he took a taxi there from Taunton, drove it to the inn, walked to the castle, then went round the base and into the orangery."

"Thank goodness the Markhams weren't there!"

"It would have done him good. He thinks he owns the place."

Judith nearly pointed out that in fact he did. She picked up the discarded rag and put it back on the newspaper. Sybil hoisted herself up, still clutching the bag.

"Thanks, Jude. I'm so glad you turned up when you did. I'll see you at dinner, OK?"

"Of course. Good luck. Though you don't need it, not now."

Sybil smiled and tugged at the doors just as Hausmann pushed them from the other side. She rubbed her shoulder. "I think I need all the luck I can get," she called back, and passed Hausmann without a word.

He was carrying a tray of tea things and staggered down the gallery. Judith went to meet him and took the thermos jug off the tray. He stood there looking helpless. She put a hand beneath his elbow and shepherded him to the sofa. He was definitely trembling.

She said in her most matter-of-fact voice, "The tea was for Sybil, of course, and she has gone. She's going to wait for Nathaniel. Everything will be all right, Robert. Sybil is not Esmée any longer. She has had nearly thirty years with a dynamic husband; whether you approved of him or not, you can see she adored him. Now she is facing the fact that she is in love again — probably always has been — with someone completely different. And the past comes up and hits her in the face." Judith made a little face at him. "Remember, she really *is* a widow! Half of her is still grieving."

He had collapsed on to the sofa. He looked broken in some way. She busied herself with the thermos.

He spoke at last. "She was sixteen, Jude. And her father — she was everything to him — why didn't he come after me and whip the hide off me?"

"Because she never told him — and anyway you weren't much older than Sybil." She held a mug of tea beneath his nose. "Breathe in. Close your eyes and breathe out slowly and let it all go. And again. Keep going." She moved the mug then put it back again. "You couldn't really have married and settled down to what you thought was an idyllic way of life. You're a painter with a mission, Robert Hausmann!" She lowered the mug of tea. "Now drink the tea. Slowly. Another sip." He choked. "Hold the mug, Robert. I'm going to drown you!"

He took the mug from her, gave her the slightest of smiles, and sipped again. He was no longer trembling. She went to the tray, sat cross-legged, filled another cup, inhaled the steam and then drank.

A wonderful silence settled over the gallery, as soft as a blanket. She lifted her gaze and looked at the painting facing her. It was one of the Hausmann pastoral landscapes: a shallow river winding through fields of buttercups, a low bridge, a herd of cows being taken in for the evening milking. It was as different from the river of gold tumbling from the watershed of Exmoor as chalk and cheese, yet it rang just as true. And it was familiar. She had seen that wide shallow river before, running so gently along the flat lands of ... somewhere. She looked over her shoulder to ask Hausmann. He was asleep, completely relaxed — sprawled — across the sofa, the mug, luckily empty, dangling from one finger.

She smiled, uncrossed her legs and crawled over to the saucers of paint on that day's copy of the *Magnet*.

188

She tidied everything on to the tray without disturbing the wonderful silence. Then she crawled to the end of the sofa and used it as a back-rest. She closed her eyes. She had told Hausmann to "let it go", and Jack had very much said the same to her. It might well have been a plea to let him — her dear Jack — go. Could she ever do that?

She must have slept, simply because she woke when Hausmann gave a loud grunt and sat up. He said, "Jude — where are you? Oh, there you are. Time we were going."

She was still relaxed; there was no more lightning, though an almost constant rumbling echoed through the sound of the wind and had to be thunder somewhere.

The sofa seemed to be moving at her back as Hausmann made terrific efforts to get out of it. She tried to get up herself, and, momentarily stuck, looked up and saw the painting again.

"It's the River Leadon. Of course it is! On the edge of the Forest of Dean." She was filled with sudden joy. "We went there. With the boys . . . they paddled . . . they loved it. Jack had an uncle living nearby . . . dead now." She twisted her body and smiled up at Hausmann. "Jack's not dead. Nobody else is dead. And you and Nathaniel rescued your friends, and you are heroes!"

He actually chuckled, then he leaned forward and ruffled her hair. "You are so like he described. Yet he said he couldn't get you on paper."

She struggled to stand up. "Are you talking about Jack now? He didn't describe me, did he? That's the trouble, Hausmann. The woman he described was the one he loved. That's the nub of it all, the heart of the matter, the —"

"Have you been drinking, Jude?"

"Tea. Lots and lots of tea."

"And you haven't told anyone else about your dream?"

"I'd almost forgotten about the dream. But I realized afterwards that Len would have let me know if Jack was ill . . . or worse." She sighed. "Nobody knows."

"I gathered as much. You've made rather a hit with my sister-in-law on the strength of your widowhood." He tried to grin, but could not quite make it.

She picked up the loaded tray and balanced it on her hip. "Never mind that. Tell me what happened last night. I know you've got a cottage on Lundy, and that you let two friends have it — both artists, I gather — and one of them became ill, and you and Nathaniel went over before the storm hit and rescued them. You might as well tell me. You're going to be pestered with questions throughout dinner."

"No one knows I'm here, except you and Esmée. I'm driving back to Taunton now." He leaned forward and stood up with some difficulty. "It's just . . . I'm hoping you will come back to Taunton with me, Jude." He sighed deeply. "It's such a mess. It was going to be the best project I'd ever launched. And it went wrong." He took the tray from her and put it on the sofa, then straightened again; it looked difficult, but at least he was no longer shaking. "When Jack phoned me on Friday, I should have told him to go straight to one of the Bristol hospitals. But I'd met you on Thursday night — well, the early hours of Friday morning, I suppose — and it seemed as if . . . as if . . . it was all being planned somehow. And then there was Lundy."

He paused and looked at her. She was staring at him, her level of concentration hitting a peak.

She whispered, "What do you mean? Jack? Lundy? What are you saying?"

He moved to the window, opaque with rain, and she could see him breathing deeply again.

He said, "I bought a stable on Lundy about ten years ago. I have made it into a home. Unconventional, but a home nevertheless. I'd been there often and always felt well. Because of the Gulf Stream it has a milder climate than on the mainland and a reputation for curing breathing problems — hay fever, asthma, bronchitis — that's what Jack thought he had, bronchitis. It has helped me . . ." He glanced round at her. "Though Irena would tell you nothing will help until I give up smoking!" He registered her agonized expression and turned away quickly. "When Jack phoned me he said he had a bad chest, and was the cottage empty? He and Matt were at home in Bristol, but you weren't there, and he had no idea where you were."

He paused again, and Judith breathed, "It was Jack. I knew it was him. He's the only one who would have a key to the house."

Hausmann nodded. "I think it was Matthew who telephoned. He asked me for the number when we were in touch." He straightened, pulled back his shoulders. "I couldn't fetch them on that Friday — we were all meeting in the gallery. But you and Esmée were going off to Lynmouth the next day, and the next tour wasn't until the afternoon, so I drove Bart's car and picked them up, came back to Porlock, took the two of them over to the cottage, and asked the farmer's wife — Kitty Davies — to keep an eye. Got back late for the Saturday tour, and you know the rest."

She cried out then, "You knew! All the time you knew he wasn't dead . . . you could have told me . . . oh my God! I thought we were friends! I trusted you!"

"I know . . . I know. I'm sorry, Jude. I was going to tell you that Friday. I tried to get you to talk to me then. But I had second thoughts. I had to be sure you felt something for him, and then he asked me not to tell you he was on Lundy. What could I do?"

She stared at him, remembered his change of mood. But her voice was still angry. "All right. But part of it was this confrontational thing, wasn't it? Letting me think he's gone for ever: no Jack in this world. And then, when I discovered he was alive, everything would fall into place. Was that the cunning plan?"

He said, "I didn't know what the hell to do, frankly. I felt that the sheer coincidence of you and Jack being in such close proximity, must mean . . . something. The trouble with coincidence is that you're not really in charge any more. Jack's condition worsened during that Sunday, and by the time we got back from our trek I found half-a-dozen messages on my phone. And the weather forecasts were all dire."

He sighed sharply and turned his back on the window. "I know about Lundy. Sometimes it is cut off from the mainland in spite of all our wonderful rescue services. Landing from the sea can be impossible. And if there's rain being driven by that wind, helicopters would be blown out of the sky. I waited until everyone had gone to bed, then told Nat the whole story." He spread his arms, as if in surrender. "I didn't ask him to come — he insisted. I haven't lied to you, Jude, whatever Sybil says. Nat knew I would not be able to manage the boat without a crew, and in the end I agreed. He could have drowned. Jack and Matthew, too. But if I hadn't gone, Jude, Jack would be dead now. And he's going to be all right. He looks pretty ghastly, but the doctor assured us that he will recover very quickly." He stayed where he was, waiting.

She closed her eyes for a moment. "Thank you," she said.

"I don't want your thanks, Jude. I want . . . I need . . . your forgiveness. I should have told Matthew to take Jack to the hospital . . . it's so obvious now."

She could not look at him. "I forgive you for trying to . . . repair things."

"Well, then . . ."

She raised her head and looked at him. He opened his arms. And she went into them, put her own arms around him, and hung on as if the wind could somehow destroy the castle walls and tear them into the drumming rain.

He held her close, so that the suppressed tears came to nothing. After a while he put his face against the top of her head and said, "Why did you tell Esmée I was gay? Were you trying to keep me safe from her? Or was it the other way round?"

"You said you loved Jack. You said it three times, I think." Her face was pressed against his oiled wool sweater; it muffled her voice.

"You think that men cannot love each other unless they are gay?"

She sobbed just once. "I don't know anything any more."

"Neither do I. We're lost at sea, Jude. We're going to a mooring now. Perhaps we'll find an anchorage."

She lifted her head. "What do you mean?" she asked fearfully.

He kissed her, slowly and carefully. Then he smiled and said, "Jack keeps asking for you. My bike is in the car park. I'm here to take you to Musgrove Park Hospital. In Taunton."

She said foolishly, "Everyone thinks I'm a widow."

"Nat will explain."

She pushed at his sweater gently and stood free. "I must tell them. Sybil. And Irena. It's the least I can do." She made a face and felt her chin quiver. "I thought Sybil and I . . . never mind."

"You'll have Jack. He needs you, Jude." He went to the sofa and pulled a bag from behind one of the cushions. "He said if you refused to see him, would I bring this back with me." He shook the bag and her nightdress fell on to the sofa.

She stared at it. "You told him about that first night? When I locked myself out of my room and you were sick?"

"I told him. I had to tell him, Jude. I love him. Remember? And you — well — I love you, too. It started then. That bloody nightie has got a lot to answer for."

She picked it up and rolled it back into the bag. "I'll take it. I'll pack a few things, stay with Jack." She tucked it under her arm, and picked up the tray. "You can come back here and take charge — it's your castle, Robert." She smiled briefly. "Give me ten minutes to talk to Sybil. All right?"

"All right. I'm going to the kitchen for some food."

She laughed, then went to him and pecked his cheek. "I love you too, Robert Hausmann," she said.

CHAPTER
TWELVE

Judith went straight to her bed and began to strip it, folding the sheets and pillow cases and duvet cover into a neat pile. She had been in the Long Gallery for less than an hour, but it seemed much longer than that. She dared not think about it; the near-death events of last night made her feel weak and would have to be put to one side.

She fetched her grip and packed yesterday's clothes — cleaned and dried by Irena — in the bottom, followed by underwear. The rinsed thermos and the contents of the dressing table went on the top and down the sides. She tucked her handbag inside the canvas bag holding sketchbook, pencils, charcoal, then slung it over her shoulder and looked at her watch again. She had kept Hausmann waiting for less than fifteen minutes.

She took another minute to think about what happened next: it was of course facing Sybil and then Irena. At this moment she discovered she no longer cared about their reactions. She thought ahead of them and let herself imagine Jack, perhaps in an oxygen tent, certainly in a hospital bed with other people all around him. What had happened to Jack? Why had he gone to

Perth two months ago? Why had he come back home — probably only one week ago from today? Was it to suggest divorce or reconciliation?

She said aloud, "He's alive. That is what matters. And now — the present — is all I can manage. Stick to that."

She picked up her holdall and opened the door; Hausmann was sitting on the top stair and looked around as she fiddled with the key in the lock, then hauled himself up by the banister and took the holdall from her. She noted how tired he looked and wondered fleetingly how they were going to manage to get back to the Taunton hospital on a bike. Mainly, though, she felt thankful that he was there.

They went up to the next floor in the lift and along a transverse landing to the west side of the castle; he tapped on the first door they came to, and after a long pause it was opened a few inches and Sybil's face peered through.

She said immediately, "Listen, Jude. I don't want to quarrel with you — especially as I am wearing your nightie." She opened the door wider and revealed herself in the enormous dressing gown. "But if you've come to heal the breach with Robert . . ." She jerked her head in his direction as if he could not hear her. "Then you're wasting your time. I would very much like not to see him again, ever."

"I've come to say goodbye, Sybil. Robert is taking me to see Jack, who is in hospital. I'm not a widow, and I have let you think I am. I apologize for that. Jack and I split up two months ago, and I haven't heard from him since, but I do know he loves someone else." She paused. Sybil was staring at her, not taking anything in. Judith ploughed on. "I did wonder — when we did our sketching trip to the Lyn — I wondered then if he had died. It gave me an insight I — perhaps — lacked before. We seemed to draw closer. You and I. So even when I was certain he was still alive, I let the misunderstanding continue." She paused again, and again Sybil was silent, hanging on to the door, staring.

Judith took a breath. "I've come to say goodbye, anyway. I'll go straight home from Taunton. Probably won't see you again. But . . . thank you. It was good to have a friend."

She turned abruptly and walked back the way they had come. Sybil said something; Hausmann answered her. Judith went on walking until she came to the lift. She did not wait for him. The lift doors closed, she pressed the ground-floor button and stepped out almost into Irena's arms.

"Oh my goodness! Someone is in a hurry!" Irena put a tray on the counter. "My dear, I am managing very well — no need for you to check up! And I promise I will let everyone know the moment Bart returns. Why don't you sit with the others? Why on earth are you in your outdoor things?"

Judith began to blurt it out, just as she had done to Sybil. She was actually saying that she probably would not see Irena again when the lift doors opened and Hausmann stepped out with her holdall over one shoulder.

That convinced Irena more than anything Judith had said.

Her voice was high and accusing. "What have you done now, Robert? I know this is your doing — did you find Judith's husband? — take him to that hovel on Lundy? I can quite see you doing it! Oh my God, what have you done?"

Judith said quickly, "Robert saved my husband's life, Irena. And I have known he was alive all this time, and yet let you believe I was a widow because I could not admit, even to myself, that he had fallen in love with someone else and had left me. Forgive me."

Hausmann said roughly, "We're going, Sis. I need to get Mrs Freeman to Taunton. Her husband has been asking for her continually since he arrived at the hospital." He suddenly put his free arm around Irena's shoulders and held her to him for a moment. "Bart will be back with Nathaniel very soon now. Try to relax — once the storm is over everything will seem better."

Judith was already by the door, tugging at it hopelessly. Hausmann caught up with her and swung it inwards, and they were through and battling down the steps to the causeway. The road was channelling the rain towards the sea.

"Not unlike the water slide!" Hausmann shouted past the hood of his oilskin.

She looked at him. "Not unlike," she agreed. He looked almost exhilarated, and quite suddenly she smiled. "Thank you, Robert," she said.

He grinned back and took her arm and they trudged up the hill towards the inn.

The journey to Taunton was a strange interlude. Judith had never ridden pillion on a motorcycle before, and was bewildered by Hausmann's directions. "You have to put your arms right round me so that you know which way to throw your body weight . . . bit like the Markhams dancing the other night . . . last night, in fact! That means your head as well — put it against my back as if you are listening to my body. Sorry if that sounds practically perverted, but in this weather it will be necessary to bond. Do you understand?"

"I think so."

He made a big thing about her clothing — it could not flap — the helmet had to be properly secured, her hands had to go beneath his oilskin and hang on to his sweater, her feet be on the rests at all times. And her bags had to be carefully stowed.

For the first few miles, until they were past Minehead, she had to concentrate; after that the roar of the bike, the warmth of her hands beneath his oilskin, the outline of his body, became part of the strangeness. She remembered sleeping in her mother's bed after her father died, and her mother saying, "Will you sit in my lap or shall I sit in yours?" Hausmann was well and truly in her lap.

The speed eased as they joined the motorway and then accelerated again. Just a few miles later they were peeling off on to the slip road for Taunton and edging slowly into the rush-hour traffic. Judith was able to sit fair and square behind Hausmann, head raised, looking around to get her bearings. The rain made for a murky early evening, but she realized Hausmann was keeping to the outskirts of the town as he manoeuvred past stationary cars towards the hospital. They came to the wide avenue leading down to the hospital, turned in at the gates and coasted unerringly into a designated parking space.

Hausmann held the machine steady with his legs while he removed his helmet, and Judith scrambled off and stood in the rain, unclipping hers and holding it in front of her. She said, "Robert. Thank you. Are you all right?"

He pulled the bike on to its stand and took her helmet. "I didn't go to sleep, did I?" In the tall overhead lights she saw he was smiling.

"I didn't notice. I felt totally safe."

"Good." He unstrapped her bags, took her arm and piloted her towards the entrance. "Listen. I'm going to show you the waiting area. That's where I'll be when you're ready to go — probably firmly asleep by that time! Does that sound all right?"

"I think so. But . . . I don't know how long I'll be."

"It doesn't matter. I can sleep anywhere. Matthew can stay with me or go to this room I've rented for him. We'll work something out between us."

Suddenly she was nervous. Everything — Jack and all the problems — was here and now. They walked up a ramp and through into a reception area. Visitors were coming and going. She looked at her watch; it was almost seven o'clock. Hausmann walked to a desk and began to talk to someone; he turned and guided Judith gently to a chair. "Take off your waterproofs. Pile them here — they'll be OK." They both stripped off what they could; Judith looked down at her dry jeans and sweater and shouldered her grip and her canvas bag again. She was going to see Jack. Jack Freeman. At least he would recognize her; she had practically lived in jeans for the past year.

Hausmann took her to a lift. He was talking. "Second floor, Jude." The lift was enormous, a small room. "Here are the buttons, OK? Now . . . turn left and follow the signs. He's in a single room. I'm going to leave you at the door. When you come out, turn right and follow the exit signs."

She glanced up to thank him; his dark face looked cadaverous.

She said, "Oh, Robert . . . you must sleep . . . seriously —"

"I'll shove two chairs together and sleep — don't worry, I'm good at it." He tried for a grin. "Here we are. Go on. He needs you."

He turned and shambled off. For a moment she almost ran after him. Then she put her hand on the door, rested her forehead on it and took a deep breath.

The bed was facing the door, and with its drip stands and the oxygen equipment looked small and cluttered. A chair fitted in on one side, and she had a glimpse of Matthew sitting in it and leaning over a newspaper spread across the quilt before he turned and saw her. His face — his dear familiar face — registered delight and relief in equal measure, then he put a finger to his lips.

Judith had already seen that Jack's eyes were closed. She came in, closed the door gently behind her, and, still in complete silence, let Matthew envelop her in a bear hug. They rocked for several moments. Every time she saw the boys she swore that they had grown taller, which at twenty-eight was ridiculous. But this time there was a difference, and she knew that she must be shrinking. She pulled away, holding his upper arms, smiling up at him, mouthing reassurances. He nodded, then indicated the door. She looked at Jack; he was undeniably asleep, but she could see how ill he was. He had always boasted about looking "lean and hungry". Now his face was gaunt.

Matthew opened the door and ushered her back into the wide corridor. He whispered, "He looked worse than that this morning — you can almost watch him recovering."

"Oh, Matt . . . I dreamt that you were chasing him and Toby . . . oh my God, why are we whispering?"

"Mum, stop crying. I'm trying to tell you he's going to be all right. He had a cup of tea an hour ago, and said that he was going to have a nap, and why didn't I look at the football results? I haven't told him that Robert was going to fetch you. He will be so pleased. This is what it's all been about. Finding you."

She controlled her ridiculous tears with difficulty. There were so many questions, and she had no idea how much Matt knew. She held her side and straightened. "We must talk. Of course. But not now, Matt. Mr Hausmann is in the waiting room. I want you to take him to his room, digs, whatever it is — he says he has rented something — and make him lie down and

203

sleep. Same applies to you. I will stay with Dad tonight and see you in the morning."

"Mum, I don't think you will be allowed to stay overnight like that."

She actually smiled. "I think it will be all right." She rummaged in her canvas bag, found pen and paper and scribbled her mobile phone number. "You've probably lost this, otherwise you would have phoned me the other evening when you were at home."

"Oh, Mum. I'd forgotten you were . . . like this." He took the paper. "Thank God you're here. Dad hid his symptoms so well — we had no idea —"

"I know how he can be. Thank you for chasing after him, Matt."

"He was like this when he arrived in July — that's why he got on so well with Robert — they were both . . . sort of . . . haunted. I think Robert kind of unloaded on Dad, and when he went back to England Dad sort of crumbled. Day by day, he crumbled. It was horrible, Mum. Dad couldn't make phone calls and he told us that neither could you. Security reasons."

"What on earth does that mean? Surely you could have let me know somehow or other how ill he was?"

"Mum, he made us promise not to. He said it was nothing to do with you, and that was the way he wanted to keep it. We thought — Len thought — it was something to do with work. A libel suit — all this phone-hacking business."

"For goodness' sake — that doesn't sound like Dad! Much too melodramatic!" She forced a smile.

"We're still a family then, Mum?"

"Yes, of course we are."

"Uncle Len kept saying that to Dad." He dropped his voice again. "Was it since Gran died? We wondered whether Dad was having a breakdown of some kind — we could not think what else it could be, unless he really is in trouble with the law, of course."

"Dad is not in any trouble with the law!"

"Well, it happened before in our family, didn't it." He stopped abruptly. "Anyway, so Dad came to Australia and met that crazy artist chap —"

"I don't know what you mean, Matt. We've never had trouble with the law in our family. And Robert Hausmann saved Dad's life. Let's stop talking like this. We're together. Everything is going to be all right." She took a deep breath. "Let's get Dad through this."

"Yes. All right."

"Go! Sleep well. Tomorrow we'll see what we can do about moving Dad back home."

He smiled properly at last. "Good old Mum!" And she watched him go slowly towards the lifts and realized that Jack had said nothing about another woman to his brother or to his sons. Whatever was haunting him was still there.

He slept for another two hours, during which time Judith sat in the chair Matt had vacated and even found herself looking at the newspaper spread across Jack's bed. At eight thirty a nurse came in and checked the drips. She raised her brows at Judith and smiled professionally. "Mrs Freeman? I think you are exactly what the doctor ordered!" She indicated the array of technology. "This is first aid. What your husband needs is complete rest and home cooking. We make allowances for his friend's anxiety, of course, but even private beds are at a premium." Her smile softened. "Your son explained the mix-up about your whereabouts, and obviously we would never have turned your husband away — but it is good that they have found you and you are here!"

Judith could imagine instantly what lay behind this obvious reproach. Hausmann had not minced words.

"It was one of those impulse things," she whispered back. "I thought I would be back home before anyone noticed I'd been away."

"Yes. Quite. Will you be all right on that chair?"

"Of course. I'm so grateful that I can stay with him." Despite what she had said to Matt, she had anticipated a battle.

"Now you've been found we don't want to lose you again." The words were a little tart, but the tone was softening all the time.

Judith tried to make her smile reassuring; she could think of nothing to say. However, less than ten minutes later another nurse, younger and uncritical, came in bearing a mug of very hot tea with no less than four packets of sugar.

"Sister said to wake up your friend and ask him whether you would like tea or coffee, and he said tea with lots of sugar."

Judith accepted the mug gratefully. "Did he say anything else?"

"He told me to go away. But then he was all right."

"Oh good. Thank you so much."

"I'm going off duty now. Can I give him a message?"

"That would be kind of you. Could you tell him to go away?" She grinned at the girl. "And to come back in the morning."

The girl returned her grin.

Judith did the usual thing with her tea; inhaling the steam, closing her eyes. When she opened them, Jack was looking at her. They stared. He tried to speak and she held up her hand.

"No words, Jack. Later, perhaps. I am here and I am staying here, that is all we need to know for the moment." She stirred the sugar into her mug. "Let this cool and then we'll share it."

He watched her every movement: from the tearing of the sugar packets to their disposal in the pedal bin by the door. When she presented him with a half-teaspoonful of tea, he pursed his lips and managed to swallow some of it. Then he closed his eyes as if exhausted. He did not open them again until she had almost finished the tea. She watched him carefully. This was Jack Freeman who really had flown the nest. She drank deeply, tipping her head to drain the mug, and when she put it on the top of the locker he was watching her.

She said, "It's gone. But I can scrape out some sugar." She offered a tiny drop of syrup and he took it obediently and licked his lips appreciatively. She tried to reload the spoon, and wondered how they would pass the night. She proffered the empty spoon, and he took it from her and put it into his mouth like a lollipop.

She said, "I couldn't believe it when Robert arrived this afternoon and told me you and Matt were the two he had rescued and taken to this hospital! I pictured you with Len. In Perth." She stood up and went to the washbasin and rinsed the mug. Then she washed her hands and face. When she turned back to the bed he had lifted himself slightly, put the spoon on a tissue, hung the oxygen mask on its hook. He said hoarsely, "I thought you might have known. It seemed to me we often shared a sixth sense."

"We did."

His face showed that he understood she no longer had a sixth sense where he was concerned. She said slowly, "I dreamed about you one night. I did not see your face but I saw Matt chasing you. It was so . . . random."

He shook his head, his voice slightly less hoarse. "But there were other times. When you were sketching. Rocks. Then trees and a cottage. Not random. Lifelines for me."

She felt her eyes stretch and looked down quickly. "For a time I thought you might be dead. The *Magnet* used your very first Fish-Frobisher strip. When I rang William he had no idea where you were."

"I wanted to be dead. Len promised he would block all phone calls."

She wanted to cry out. She swallowed and kept staring down at the blue cellular blanket. At last she said, "How could you . . . how could you wish that?"

"Because I hated myself. And still do. But there was Matt and Toby. And then Robert had this grand plan."

She glanced up and saw that his eyes were closed and a ghost of a smile lifted his face. She looked down again and felt her own eyes fill stingingly.

Jack whispered, "The air on Lundy and you just across the water. We would stay there. Together. And everything would be all right."

"I know. He specializes in those sorts of plans."

"He needs someone like you to keep his feet on the ground."

She knew he had opened his eyes and was watching her downbent head. She said, "This morning. When you arrived here and they connected you up to all this . . . stuff." She risked looking up as she indicated the drip stand. "Can you remember anything . . . I don't know . . . anything happening?"

He stared at her and blinked fiercely, concentrating.

"I was pretty delirious at times. I tried to picture you. Robert said he would bring you to the hospital, and I tried to imagine you away from home. Different place. But still . . . you. Doing things. Ordinary things."

"Making tea?" she encouraged.

"Yes. Making tea lots of times."

There was a long pause. She looked up and their gazes connected.

She said, "Something else?"

"A space. An exhibition space? Thunder — but that was here, too. You held something. Not one of your pencils. A charcoal stick. And you started to draw. Quickly. You'd done it before — rocks and cliffs. This was different. Brief." He drew a sharp breath. "We were together. Jude, we were together."

He fumbled one hand towards her and she took it and held it between both of hers. "The Fish-Frobishers!" His whisper escalated roughly. "So ordinary, Jude. Our bread and butter. Tell me how it turned out."

She told him, and added that the strip was on its way to the *Magnet* offices. When she stopped speaking he was smiling. He turned his hand within hers and lay back, and within minutes she saw that he was asleep.

Time went slowly. There were too many questions still to ask, but she understood that he had established something for them both: their closeness had somehow survived these past weeks and months. She rummaged in one of her bags and came up with a pencil and her sketchbook. She captured Jack in five lines, then added two more to take in his hair, which was standing on end. She drew a pillow and a bedhead to frame him.

It was past midnight when the night sister came in. She brought a carton of soup and some supermarket bread and saw the cartoon drawing on the cellular blanket. She nodded.

"You've got him exactly. But he will look better soon — I promise you."

"He's looked like that most of this year. I didn't see it until now."

The sister shrugged. "When you see someone every day you often don't notice changes — they come gradually. He must have been very low to become so ill. And so suddenly, too." She went to the drip stand and started to dismantle it. "He probably felt terrible and hid it."

She removed a cannula from Jack's arm; he smiled but did not open his eyes.

"Why don't you use the bathroom while I'm here? You might be able to sleep for an hour or two. That soup is scalding hot."

Judith found her sponge bag and went into the tiny bathroom. She swilled her face with warm water and did her teeth. When she came back into the room the sister was leaving. She had pushed two chairs together, lined them with one blanket and placed a pillow and more blankets on top. She smiled and was gone.

Judith sipped her soup and chewed on the bread, and felt drowsiness spreading from her eyes and face, through her arms and legs. She remembered putting the carton in the flip bin and settling herself into the pillow and knowing she would sleep.

When she woke it was disappointing to glance at her watch and see it was only just gone 2 a.m. She shifted so that she could see Jack; every muscle in her arms and back protested.

Jack was sitting almost bolt upright, the blanket pushed down to his waist. She groaned.

"Oh, Jude . . . you looked so relaxed."

"I was. But I thought it would be about seven o'clock and it's only two."

"And you're stiff and uncomfortable."

"You could say that. How come you're awake, sitting up and talking normally?"

211

"I woke up, went to the loo, drank some water and came back to bed!"

"Brilliant."

"It is. I'm better!"

"Rubbish. Go back to sleep."

"Only if you come and share the bed. Come on. It's just about wide enough. You can sit on my lap."

She lifted her head sharply. "Oh, Jack."

"I know it's what Eunice used to say — you've said it practically every night since we went to Paris. Come on — it works, and there are no bits and pieces of tubing to get in our way. Bring your own pillow."

She stumbled away from the chairs, pulled her pillow to her chest and collapsed next to Jack. He moved carefully to make room for her, then put his cheek against the nape of her neck and whispered, "Sleep tight, darling."

She thought, totally bewildered: There's no other woman. Nothing, no one between us.

And she closed her eyes again and was gone.

CHAPTER
THIRTEEN

They went home the next afternoon. Jack was weak, but all his tests were positive and he seemed utterly content. The last two months might never have happened. The doctor who discharged him assured the four of them that all Jack needed was rest and a good sensible diet. It sounded routine . . . easy.

Judith seemed alone in finding the whole situation bizarre. Robert drove them in Bart's car, which made it odder still. He had to have been back to Castle Dove to fetch it, clean himself up and change his clothes, but although Judith asked him twice about Nat and Sybil she learned nothing.

All Robert said was: "I saw Bart when I collected the car keys. No one else." Matt, who sat beside him, made no attempt at conversation, and Jack was not strong enough to make more than appreciative noises at the autumnal trees and the first glimpse of the sea as they came off the motorway. These escalated to near-ecstasy as they manoeuvred on to their own drive.

Robert came in with them, and while Judith settled Jack into his armchair next to the gas fire he switched on the heating and told Matt rather brusquely to make some tea. He shook his head at Matt's offer of a mug and left soon after. Judith thanked him and held the door open while he scribbled something on a piece of paper and put the paper by the telephone.

"Ring me if you need me," he said. Then he was gone, and Judith was left holding open the door, looking at the empty road and feeling bereft.

The rest of that week seemed to belong to some kind of time warp. Judith found herself checking the calendar, glancing at her watch, frowning with disbelief as she read the account of Arnold McCready's funeral in the weekly newspaper. Matt's presence in the house was as strange as Jack's, yet just as normal. He picked up the threads of his Englishness, as both boys did every time they came home. He accepted his father's "breakdown" and subsequent illness as "one of those things". He said in his serious voice, "Mum, we've got to put it behind us. Otherwise it makes it worse for Dad. He's been ill, and now he's better. It always helps to simplify things — like Dad used to say, one line is better than two." He followed his own advice and settled into local life, as he and Toby did twice a year. Judith heard him on the phone to Perth and unashamedly listened in.

"It was hairy, of course. But that artist chap — Robert Hausmann — he arrived soon after we got home . . . yeah, he sort of took over. What? Batty? Well, I guess so, but he conjured Mum up, and then of course everything was OK." There was a long pause while he listened, then he said, "That's fine by me, Tobe. I'll do the rescue stuff, I'm kind of into that now. Tell Doc Zack I carried my dad down the side of a cliff

214

in a hurricane last Monday — that should impress him!" He laughed, and Judith had a sudden memory flash of the Long Gallery creaking in the winds from the Atlantic. She turned into the kitchen, where she was preparing vegetables for the evening meal. That time and place felt more real than this one — the storm and the lightning and Sybil hiding her face. Not this house and the blandness of meals and bed-making. She stared through the window at her beloved garden, bathed in typically mellow September sun; was she no longer a nest-maker?

The rain had stopped at last, and the countryside was clean and washed bare of the fallen leaves. The house was not quite as tidy as she had left it: Matt's predilection for reading newspapers in the bathroom meant that the laundry basket was piled high with the previous week's sports news. Her computer was loaded with messages from Martha Gifford, which she high-mindedly did not read. Likewise with messages going to Martha. She tried to be interested, speculating as to whether they kept up a regular correspondence, and whether Martha might become a nuisance, as she so often had in the past. She had been very much younger than the boys, always trying to play football, always in the way. But Matt was nearly thirty now. Might there be something in it? Might she go to Australia to be with him or . . . might he come home?

Not even that prospect made much impression on Judith, however. The house had waited for her return, yet failed dismally to wrap her in the usual comfort of homecoming. Castle Dove and the countryside around it had been strange but exciting. Home was even stranger and not exciting. There were times when it became worse than unexciting: full of unexpected fears. She waited for Jack to talk to her, yet dreaded to hear what he might say.

On the Saturday, after four days of living in this limbo, Matt went into Bristol city centre to meet with a school friend, and Jack and Judith had the house to themselves. They went through the motions: Jack was in the bathroom for a long time while Judith cleared the breakfast things and tidied generally. The post came, and there was a slip of a letter for her and a thick one for Jack from the *Magnet*. He had already fielded an email from William about Judith's contribution which had said simply, "Keep 'em coming!" so the gap of his two-month absence had been bridged. She weighed this large envelope in her hand and wondered what was in it, then put it on the hall table without further interest, stuffed her letter into her pocket, and went into the living room to look at the garden. The wind that had rocked the Long Gallery at Castle Dove had wrecked most of the late flowers here, but surprisingly she noticed a group of dahlias against the wall still holding aloft their blossom heads to dry in the sun. That's what she would do with this long empty day without Matt: she would spend it in the garden. Jack no longer needed constant "surveillance"; he might even make them some lunch. And there was his letter from William . . . She went into the utility room and put on her wellingtons and an old fleece, found gardening gloves and went outside.

Two hours later, with four green bags of weeds and an aching back as evidence of her labour, she went inside again. Earlier, Jack had waved from the kitchen and held a coffee mug on high, but she had shaken her head and continued to trowel around the perennials and clear beneath the shrubs. Now, she realized she needed some coffee and probably a sandwich or some soup. Or something. She was tired and aching.

The kitchen was as she had left it, except for Jack's coffee mug on the draining board. She stared at it in disbelief. Was this how it was going to be? They had done everything — everything — together, hadn't they? And Jack was well enough to have made some sandwiches, wasn't he?

Angrily she washed her hands at the sink, reached for the roller towel, found it very damp, and practically tore it down and threw it into the machine. Suddenly she wanted to cry. She held on to the edge of the sink and squeezed her eyes tightly shut and let the questions hammer inside her head. She blanked them all out . . . but, even unacknowledged, they were still there, and were the kernel of a much bigger question. How long could they go on without some kind of explanation? Once Matt went back to Perth, how would they spend their days? All right, like Matt, she accepted that Jack's mind and body had broken down, but had his memory gone as well? Was he expecting everything to go back to how it had been?

She found a clean towel and hung it up, then began to assemble crockery and food on the kitchen table, made herself some coffee. Perhaps she should look for a job. She sat down with a bump; who on earth would employ a middle-aged woman without a single qualification?

The door of the study opened and Jack's voice — quite strong — came down the hall. "That you, Jude? Is it time for lunch?"

And suddenly the anger — simmering everywhere, it seemed — overwhelmed her, and she yelled back childishly, "Food and skivvy await the master!"

It did not help one bit when he took it as banter — as it might well have been in the old days — and came into the kitchen grinning widely and looking, she had to admit, very like Jack had used to look: energized, almost excited.

He sat down carefully, however — his movements were still conscious efforts — and moderated the grin. "William has sent a bundle of newspapers. Seems a few journalists have been messing about with all the rules and a scandal is about to break. The suggestion is there's been a mole — not quite Establishment, but hanging on in there. I thought I'd call him Maurice the Mole. I've got an email ready for William: a bit of a storyline with some attachments — sketches, notes. That was why I was waving at you."

He put his hands on the edge of his chair and changed his position slightly.

She said, "You've been sitting for too long." She stood up and put both hands beneath his elbow. "Come on. A turn around the garden, then I've got some soup."

He groaned. "How long does soup-time go on for?"

218

"This is Mexican bean soup with chillies." She opened the door with her back, just as Sybil and Robert had done at Castle Dove. "Puts hair on your chest."

"Oh goodie," he responded, following her on to the patio, stopping, drawing in long appreciative breaths of the autumnal air. He lifted his head, closed his eyes, and then moved away from her and leaned on the rail where Matt had flung his wetsuit after a dip in the Bristol Channel the day before. She felt a dull acceptance somewhere in her chest, and thought that it was not that difficult, they could keep it up, perhaps even pretend nothing had happened.

Then he said, "I'd love to see Lundy Island. All I remember is wind and rain. Robert says it's microcosmic, a state of mind."

She came and stood beside him, gripping the wrought iron hard.

He said, "When I ran away to Perth — after it happened — there was Robert, in hospital after he, too, had tried to run away! So I knew that didn't work." He shook his head. "He kept on and on about Lundy. Wanted to take me back and show me. But by then I knew nothing was going to work without you." He glanced sideways at her and gave her a wry smile. "Stuck it out for weeks, as you know, told myself it was better for you — fresh start — that sort of thing. Then I had an email from that master of understatement — Arnold McCready — he'd seen you somewhere and said you 'weren't good'. So I told Len I was going home, and he said he'd come with me, and I didn't

219

want that, so I walked out. Matt caught me up at the airport." He shrugged. "All the wrong things . . ."

He turned and leaned his back against the railing. "Jude. I'm sorry. I see now that you must have known all the time, and you were trying to make the best of a bad job. I would have gone along with that for ever, my love, but . . . it wasn't right. I was responsible for her death, Jude. The only other person who knows that is Robert Hausmann. It was one of the reasons Robert wanted us to go to Lundy. Apparently you learn acceptance there."

He stopped speaking. She found she was gripping the railing much too hard. A death? Who had died? She relaxed her hand with some difficulty. He was not talking sense; she must be . . . reasonable.

"Jack. You've got it wrong. I have *not* known what was happening. I *still* don't know. I was wrapped in sadness about losing Mum. I was devastated at losing Naomi. I admit I wasn't putting much into anything. And then you left. I hated you; but when I thought you were dead . . . oh my God, Jack, I was poleaxed." She tried to smile and felt her mouth tremble. "Perhaps this isn't such a good time — you're still pretty weak and this new project with the *Magnet*, it's something upbeat at last. But, I do need to know. Who died?" She saw his distress and strengthened her voice. "Listen. Let's go and have that soup. And then, perhaps . . ."

He nodded. "That sounds good. Things never seem so bad on a full stomach!"

It was a pathetic attempt at one of their old exchanges. She held the door open for him and they went inside.

Amazingly, he managed a full bowl of the soup; it was strong stuff and he drank a glass of water afterwards, then put his bowl into the sink and sat up very straight in his chair. It made her nervous, and she started to wash up noisily. When he asked her to sit down she suggested they go into the sitting room and "make themselves comfortable" as if they were guests in their own house.

He repeated quietly, "Sit down, Jude. Please."

She sat opposite him this time. He was out of accidental reach, no fear of their knees touching. She put her hands on her lap beneath the table and pulled at her fingers as if trying to lengthen them.

He said quietly, "I cannot believe you had no inkling. We weren't easy together any more." She said nothing and he took a breath. "It happened at the office party, of course. She was — she was so unhappy. Everyone was at it — you remember from other years. She said it made her feel the odd one out even more. I got some more drinks . . . Jude, please believe me when I tell you it was impossible not to . . . not to . . ." She made a sound and he said, "OK. I knew immediately that I'd done the wrong thing, simply because she was so happy — Naomi seemed contented enough when I met her here, but I'd never seen her like this. She lit up. I wasn't surprised when she came round on Boxing Day with that champagne and the chocolates for you. I was surprised — and aghast — when she came into the study and . . . well, obviously thought there had been much more to the party than I had."

He had not heard the tiny scream of protest as he spoke Naomi's name. He was somewhere else, deep in a time from which there was no escape. He rested his elbow on the table and put his head on one hand. "Yes, all right, I could have — I should have — clamped down that day. But I thought she'd come to her senses of her own accord. Oh, I don't know what I thought, Jude. Only that I was sick with myself for letting you down. You were still so fond of her — dependent on her — and far from easing her away, my efforts to talk to her properly seemed to make her dependent on me." He stopped talking. Strangely he left an echo circling oh so gently around the kitchen. Naomi. Like a chord played on a guitar. Naomi. Naomi. So obvious. Yet never suspected. Never imagined.

Judith held on to her thumb and forced herself to make an effort. Naomi and Jack. It did not work. Naomi wouldn't have let it happen. So . . . Naomi was someone else, not the Naomi she had known. Naomi was a widow who had nursed a sick husband for — how many years? She had never spoken of him, never described him. She had said once, "I was Naomi Shannon — I might go back to that name. Naomi Parsons is so hard. I never liked it."

So was it Naomi Parsons or Naomi Shannon who fell in love with someone else's husband? She had warned Judith about it — tried to put her on her guard, perhaps? Judith found, quite suddenly, that she could indeed imagine someone called Naomi Shannon falling

222

in love with Jack. She could almost see the long neck, the head tilted back, the brown eyes as clear as milkless tea. She looked up and said, "So. I was betrayed twice. By my husband and then by my friend — my only friend, actually."

"I've said that to myself so often, Jude. That's why I went to see her in London during the spring bank holiday."

"Ah, I see. When the boys were here." She wanted to hurt him. She could not remember the holiday, but she said in the same level tone, "Yes, of course. That was the day they went to Woolacombe for the surfing championships. I thought of walking down to Arnold McCready's and seeing if Arnie wanted to come and play but —"

"Jude, please don't."

"All right. Is there much more? Only I've got one or two jobs —"

"She arrived. She had insisted we meet at the Ritz. Tea at the Ritz. She had an overnight bag — said she thought I had booked us in for the weekend. It was horrible. Horrible. When she saw my face she began threatening again. I told her she could do what she wanted — tell the whole world — it would make no difference. I would not see her again. At last she believed me. And she looked at me, picked up her bag and bolted. If she'd left the way she had come she would have gone into Green Park. As it was, she ran out into Piccadilly, which was packed with holiday traffic and . . . and . . . and . . ." He opened his hands, then clenched them and put his fists on the table.

"They said the car mounted the pavement. But it killed just Naomi, and there were other people all around her. It had to be deliberate, Jude. And it had to be because of what I'd said. I can't even remember . . . I had told myself — schooled myself — to be brutal. I couldn't go on any longer. It had to be final. And it was."

She was aghast. This was most definitely not the Naomi she had known. Naomi's serene ambience had been part of her, never deserting her, not even when her long legs were twisted inextricably behind her washing machine. This was a different Naomi. Naomi Shannon. Passionate rather than compassionate. For a moment Judith saw those same long ungainly legs, unrecognizable beneath the wheels of a car. She coughed, then choked.

He sat there, stone-still, probably seeing it all again like an endless strip of film. She saw it herself. And more; it had been she who had urged Jack to take Naomi to that office party, and she should have known only too well how easy it was after a few drinks to let a flirtation become something more.

She stood up abruptly and ran water into a glass and drank it. She leaned over the sink and choked again, drank again. Stood upright.

Jack was sitting there. Staring.

She said levelly, "Why didn't it come out at the inquest? Did you give evidence?"

He looked up at her and said drearily, "I didn't know. Not then. I left immediately and went through the park and on to Paddington for that six o'clock train. I heard it on the car radio the next day. When I got in you had heard it, too, and told me. If I'd had to tell you I would probably have started from the beginning. I don't know."

"You said nothing? To the police? To — to *anyone?*"

"No. What was there to say? I thought it was over — I told myself it was her choice. But it was just beginning."

"Someone might have seen her — been able to tell you it was an accident." Judith heard her own voice, offering what? Some kind of comfort? She gripped the sink again, battling with another wave of nausea. After a moment she ran the tap, splashed water on her face.

"I don't think I'm taking this in, Jack." She turned and leaned her back on the edge of the sink. Jack had not moved, but his stare had slightly changed, and he looked defeated. She said, "I learned something from my weekend at Castle Dove — people are rarely what they seem to be. Behind every bully there's a victim. Hiding. And behind the victims there are many bullies. Manipulators — that's probably what I mean." She shrugged. "That's obvious, isn't it?" She leaned forward. "But . . . oh, Jack, I thought we were above that. I thought that moment in the lecture room — and then the few days in Paris — I thought that's how it would be always. Always and always." She sounded childish, silly. She raised her brows self-mockingly. "Same applies to Naomi. Naomi had nursed her husband for ten years — I remember now, she told me it was ten years. She missed him terribly. Just as we missed Mum. But Naomi must have seen it as an escape." She could not look at Jack any more. She closed her eyes. "Oh God. Oh, Jack . . . you should have told me . . . after the party . . . you should have told me."

"Yes." The single word seemed to fall heavily to the floor. They had come full circle. Another silence filled the kitchen as the sun began to make for the sea.

It was warm; somewhere a fly was buzzing and she hadn't turned the tap off properly, it was dripping.

She said, "I have to walk round the garden, Jack. Perhaps you should go and sit in an armchair, you don't look safe there."

She went through the utility room and out on to the patio, then straight down by the border that fourteen days ago she had tidied so carefully before deciding to answer the advert in the local paper about the exhibition at Castle Dove. She dropped down the steps into the vegetable garden and walked alongside the single row of bean sticks to the wall that overlooked the sea. When she came to the gap where the top stones had fallen away during the year of the snow, she leaned her elbows on the opening and looked across the roofs towards Wales.

She said aloud, "He's ill. He could go one way or the other. I'm not ill, but I could also go one way or the other." She heard her words, closed her eyes and saw them written in the sudden darkness. She thought, for just an instant, that she was offering herself a choice. Then she saw there was no choice.

She had no idea how long she stood there trying to accept that truth. At some point she realized it was colder, and turned with some vague notion of fetching a cardigan. Then Matt's voice came from the patio.

"Mum — are you coming in now? What shall I do about the oven? And can I hang my wetsuit in the utility room?"

She climbed the steps on to the lawn and stood looking at him. Already life had gone back to normal for him.

She said, "Yes, I'm just coming. Don't know about the oven. And yes to the wetsuit, so long as it's not still dripping."

She trudged on to the patio and into the house. She had thought it might feel like shouldering a heavy load, but it didn't. She locked the back door and went on into the kitchen. There was a wonderful smell coming from the oven and the warmth told her that it had been on for some time. Matt followed her.

"It's one of Dad's curries, isn't it? How long did it take him to make that?"

"I don't know. He wasn't too good when I went into the garden."

"When was that?"

She looked at him wide-eyed. "I don't know."

"Mum — you check up on him every five minutes!" He paused and then blurted, "Did you have a row?"

"Of course not! Well, there was a stumbling block."

"He told you to get off his back, and you did!" Matt was grinning. "And it was the right thing to do, Mum! He made one of his curries and it smells good!"

She nodded wryly, surprised that it had taken her so long in the garden to realize that she had no real choice. She put on oven gloves, opened the oven door, blinked at the rush of heat and eased out the cast-iron casserole. She prodded the contents with a knife, then replaced the pot carefully and switched off the oven.

"It can finish in its own heat," she said. "I'll see to the rice in a minute."

She fetched mugs — washed and put away — and made tea. "I didn't expect you back so soon, actually."

"I did tell you. I didn't think you were listening. You were worried about Dad. As usual."

"Yes. Yes, I was. Strangely enough, I don't think I am now — not in the same way."

Matt made a face. "One curry doth not a menu make!" He burst out laughing. "Hey, listen to the son of the two artists! A quip, no less!"

She registered the "two artists" and that Matt's Australian good temper had escalated into an English excitement.

She sat opposite him, pushed his mug of tea across the table. "What's happened today — something good?"

"Artist mother very acute or astute?"

"Both. Come on. You're different. You've reverted to being eighteen."

"Two things. Shall I save them till Dad wakes up?"

"Where is he?"

"On the sofa in the living room. That's how I know he's asleep."

"He'll be awake by now. Let's go in." She poured more tea and they took it in with them. Jack was awake and had pushed himself up. He looked awful in one way, totally drained. But also peaceful.

"I can smell it from here," he greeted them. "Did I set the temperature too high?"

"It's great, Dad. Like old times." Matt sat on the sofa and held Jack's mug towards him. "Mum's investigated. She's going to do the rice in a minute."

Judith watched Jack as he took his mug of tea and inhaled the steam just as she did. They had grown up together, the two of them. It was worth trying, surely? But it was her turn to say something, and that was going to be difficult.

But it came to her very naturally, and she said, "Matt's got some news to tell us, Jack."

Matt made a face. "Sounds suitably condescending, Mother dear." He grinned at her. "First things first. Martha has done her first year — NQT it's called, which means newly qualified teacher. So we thought we might make it official."

Jack stopped inhaling and said, "Not Martha Gifford? Little Martha Gifford who stole your marbles when you were ten years old?"

"She wanted me to notice her, Dad. And she never — not once — got me mixed up with Toby. And she's not little any more." He looked at his mother with some defiance. "She was six at the time, please remember."

Judith discovered she wanted to laugh. "When you went off to Perth with Uncle Len she came to see me. She suggested that I use my maternal influence to put a stop to the whole thing. I'd forgotten all about it. She was fourteen. Hot pants and a drawstring top."

Matt drew his top lip down. "She wears conventional clothes now, of course."

"Yes, I suppose she would. What a shame."

"She's allowed to wear trousers at work — more practical, of course — but one of the boys told her she had a nice bum, so she's worn skirts ever since. It was quite innocent, too, he's eight years old."

Judith avoided Jack's gaze.

"I think that was jolly decent of her!"

Matt looked at her suspiciously. "Mum, please be serious. We're engaged."

She was suddenly very serious; she looked at him, loving him so hard she wondered he did not reel back into the sofa. "Matt! Darling Matt! How absolutely wonderful! She was such a character — she'll be just great for you! Is it really going to happen? Is she going to chuck in her job and leave her family — for you?"

"No." He was delighted with her reaction, taking Jack's mug and putting it on the coffee table with great care before leaning over to take her hand and swing it crazily. "That's the other bit of news. Last time we were over, Tobe and I had a look at a transport firm operating from Filton. Len was interested — he thinks it's time he came home — wanted our opinion. It's a small outfit, but plenty of opportunity for expansion. They stand in for the ambulance service and coastguard rescue; even the police use them. They need other machines and other pilots. Toby and Len are coming over and we're going to get round the table." He released her hand and she massaged it. "What do

230

you think? Martha and I went and had a look this morning. She was dead impressed."

Judith really was stunned into silence. Jack said tentatively, "It's a bit much to take in — why haven't you mentioned it before, for Pete's sake?"

Matt opened his eyes wide. "It did not seem quite . . . appropriate?" he suggested. He added soberly, "Last time, there was Gran. This time there was you, Dad. We won't go any further until you get strong again and can come and look round with us."

Jack said, "I don't know a thing about the transport business. But if Len OKs it that will be enough for us." He sat forward with some difficulty. "Are things looking up? Martha Gifford. This opportunity for all of you to come back home — is it what you really want, Matt?"

Matt said, "Well, of course. I mean I've always known about Martha. Haven't seen much of her in these last few years, of course, but she's been kind of built into my life. And she was so young — just as well Len took us off your hands, Dad. We needed space and physical work. Anyway, Len made it plain to us right from the start that he would be coming back one day."

Jack said, "Jude?"

She swallowed. "It's wonderful. Perhaps . . . it will be possible."

Matt was surprised. "What's not possible, Mum? Len will sell the Australian business, no problem. And part of the deal is that we come with the new helicopters. We've had our licences for years now — you know that."

Judith nodded. "And Dad has a new project, too. It could be possible. It could actually work."

"Mum, you sound distinctly odd. I'll go and see to the rice and shout when it's ready. You're probably faint from lack of food." He almost leapt up, then paused at the door; Judith could almost feel the energy fizzing from him. "You know, if we'd been here Dad wouldn't have been ill. And even if he had, we could have looked after him — we plan to live here, you know. It's twenty minutes along the motorway to Filton. And Martha likes the local schools — actually she hates driving into Bristol every day. We've been looking at houses. There's an old cottage on the Somerset Levels — we could do it up. Your turn to leave home next, Mum!" He laughed. "If you feel the need to do a runner — you could walk that far."

She picked up a cushion and flung it in his direction. She was very close to tears. All this time, when she had thought herself isolated, there had been plans being made for the future that involved her. And Jack.

Jack was actually smiling. And waiting for her to say something.

She leaned forward and whispered, "Martha Gifford!"

He nodded. "She went a bit wild? I remember her coming to tea, bringing flowers for Mum."

"Angling for news of Matt? She thought Australia was all sex and sea."

"She looked through the latest snaps — they were of the boys working."

"Was it after that she buckled down and began her training?"

"Four years ago. Yes. Probably."

"We didn't take her seriously."

Jack drew down his mouth. "We should have done. After the theft of the marbles, we should have known she was very serious!"

And, incredibly, they both laughed.

For the rest of the evening she thought it was going to be all right. Even easy. Matt did most of the talking, but both she and Jack had no difficulty in chipping in now and then, and when they did Matt became even more vocal and told them jokes from the outback that made them laugh again.

He said, "Len's got quite a talent for fitting in — everyone gets on with him. That doesn't always apply to Poms setting up a business over there. He's very straight — tells it how it is. Tobe and I got roaring drunk our first night out in Perth. He made us work twice as hard the next day, stripping down one of the engines in a hangar. We were in a bad way. He said hard work was the best detox there was." He grinned. "We didn't make it a regular thing — I can see that's what you want to know!"

"I never thought it was going to be a proper apprenticeship." Judith heard her own words, and realized it was the first time she had voiced the bewilderment she had felt at the time. "And then it went on and on. Ten years, Matt. You and Toby were eighteen when you went out there."

"Didn't Dad tell you?"

"Tell me what?" She looked at Jack.

He said, "Thank God there was no need. Len always believed in hard work. He got me my first job on our local paper when I was messing around after art college. He stood in when Mum and Dad were killed."

She turned to Matt. "What didn't Dad tell me? And why?"

He said, "Loyalty? I don't know. But Toby and I went through a wild time, told Dad we'd had enough of studying and had no intention of going in for higher education. We tried some cocaine and thought it was OK. The dealer took an interest in us — nobody could tell us apart then. He told us we could make money from our twinship — that's what he called it at first, afterwards we were not allowed to use the word." He turned down his mouth. "We provided an alibi for him. One of us had to be by his side when he was doing a drug deal — on show, definitely on show. And the other had to be just as obvious, but somewhere else. Witnesses were confused and unreliable, and it would wreck any case the police might be building against him." He shrugged. "It was a joke to us. We were so stupid it was unbelievable. We weren't allowed to use the word 'twins'. We were policies. Insurance policies."

"Nigel Thorpe said something to me one night — warned me, I suppose. He still lives down the road — d'you remember, Jude? He was the local bobby for ages. I think he's retired and works for a security firm now." Jack sighed. "And Len happened to be over here for a couple of weeks. He offered to take the boys back with him, and they jumped at it."

"We'd got in over our heads, Mum." Matt was making coffee after the meal. He brought it to the table and stood there, remembering. "We thought we could make a bit of money and set up . . . something. We thought we were using him. When he let us know that he was using us, and that with that first job we were up to our necks and couldn't back out, we were really scared."

She was stunned. Again. Matt said, "It was a long time ago, Mum. Don't look like that."

Jack tried to take her hand. "It happened so quickly, Jude, and when I got back from settling them in, Mum was —"

"I know." She withdrew her hand and poured the coffee. "Take no notice. It's as if — looking back — I have gone through life wearing a blindfold." She glanced up. "Is there anything else? Has Toby got someone like Martha Gifford? Is Len proposing to take on other protégés whose parents are unable to cope?"

"You coped so well, Mum!" Matt frowned. "And of course Toby has got a girlfriend. You've seen pictures of her."

She sighed and shook her head helplessly. If she had known why the boys were leaving home, she would not have been able to cope with Eunice, probably.

She drank her coffee, and Matt said he'd go to bed because he wanted to swim in the tide early the next morning.

And then it was time to lock up and follow Jack upstairs. And it was then she thought of Naomi and suddenly discovered that she could no longer sleep with

Jack. It was quite simple. She had got into bed with him back in Taunton, and ever since then had slept by his side so that she was there "in case". Now he did indeed seem better. And he had told her about Naomi.

She said she would have to sleep in her mother's room; no explanations, but of course he knew why, and almost winced. "I'm sorry," she said lamely, picking her pillows up from the bed. "I can't do it. I don't think I'm going to sleep very well, and I need to be able to get up and move around the house."

He nodded. "I . . . understand. It's just . . . it's been so good tonight. I thought we might talk about that . . . being a family again. And anyway, I'll miss you."

She went into her mother's room, made up the bed, and began to undress. It was then that she found the flimsy envelope that had arrived that morning, still in the pocket of her jeans.

She sat up in bed and ripped it open and fished out a single sheet of notepaper. It was from Sybil, her address in Kingston upon Thames at the top, her signature at the bottom, and in between, starkly, "Guess what? He says it's too soon, and we must wait until Moss is out of my system. As if!"

She put it back in her pocket and lay down. The thought of Sybil in Judith's nightdress, much too short for her, perhaps setting up a scenario as the Markhams had done — it had seemed romantic and wonderful. But if Nathaniel had rejected it, the whole thing immediately became sickly sentimental. He had his

236

reasons, of course. But reason had nothing to do with it.

She felt tears behind her eyes and let them come. They were for Sybil, who had been rejected. And they were for herself, too.

CHAPTER
FOURTEEN

When she went downstairs the next morning, Matt was already there, window wide open, head outside, kettle just beginning to sing.

"Did you hear the bells? They were doing a complicated ring, unusual for the early morning service."

"It's a recorded peal. I told you they couldn't get ringers — ages ago — took a vote on it, electronic bells just got in."

"Oh. Yes. I do remember. What a shame." He withdrew his head and closed the window. "Plenty of autumn mist. If the sun gets through it will be lovely." He grinned at her. "I bet you slept well last night, didn't you? All that fresh air, and Dad's new thing, and the Freeman Rescue Copters moving operations!" He swilled the teapot with boiling water and put in teabags. She sat down and watched him, the sense of displacement surfacing for a moment.

She said, surprised, "Yes. I slept very well." She thought back and remembered the look on Jack's face when she had said she could not sleep with him. And then the stark little note from Sybil Jessup. She had thought then that she would not be able to sleep at all.

238

She said to Matt, "Since I decided to go on the Exmoor weekend, I've slept really well."

"Not before? You must have been so worried about Dad."

"Actually, while I was away I was almost convinced he was dead."

Matt was shocked. "Why? He said you knew where he was — why on earth would you think that? If he'd been that ill, Mum, we would have sent for you. You know that, surely?"

She was angry. "Matthew, he . . . left. One suitcase and a backpack. I thought if he was going to you he would tell me. Or, perhaps *you* might drop me a line or give me a ring. Can't you begin to imagine . . ."

She closed her eyes for a moment, recognizing the utter futility of it all. She had been just as bewildered herself, until Jack had opened up yesterday.

She said, "Sorry, love. The *Magnet* was running his old cartoons . . . it's all been . . . confusing."

"Especially meeting that crazy artist — we actually picked him up from the middle of nowhere, raving mad. Dad stayed with him all that first night — he would have discharged himself otherwise. Dad was never as bad as that, I can assure you. We would have considered all promises null and void." He put a mug of tea in front of her, then the sugar bowl. "What is it about artists, Mum? You're an artist, but you don't go bonkers when it's a full moon!"

"I don't have to earn a living by painting, love." She looked at him ruefully. "I couldn't do it. Robert Hausmann and Jack Freeman can do it, but they are never confident about it. It's the uncertainty that makes them . . . anxious."

"D'you know what you're talking about, Mum?"

She spooned sugar into her tea and grinned at him. "No. Not really. I felt Dad was superhuman. A rock. But when I talked to Hausmann, I got to understand how fragile artists are."

Matt was laughing. "Fragile? Robert Hausmann fragile?"

She remembered the first time she had encountered him. Fighting with the heavy door, muttering to himself, lumbering towards the lift. He had been huge and hairy, and she had to have been desperate to stop him. She laughed too, but nodded. "Yes. Especially Hausmann, who sees his work as a responsibility."

Matt said, "I don't get it. I can see that as an aero-engineer I am responsible for the safety of people. It's simple. I go over everything. I listen, I check for odd smells. I know when an engine isn't working as it should. I can't see how that applies to painting a picture."

"Can't you?" She drank her tea. "Come on, Matt. We're all responsible for one another. It's when it's a burden . . . that's the prob." She put on what she thought was his Australian accent, and he screwed up his face as if in pain. She went on, regardless. "You check everything. It's OK. You sleep well. Artists . . . there's no check on how much damage an artist can do. Damage to self-esteem, lifestyles — think of some of Dad's cartoons. And Hausmann — he's dealing with immortal souls. What sort of burdens do they have to carry?"

"You're getting in too deep there, Mum. We all live our own lives —"

"That's it! We jolly well don't! If we do things properly we fit together like a jigsaw puzzle. A perfect picture! If one piece is missing or rammed in the wrong way, there's no bloody picture!"

She registered his expression of shock and laughed. "Sorry, love. Go and put on your wetsuit. Time and tide are just about right. And if it's really foggy down there, for goodness' sake don't swim out of sight of the shore!"

He came to her, hoisted her out of her chair and wrapped his long arms around her very tightly.

"Mum, I don't know what's happened, but you won't leave us, will you?"

She managed a muffled laugh and he loosened his grip enough for her to look up at him. She was about to make a flippant remark, and then stopped herself.

"No. I'm here for keeps. There's more to it than pieces of a puzzle. I have to mix some different colours, lighter perhaps."

He went on staring at her, and then suddenly tightened his hold, kissed the top of her head and put her back in her chair. He paused at the door of the utility room and looked back. "Meant to say, I asked Martha to lunch, is that OK?"

"Fine. Sausage and mash? Oh, sorry, we're out of sausages."

"Mash will be fine, Mum. Just be here."

241

She heard him pull his wetsuit from the clothes horse and bundle it into a bag, and then he was gone. She stood up again, more slowly this time, fetched a tray from the side of the fridge and began to assemble a breakfast for Jack.

The lunch for Martha Gifford proved to be a lifeline. When she took in Jack's breakfast tray half an hour later, Jack had already shaved and showered and was getting dressed. He had looked thin and ill in the hospital bed, but as she put down the tray she saw the enormous effort he put into getting his jeans over his legs. He stood up and his thighs were skeletal. His legs looked wasted. She stopped herself from rushing forward to help him, and set out the toast and boiled egg on the bedside table.

He said breathlessly, "I was just coming down." He cleared his throat. "The three of us in the kitchen."

"Matt's gone for a before-breakfast swim. Have yours here." She sliced off the top of the egg.

He came slowly round the bed, sat at the table and stared at the egg.

"Thank you." He scooped at the discarded shell-top. "How did you sleep?"

"Very well. What about you?"

"Not badly. Those pills are good." He swallowed and scooped again. "We have to talk, Jude."

"Of course. But not today. Apparently Martha Gifford is coming to lunch. I'll do a cassoulet. We'll eat in the dining room. If you're up to it, you could go on working in the study for an hour? But you must rest this afternoon, Jack. Is that a deal?"

He nodded and she felt a sudden rush of irritation. He looked hangdog. This was exactly how he looked when he had the slightest thing wrong with him, and was put on to gain sympathy. Those times had gone. She folded his pyjamas briskly, and actually straightened the side of the bed he had slept on.

"See how you feel at coffee time. Perhaps you could make one of your citrus tarts for pudding? We've got lemons and plenty of eggs."

She paused before closing the door and saw his face light up. Just for a moment she felt a touch of the old overwhelming tenderness, and then Naomi's face came between them and she closed the door with a click.

After that, the day belonged to Martha and Matt.

Martha Gifford was the kind of girl whose complexion changed when she was happy. She built up warmth and beamed it out to other people. Judith recalled feeling worried about the way she had made a beeline for Matt when she was a child. When both boys were whisked off to Australia — obviously it seemed now, as yet another rescue operation — there had been a fleeting moment of relief that Matt was removed from the determined fourteen-year-old. Plenty of time for her to grow up and meet other boys. But apparently she had carried on her campaign at long distance and, as she told Judith and Jack joyously, she had been the first person on their road to use Skype. "It was just great!" she announced, waving a bit of potato aloft. "You can see but not touch!"

Matt looked embarrassed for just a moment, and then joined in the general laughter. Judith wondered wildly what exactly that might have meant, and how old Martha might have been when she was introduced to Skype. Then she met Jack's dark eyes and remembered the hotel in Paris when she had been nineteen. His mouth twitched and the next minute he, too, was laughing. She ladled more cassoulet on to his plate and hoped her face did not look as hot as it felt.

After the citrus tart, Matt bundled his parents into the garden and he and Martha washed up and made the coffee. Laughter floated from the open kitchen window.

Jack said, "They sound all right. Don't you think?"

Judith nodded, then added, "Yes."

More laughter, abruptly cut off. "They sound like us." Jack waited, and when Judith said nothing he added, "Like we used to be."

"Yes." She pulled at her fingers. "That was thirty years ago."

"Not till next year. Don't you remember what Mum said when we told her you were pregnant?"

Judith quoted, "She said we'd only just made it into the respectability stakes." Tears spouted unexpectedly. "She . . . she . . . oh God, Jack, she would be so disappointed now!"

He made a sound somewhere between a gasp and a cry of protest, then put his hand over hers so that she could no longer pull at her fingers. She tried to release her hand and could not. Skeletal he might be, but he was still stronger than she was. She let her tears drip, and knew he too was weeping.

Suddenly the sound of an almighty crash came through the open kitchen window. Judith leapt up just ahead of Jack, so saw, just for an instant, that Martha Gifford's sandalled foot was upside-down on top of a pile of saucepans. At Judith's side, Jack stumbled and grabbed at the back of the deckchair, which immediately collapsed on to the lawn. They both fell down just as the foot disappeared, to be replaced by Matt's face, much too low for him to see his fallen parents.

"It's OK, Mum . . . Dad! Bloody saucepans weren't balanced properly on the drainer and fell into the sink — don't panic!"

Judith picked herself up, found a tissue in her jeans, and began blowing her nose frantically. Jack stayed where he was.

Martha's face appeared. "Nothing broken, Mrs Freeman . . . omigod . . . is Mr Freeman all right? Matt . . . can you just . . . no, not there . . . by the door . . . thanks . . . darling, your dad seems to be —"

"Hang on!" Matt's voice seemed to fill the garden. "Just coming!"

Judith crouched by Jack. "Jack. Listen. That sounded terrible, I know. Mum — of all people — she would be on your side, Jack. I should be, too. And I'm not. Please stop crying. Matt mustn't know anything is . . ."

She stopped speaking. Jack's face was as contorted as before, but now he was laughing. She knelt by him and shook his shoulder none too gently.

"Stop it . . . you're hysterical . . . are you hurt?"

"Jude, don't you see? Those saucepans didn't fall by themselves! Can't you remember . . . the back room at number forty-seven, when you sent the aspidistra flying? Mum came rushing in and gave you a good dressing-down, and I tried to take the blame, and suddenly she started to laugh and said she'd never liked it because your dad had bought it for her after one of his nights out?"

"For God's sake, Jack! Does that make it all right? Dad went out with his mates and got drunk occasionally. How does that make our situation more . . . more acceptable?"

It was as if she had slapped him. He stammered, "It was just . . . I was thinking of Matt and Martha. And the saucepans. And then . . . us."

Why did she constantly feel wrong-footed? She said, still furious, "Wrong place, wrong time. Are you hurt?"

"Of course not. The grass is like a sponge. Too much rain."

Matt arrived, and between them they got Jack into the other deckchair. Martha joined them. She looked sheepish. She said, "The coffee seems to be ready. Shall I pour it and bring it out here?"

They looked at her blankly, then Judith said, "That would be really nice. I think I'll go for a cardigan, the sun has gone in."

She took the stairs two at a time, went into their shared room and took a cardigan from the wardrobe. She said quietly to herself, "There's no middle road, I either accept it or I go. And I can't go."

246

She looked out of the window as a car drew up outside.

Robert Hausmann got out.

He was unusually polite. Matt answered the door; she heard the surprised greeting and then Matt's pleasure at seeing him. She moved on to the landing.

"Mum's upstairs fetching something. We're in the garden — yes, Dad too. Come on through. Why didn't you phone? You could have come to lunch."

"I didn't want to bother you. On my way to Cardiff —"

"Oh, of course, that's your home, isn't it?"

Their voices disappeared into the utility room. She went to the end of the landing and peered through as they emerged on to the patio. Jack yelped a welcome, Martha got up from the grass and was introduced. Lots of handshaking. Hausmann was wearing an open-necked shirt under a sports jacket. His voice was different, too. Not gruff. Not aggressive. Quite unlike Robert Hausmann.

She went to the head of the stairs and held on to the newel post, frowning, remembering the absolute pathos of Sybil's note, still in the pocket of her jeans. Was Hausmann working at some "cunning plan" yet again? Had he learned nothing?

By the time she reached the kitchen Matt had fetched more chairs and Martha was on her way in.

"Mrs Freeman . . . it's the artist who went to Australia . . . he's having coffee . . . I'll top up the jug."

She smiled. "He's really nice, isn't he? Matt said he was sort of wild and unkempt."

"Well, he can be. But not always. And I think he would prefer tea, actually. I'll take out the rest of the citrus tart and the biscuit tin."

But she had never seen him other than unkempt, and felt she was meeting him for the first time when he pecked at both her cheeks. Then he took the biscuit tin from her and opened it up. "D'you mind? I missed breakfast."

Quite suddenly, she felt herself relaxing. She said, "What do you think of the patient? He made the citrus tart for lunch. And he's started work again."

"What? Well done, Jack. But steady as she goes. This time last week they were varnishing a coffin for you down in Porlock woodyard!"

Martha, coming up with the tea tray, looked shocked. Matt said, "Charming. Guaranteed to make a recovering patient feel heaps better."

"Cheers him up — listen. That's a Jack Freeman laugh!"

It was indeed; Judith smiled at Jack, knowing that Hausmann had brought the same reassurance to both of them. He stopped laughing, but his gaze fixed on Judith became different.

She turned quickly to Hausmann. "You're going to see Nat in Cardiff?"

He lifted his eyebrows. "How do you know that? Oh, of course, the dream. And other things."

"I heard you talking to Matt."

"Ah. Well. Yes. Yes, I thought I might look him up. Everyone disappeared last Tuesday morning before I got back from the hospital. Apparently there was a bit of a fuss with Nathaniel. Thought I might be able to smooth it over."

Judith found Sybil's letter in her pocket and passed it to him without a word. He read it, folded it into its creases and handed it back.

"I thought perhaps it was the other way round." He looked at her and shrugged. "All I intend to do is to talk to Nat."

She smiled. "Of course."

"Seriously, Judith. What else can I do?"

"Nothing."

"If you mean I should step right back, then nobody will do anything, and Nat will go on being alone, and Sybil will marry someone like her husband — who will stifle all her real personality."

"But perhaps Nat would be happier on his own, and Sybil needs to be kept in wraps?"

"Do you believe that?"

She did not reply and Jack said, "Of course she doesn't. Jude believes in family."

Hausmann said quickly, "Also it was a chance to see you and ask whether you are ready for Lundy yet."

Matt broke in. "Lundy? You didn't say anything about Lundy — Dad can't go back there, not after last time."

Hausmann said strongly, "He barely saw the place. The weather is set fair. You both need a proper holiday. Matt will go home and —"

Matt said, "I am not going back to Perth, Robert. Len and Toby are coming here. We've bought in to an auxiliary air service — four copters based at Filton Airfield."

His voice had changed, and Hausmann looked at him, surprised.

Jack said quietly, "I am ready, Robert. I am not certain about Judith."

Matt was definitely angry. "Dad, how can you consider going to that godforsaken place again? Mum can cope here all right, but in an emergency she will need help. You have no idea what it was like last time. Robert's cottage leaked in three places!"

Jack said, "I was there, actually." He smiled as if they were discussing just the weather. "I could work there. And I could repair the leaks, too. And we could walk down the combe and watch the birds. And Mum could plant the garden for next spring. And paint." He looked at Judith. "You would have time there, Jude. You should start to paint again."

She was silent, realizing that Hausmann was determined not to interfere this time, hearing Matt take his place and sink Jack's arguments.

Unexpectedly it was Martha Gifford who spoke.

"Matt showed me some of your work, Mrs Freeman. And Lundy is sort of magical. I went there once on a field trip. They grow prehistoric cabbages."

Everyone looked at her and then burst out laughing. Hausmann explained about the cabbages, which indeed were ancestors of the modern, hearted variety.

250

He then stood up and announced he had better get on the road to Cardiff.

"Nat is expecting me. He's doing macaroni cheese for six thirty prompt!" He shook Matt's hand. "Sorry, Matt. And congratulations on the new business. Really good news."

He moved to Jack. "Will we see anything of your new stuff in the near future?"

Jack nodded. "Hope so. I'll be in touch. Take care of yourself."

"Likewise you."

Hausmann grinned at Martha. "Every time I see one of those forlorn cabbage leaves, I'll think of you!"

He followed Judith up to the patio and through the house. The car — borrowed from Bart as usual — looked terrible. It was still streaked with mud and caked with salt. He followed her gaze and grinned.

"Irena was beginning to love me till she saw the state of their vehicle."

"What a shame," she said.

"I wasn't comfortable with her approval."

"I can imagine."

He unlocked and opened the driver's door, then held it against his body like a shield.

"He has told you?"

There was no point in pretence. She nodded once.

"What are you going to do?"

She said, "I suppose we should do something . . . official. I did think I would try to contact some of the witnesses . . . but even if she didn't deliberately kill

251

herself, it would make little difference to Jack's sense of guilt. There's more to it than that."

"That is why I asked you what you are going to do."

"Absolutely nothing." She looked up at him. "We are complete opposites, Robert."

"You mean, you will stay with him?"

"There is no alternative."

"The alternative is that you leave him. Make your own life."

"No. That is not an alternative. He needs me. The boys need parents who live together and run a home together. Someone has to make a safe place."

He nodded. "You are good at that."

"Did you know that my maiden name was Denman?"

"No. Is it relevant?"

"Very. Think about it on the way to Cardiff."

"All right." He eased himself into the driving seat and fastened the seat belt. "I am not about to interfere with Nathaniel's feelings. But I need to know they are genuine. I can't ask Sybil to wait for him if he's simply got cold feet, can I?"

She smiled and shook her head as if in despair.

He started up and revved the engine, then clutched and used the gearstick and began to ease away from the pavement. In the comparative silence he said, "Thank you, Jude. You know I will always love you."

She watched him go. He had given her time to tell him that she loved him too, but she had said nothing.

CHAPTER
FIFTEEN

The next few days coined a new adage for Judith and Jack Freeman. Whenever anything went particularly wrong or particularly right, one of them would glance at the other, nod knowingly and say, "I blame Martha Gifford for this," and then they would laugh. It was a small and silly bond, but it was a bond. And Martha seemed to encourage it.

It started that evening after Bart Mann's muddied car had disappeared round the corner to join the motorway slip road going south-west, and Judith had gone slowly back through the house and into the garden, where the others were discussing Robert Hausmann avidly. She had leaned on the patio rail and heard Martha say, "I don't know why, but I feel sad for him — all that lovely work. I took my class to see his stuff at the West of England Gallery and they enjoyed it so much . . . it . . . it's absolutely accessible to children and adults alike. And yet there's no pleasure in him. I mean, he gets no satisfaction from his work."

Matt added, "Just the opposite. It's driving him round the bend. When we picked him up from the desert floor I could have sworn he'd gone there to die." He looked at Jack, sunk again in his deckchair. "He might still have done, if it hadn't been for you, Dad. I remember seeing you holding him . . . literally holding him in your arms in that hospital bed. Not letting him go. He was trying to discharge himself, wasn't he?"

"In a way I suppose he was. But actually, I think I was trying to hold him together. Stop him from disintegrating."

There was a silence and Judith walked down the steps and across the lawn.

"Has he gone, love?" Jack lifted his head and for a moment Judith felt his fatigue as her own.

"He has. He's driving his brother's car."

"Thank God. I thought he would have been on that motorbike."

"Yes, I wonder why he was not? It's quicker, especially on a Sunday, when so many cars are on the road."

Matt said, "He was hoping he would be taking you both back with him. I'm glad I put the mockers on that one! He's definitely losing his marbles!"

Martha chirped quickly, "Bit like you then, young Matthew!"

They both laughed, but Jack said, "You were only too glad to see him last week, Matt! And when he brought Mum up to the hospital you thought he was some sort of conjuror!"

Matt sobered. "He's terrific at times. Just . . . over the top, I suppose."

Judith started to gather the tea things on to a tray. She paused and balanced the tray on her hip. "But his painting . . . he needs to paint memories. The

254

memories of his family, terrible memories. But all his 'scapes are future paintings of the past." She shook her head. "That doesn't make sense, I know. What I mean is, he's painting the present from a viewpoint somewhere in the future. When all our beauty may well be gone. That's what gives it that poignancy. We think of it as everlasting. And he knows it is not."

There was a silence, then Martha Gifford breathed, "Oh my God."

And Jack said, "You've got it, Jude. That's why he was being torn into pieces and wanted to end it all." He turned to Martha. "You understand that too, don't you? He's painting for the kids in your class. Maybe for your own kids."

Martha said tearfully, "But it's so sad, because he won't be here to see it happening. I feel that I should tell them . . . explain to them —"

"Nature walks. More of them." Matt spread his hands at the sheer simplicity of his solution. He registered her response to his suggestion, and added irritably, "Listen, Martha, you're not to blame for the world going to pot!"

Quick as a flash Jack quipped, "Why not? Let's blame everything on Martha Gifford."

Judith held her breath, wondering if this girl could take that kind of banter. Then, quite suddenly, into the startled silence came the rush of starlings as they swept towards the sea in perfect formation for their evening dance. They watched as a family, very aware of the ephemeral. Then Matt said roughly, "Let's go inside before Dad catches another cold, then pneumonia, and we're back to square one!"

Martha swept them all with a grin. "I might be held to blame for that, too. So come on, Mr Freeman, give me your hand!"

Judith watched as Matt and Martha pulled Jack out of the deckchair. She walked behind them to the patio, very conscious of them as a family; she could see that ever so gently they could drift into something resembling just that. But something had to happen first. Forgiveness? How could she forgive herself for drifting away from her husband and her sons? She could justify it, but not forgive it. And Jack, how could he forgive himself for Naomi?

She thought of Hausmann, who was always fighting for some kind of redemption. Were they all doomed to disintegration?

She shook her shoulders as if to rid herself of such pessimism, and followed Jack into the living room, held the cushions in his chair so that he could settle into them, then went across to the windows. She held the curtains for a moment, staring out at the darkening view. A lighthouse in Wales flashed and was gone. The answer came to her with the light. They should go to Lundy. Not only for their own sakes but for Robert's. He loved Jack; he had said he loved her. Certainly he had done what he could to hold them together. They might become his form of redemption.

She laughed aloud at the thought, almost hearing him furiously renouncing such a pious motive for doing a good turn.

256

Jack said, "What's funny, honey?"

It was a line from one of his cartoons, and she turned and smiled at him. "All of us, this afternoon. It's Fish-Frobisher stuff — pure and simple."

"Yes. We'll have to fit Martha into the Frobishers — give her a name. Daisy, perhaps."

"Doesn't fit with the other one — Stargazer." She wondered if that might be their solution; to reduce real life to the size of a cartoon. She closed the curtains and went back to Jack.

But that night she still slept in her mother's room.

The next morning she overslept and went downstairs still weary, limbs heavy, mind dull. Martha had already left for school and Matt was sitting at the kitchen table, obviously at a completely loose end. Judith was so used to seeing the twins as a twosome that at first she thought it was Toby's absence that gave Matt that lost look, then realized that the missing half was now Martha Gifford. For an instant she felt a pang of — what? Envy? Because that was how it had been for Jack and herself and could never be again? At least she knew how Matt felt, and she made herself smile down at him. "What about your swim?" she asked.

"Tide's not quite right. And it's really cold this morning."

"Is it?" She actually sniffed at the air, then grinned again. "I don't think it is, my little lost lamb."

"Lost lamb?" He sounded outraged. "And why are you looking sort of . . . smug?"

"Because you look lost, incomplete. And that's probably how you feel. And I'm looking smug because I know the reason for it. I blame Martha Gifford."

"Mum, for Pete's sake. I'm meeting her out of school, and I'm hoping you and Dad will join us, and we'll go and look at Len's new project." He glanced at his watch. "I don't think I should feel lost when there're only six and a half hours until the school bell goes."

She busied herself at the cooker; made fresh tea and put bread in the toaster. She waited a while before she said, "Unfortunately, logic has nothing to do with emotions. So I still blame Martha Gifford." She put a poached egg on top of his toast. "I think she'd be tickled pink, don't you?"

He acknowledged that with a rueful grin and started on his breakfast. She sat opposite him and let an unexpected content soothe some of her weariness.

She said, out of the blue, surprising herself, "I really like her, Matt ... I'm so ... pleased." It was inadequate, and she added, "She's strong and gentle and fun." He reached a hand to cover hers and, even more unexpectedly, she felt her throat contract against a sob. She tried to retrieve their usual lightheartedness. "It's great that you're coming home again, Matt."

"Well, you can't blame Martha for that, Mum! Len's been negotiating at arm's length for ages to get a foothold in Bristol. He's always had a complex about kidnapping us at a tender age!"

"Oh my goodness — and he was actually rescuing you. Thank God for Len! How come you kept it such a dark secret?"

"It was just before Gran had her stroke, if you remember. You must have known something was wrong with her, you were there nearly all the time. Dad thought it best not to tell you anything about it."

"Oh, he did, did he? I wish he hadn't. I remember feeling horribly cut off."

He said nothing to that; he finished his egg and sat back apparently replete.

She lifted her shoulders in a brief shrug. "Well, I can't blame Martha for that, can I?"

"It wouldn't have happened that way if Martha had known. She would have told you. She believes in things being in the open — however painful and embarrassing that might be."

She thought of Naomi and nodded. "True."

He looked down and said awkwardly, "Mum. I know we've lost out over these last ten years. And I know nothing stays the same. But . . . all this business with Dad . . . you're all right now, are you?"

She nodded. "Of course. It was . . . let's say it was difficult. After Gran died I went into some kind of depression; I realize now that Dad was ill as well as depressed." She smiled. "Actually, it's so obvious that he would have gone to you to sort himself out. At the time . . ." She hesitated, remembering. "I suppose I was angry." She shook her head. "I don't know, Matt. I wrote off the idea of Dad going to you because none of you got in touch —"

"Mum, honestly, if you'd heard him . . . he made us promise —"

"I know, I know." She smiled again and reached for his hand. "How about putting it all behind us? Lots of new things happening — it shouldn't be too difficult, should it?"

Matt visibly relaxed. "Not now. You're back. It'll be all right now." He turned his hand within hers then shook them both. "Sorry to be so . . . I don't know. I feel embarrassed now. Don't laugh — yesterday I even found I was trying to blame that crazy Hausmann! When you talked about his stuff — made Martha cry — you were making allowances for him that I felt you hadn't done for Dad!"

She said soberly, "He was the one who saved Dad, remember."

"I know. If it hadn't been for the weather he was going to bring you over; he knew Dad would recover if you were there." He freed his hand and waved it helplessly. "He knew you'd put it right. Like you always do." He gave her an upside-down smile. "He knows you sort of intuitively, somehow. Everyone thinks Dad is the one who runs everything, and of course he does on one level. But you are the one who makes everything work. When you arrived at Taunton last week I knew you'd make it work again, and so did he. And then . . . and then . . . when Dad was really improving, and you and me were . . . it was like old times. I couldn't wait to tell you about Martha. We were all laughing together, weren't we? Then Robert the Grim turned up, and I suddenly saw him as a threat."

She wondered whether Jack felt the same way. She forced a laugh. "He is mainly concerned about Dad. I think they might have a pact to keep each other alive and fairly sane!"

"Possibly. But, Mum, it really is primitive over there. I wasn't making that up. And if you do go it will be coming to the end of autumn — gales galore."

"Dad wants to go, darling. He really does. And I think it would be good to be away when Len and Toby are here and everything is happening. Dad has got something new to work on. He needs to think it through. You know how it is when he gets his teeth into something."

He nodded reluctantly. "It all seems a bit crazy now, doesn't it? Dad in the outback and you in your Gothic castle. From the bits you've told us it all sounds like a French farce!"

She burst out laughing. "Actually it was a bit like a French farce. And it certainly was a Gothic castle, full of passages and unexpected rooms. There were only seven of us, plus the driver of the coach, and one couple were really working on creating romantic situations . . ."

She came and sat down again, and in the middle of telling him about Stanley and Jennifer, she started to cry. He was appalled and knelt by her, pulling her head on to his shoulder and ruffling her Shirley Temple curls.

"But it was lovely, Mum — surely you saw that, too?"

She raised her head. "Of course I did — and I am so glad you are seeing it, too! It bodes well for your happiness, love. Sometimes you actually have to work at being in love."

"May I tell Martha about those two? She would love it. The thought of them dancing in the dark —"

261

"The orangery was full of candlelight."

"Yes, but they were still dancing in the dark, weren't they?" He grinned at her and let her wipe her face with a tissue. "Just like all of us."

That started her off again, just as Jack appeared at the kitchen door. Matt stood up and almost pushed his father into a chair and began telling him about Stanley and Jennifer Markham. And then made more tea. After they had finished with the story, they were all smiling. Judith lifted her mug and suggested a toast.

"To Castle Dove and all who sail in her!"

They echoed her solemnly.

Later she went upstairs with Jack and sat on the laundry box while he shaved. He protested gently, "Jude, you know I can manage."

"It's whether *I* can manage! Matt has been making enquiries. I have to tell you, because we must try to tell the same story!" She laughed, trying to make it sound comic. "I've shifted the blame from Martha and put it on the stress of Mum's death — she wouldn't mind one bit. Then — as you know — I changed the subject to Castle Dove."

He was silent, staring at her. Eventually he nodded and turned back to the mirror. "I didn't know about the orangery incident. That was rather special. Robert didn't mention it — nor the Lorna Doone Project!" He grinned at his own reflection.

"He hasn't had an opportunity to talk to you properly. He was speechless . . . it was quite a moment, in fact." She paused, then confessed. "I cried, actually."

262

He stopped "scrapin' his face", as she had called it when she had first watched him shaving, and looked at her, concerned. She shrugged. "Can't you remember being almost fifty years old?"

"Hey! You sound like a cheeky schoolgirl — I blame Martha Gifford!"

She laughed inordinately. "Oh, Jack, she's really nice — imagine sticking with someone from the age of four."

He finished beneath his chin, rinsed his razor and laid it carefully aside, then sat on the stool. "We would have done, if we'd met that soon." He looked at her; she wondered how a human face could reveal such sadness. "I threw it all away, Jude. I have spent so much of my life showing what fools men and women can be, and it turns out that I am the biggest fool of them all."

She shook her head. "What about that woman called Judith Denman? She was guilty of overdoing the nesting bit, surely? She should have gone to that party, Jack."

He shook his head despairingly. "If I'd told you . . . I'd got into the habit of trying to shield you . . . oh, it's so absurd —"

"No — no, it's not, Jack. But I need to know things like that. Everything between us has to be in the open now. How can we forgive each other if we don't know what there is to forgive? I took on the role of homemaker, and when the boys left for no apparent reason that made any sense to me, I almost embraced Mum's illness. You were still with me on that. But insidiously we were moving apart — the Australian visits especially. And Naomi, she was my friend, yet all we had in common was that she had nursed her husband. I knew nothing about that time. I just assumed she was devoted and kind. Yet she told me that widows were not welcome into married households — and that's not true, Jack. But it was for her."

She stopped speaking, exhausted. She saw things clearly, simply. She leaned forward and took his hands and held them tightly.

"Listen, Jack. You had no hand in her death. You have got to believe that. Whether it was a genuine accident or an organized one — yes, I mean that, because Naomi sought attention — it was not your doing." She took a deep breath. "For a while — during the weekend at Castle Dove — I thought you were dead, Jack. It was only for a few hours, actually. But in that time I realized that death really is final; nothing can be done about it. And I wanted you to be alive more than anything else — even if I never saw you again. Just to know you were on this earth would have been enough. And you are here, and I am here, and our son is in love with someone we can love, too. And both our sons are coming home. Jack, we've got another chance."

"Jude, you know I love you. Do you love me?"

She tried to smile. "I don't know. But — oh, Jack, we're still together. We're holding hands. We've got to try."

She felt his grip tighten, and it seemed to give her strength. Her smile widened, and she said, "Jennifer and Stanley Markham — Matt called it dancing in the dark. But they were taking the whole thing seriously, making their efforts to have a child into sheer romance." She shook his hands gently. "Let's go to Lundy, Jack. Just a couple of weeks. Live from hour to hour while we explore. No heavy stuff about what has happened; simply *be*, side by side, soaking up a new environment. You can still work on your new project, and I can paint again. But mostly I can indulge my nesting instincts to the full!" She tried to laugh. He leaned towards her and pressed his forehead to hers.

"Will it be like that couple at Castle Dove?"

"Jack, I don't know. It won't be set up — a game of pretend. And we've never done much dancing. But you've got a thing about the place, and it seems to me we should try."

He straightened and looked at her. "I would love to go there with you, darling. I might have been a bit delirious, but I felt even then that it was our place."

As she stood up she felt an urge to lean down and kiss the top of his head, but then she did not. She went into their bedroom and opened windows, made the bed and fetched her pillows from her mother's old room. She said quietly, "The trouble is, Mum, I know him so well — he is so darned familiar. I have to remind myself that he is a stranger."

And in her head she could hear her mother's chuckle as she came back immediately, "That's what makes it exciting!"

Judith went to the open window and leaned out, looking at the fading glory of the autumn garden. Her mother had lost speech after her second stroke, and to hear it so clearly now was unusual. Judith whispered,

"Eunice Denman, you're still saying the unexpected."
She waited and nothing happened. She smiled down at
the fig tree. "OK. So I've made a lot of mistakes, and
I've got to get on with it — that's what you'd say. And
like a dutiful daughter —" A sudden breeze whipped
through her curls, a gentle reprimand. "Sorry. A dutiful
wife?" No more breeze, and she put the window on the
latch and turned as Jack came into the room. He
spotted her pillows immediately and sat down on the
end of the bed.

"Thank you, Jude." He was out of breath after
showering. "Will you phone Robert?"

"You do it, Jack. I think this is part of his thanks to
you for holding him together in Perth."

"It was mutual, actually." He nodded. "I've got his
mobile number and he's always got his phone with
him."

Judith thought wryly of the Lorna Doone trip just
over a week ago. Had he had his phone then, in spite of
professing not to? And was this Lundy thing another of
his plans?

She went downstairs and found Matt in his wetsuit.

"Thought I'd give it a go — the tide should be up by
now." He pulled up the zip and went to the door. "I've
been talking to Len. He's raring to go. I said he could
come any time."

"Here? Len and Toby? Well, of course. And Dad is
going to ring Robert Hausmann and fix something up
about going to Lundy. You can all manage here for a
couple of weeks, can't you?"

Matt nodded and screwed his face up. "It really is basic on Lundy. Just one room. You wash in the sink. The loo is the size of a small wardrobe."

"I can see you must have hated it. Dad being so ill and that terrible storm. How will it be now that Dad is getting better?"

"Mum, I don't know. Will Robert the Grim be around?"

"No," she said very definitely.

He relaxed. "If it's unbearable you can always ring, and I'll take you off in one of the copters." She laughed, but he said, "I'm serious, Mum. In fact I can fly you there — there's a landing pad next to the hotel."

"Actually, that would be great, Matt. Much easier for Dad."

It tipped the scales for him; he grinned. "I can tell you're thinking of it as a haven, aren't you?"

"I'm not sure. But on a practical level it might be better to get Dad away from the house here until Len and Toby are settled in."

"That sounds a valid reason to me; if it is a haven you are hoping for, you will be disappointed."

He ruffled her hair again, and she ruffled his. They smiled at each other, and she shook her head at him. He said in his little-boy role, "Sorry, Mum."

She slapped his wetsuit, opened the back door and watched him go down the drive to the footpath. He was twenty-eight and already set in his ways.

She said aloud, "Thank you, God, for Martha Gifford!"

Then, on an impulse, she went back upstairs to tell Jack that Matt must have always needed Martha Gifford.

CHAPTER
SIXTEEN

The first morning Judith woke up on Lundy, she knew they had done the right thing. She lay very still, orientating herself, conscious of the warmth of the enormous duvet provided by Kitty Davies, and the closeness of Jack, whose head was softly lodged on the back of her neck so that she felt every breath he exhaled.

The oak shutters were supposed to be "draught-free", but somewhere light was creeping into the cottage. She sneaked her arm over the duvet and squinted at her watch. Almost eight thirty. She had slept — and hopefully so had Jack — for nine hours. Mrs Davies had warned them that the birds would wake them up at the crack of dawn, but though the light was still grey, it was well past dawn and there were no birds about yet.

Then, as if in response to that thought, they arrived. They sounded like a breeze coming from the top of Millcombe combe, then a wind; then came an unholy scream, and they landed on Hausmann's slated roof. Jack had told her about the landings. "Considering their feet are webbed, it's amazing. They could be wearing hobnailed boots. It wouldn't be so bad if they stayed where they were for the morning conference. But no, they walk about — all the time stamping and yelling fit to burst! I might have been delirious, but I didn't imagine that!"

That first morning, in spite of all warnings, Judith sank her head beneath the duvet as the successful landing was followed by shrieking commands from half the arrivals — probably at least thirty of them, by the sound of it — and the other half began a stamping march around the squat chimney. Some latecomers appeared to be wailing helplessly as they slid from the ridge down the steep roof to the gutter above Judith's cowering head.

Jack protested as he rolled on to his back, "My God, I'd forgotten what noisy blighters they are!" He thrust his arms above his head and stretched luxuriously. "I'm back, boys! It's only two weeks since I was here last, and you're still having the same arguments!"

Judith emerged from the duvet and hoisted herself up. "Is it only two weeks? Yes, it is. Oh, Jack, I think Hausmann is right and this is a magic place. Listen to them — they're welcoming you back!" There was a momentary silence from the roof, then a single squawk, as if in agreement. Judith laughed and called, "Me, too? Am I welcome, too?" Another silence, then another squawk. Jack moved an arm from above his head to around Judith's shoulders and they both laughed; it was absurd, but it was another moment shared in many that had happened during the past week of planning and arranging and phone calls between Bristol and Australia.

269

She had fussed and fretted about Len and the boys taking over the house, and had insisted on walking Matthew around, pointing out the contents of the airing cupboard, the whereabouts of her special drain cleaner, the sell-by dates of foods in the refrigerator. She had written lists about watering the plants and sorting the rubbish for recycling. Matt had said without intentional irony, "My God, I didn't realize running a house was worse than running a business! I'm booking the helicopter for tomorrow, and you are going to Lundy — OK?"

And here they were, no more lists. Just birds. And once started, neither of them could stop the ridiculous dialogue with the gulls. They called comments up to the roof and it seemed that the birds responded. The hobnailed boots marched around outside, waiting for a pause in their laughter before yelling a response. Then, just as suddenly as they had arrived, the birds left. There was a short interval of chattering, quite a different sound during which their beaks audibly clicked. Then some kind of assembling, then a mighty shriek, and they all flew off at once, and the roof seemed to lift very slightly and to creak with relief.

Judith shook her head helplessly. "D'you know, I had a dream that Matt had boiled my favourite undersheet and completely ruined it — how could my subconscious become so . . . so *trivial*!"

Jack stared at her. "You've got a favourite undersheet?"

"Yes. The corners are deep enough to go under the mattress properly — no good you laughing, Jack." But

270

she was laughing, too, and then reminding him of their one and only weekend at the Whortleys' country house, when Jack had been paranoid about forgetting his dressing gown, and then had met William's father-in-law outside the bathroom wearing only socks and a badly draped towel.

Eventually, she went to the wardrobe-like cubicle housing the lavatory, and was at the sink washing her hands prior to filling the kettle when Kitty Davies announced her arrival with a brisk tattoo on the door.

"You awake then, my 'ansoms?" She opened the door a crack and bellowed through it. "Kin I come in, then?"

"Come on, Mrs Davies. Just making tea." Judith hugged her coat around her as a blast of October air filled the single room. She noticed Jack prudently pull the duvet up to his chin; he looked incredibly prim. "We'd be asleep still, I think, if it weren't for the gulls."

"Oh, call me Kitty and I'll manage, Judith. Your husband and son were Jack and Matthew straight off, and no messing." She was the shape of a cottage loaf, and as wholesome looking. "So you're well on the way back to health if you've slept like that — the wind was something awful about two o'clock this morning. Settled down now, and the cows is all standing, so we won't expect no rain for a bit."

She went over to the rank of cupboards above the fireplace. "Robert did put a few groceries up here. Porridge and eggs for breakfast, he said . . ." She pulled down a package of porridge oats. "An' I got the eggs in me pocket safe and sound." She placed a carton of eggs on the table next to the porridge, opened the tiny fridge and took out a jug of milk. "Now, I got his list here." She fished in another pocket and held up a piece of paper, frowned in the half-light, and went to the shutter by the door. "That's better. I told Robert he should have curtings for the summer months, but he didn't seem to know what I was talking about." She gave an indulgent laugh and consulted the list. "Dave will be coming over today with the milk." She looked back at the other two. "That's my husband — David Davies. He's Welsh and I'm Cornish. It's a good mixture. He's a farmer and I'm a cook." She went back to the list. "You still got bread from what I left in the crock, I expect, but he'll bring some more. Robert did say as it's chicken and fish only — Dave will bring what you need in that line — and there's plenty of vegetables. Believe it or not, we're still picking beans — a great year for them — and tomatoes. The kitchen garden is sheltered, else every vegetable on every stalk would be blowed over the cliff by now! Robert did say — plenty of vegetables. He's fussing as usual, and you are looking 'ansome, I have to say, Jack. But I won't forget that night. Your son — poor lamb — he was frantic." She looked at Judith. "How is the poor lad now?"

"Well . . ." Judith widened her smile as she began to pour tea. "He's going to marry a girlfriend he's had since he started school. And he's moving back to Bristol." It sounded so simple, so completely ordinary and right. She passed this wonderful Kitty a mug of tea. "Kitty, thank you so much for looking after us like this.

It's the perfect place for Jack to convalesce, but I had wondered about the day-to-day living."

Kitty took the tea and sipped appreciatively. "It's Robert what arranges it all. All these lists — as if I don't know what people need to keep body and soul together. I told him straight coupla year back, when he had a young artist chappie here: 'Stop fussing around him. The island will heal his poor brain and I will keep his body going.'" She helped herself to more sugar, and stirred vigorously. "Robert wanted to be here to welcome you in. I said, 'Leave them be.' But he didn't like it when Matthew brought you over in that helicopter." She laughed and sighed at the same time. "Trouble is, he wants to look after the whole world, and as Dave says, look after number one and it gives you the strength to look after others!"

Again Judith was struck by this simple analysis of the complicated human being that was Robert Hausmann. She sat down at the table, and smiled up at Kitty Davies.

"Perhaps underneath it all, Robert is the original old hen fussing around his helpless chicks?"

Kitty laughed inordinately. "Oh, he wouldn't like that at all, Judith! Don't you go telling him he's an old hen!"

"I wouldn't dream of it. He's given us all this . . ." Judith gestured widely with one hand, ". . . for as long as it takes to get Jack back on his feet. How could I ever call him that?" Suddenly she recalled Hausmann as she had last seen him, using the car door as a shield between them, saying, "I will always love you." And she had said not a word in reply.

Kitty left, and the day began.

They started with the breakfast: porridge stiff and stodgy and then creamy with the milk from the farm, then scrambled eggs containing chopped tomatoes, finishing with a slice of toast and some of Kitty's marmalade.

"Four-star stuff," Jack said appreciatively.

"D'you know, Jack, I was about to say it's the best breakfast you've had since the beginning of the summer, but I think it's been much, much longer than that. I do not remember when we last ate breakfast together — is it fair to say that you were busy and I was dreary? Oh, Jack, I'm sorry. Didn't we even do breakfasts any more?" She looked at his face and was aghast to see the grief there. "Jack, I shouldn't have talked like that — I was determined we would live in the present, and here I am, looking backwards again!"

"My God, I am so glad you can! We must be able to talk again about anything and everything. It's because I didn't talk about Naomi that a ghastly mistake turned into a tragedy. Sorry, sorry, love. I know that's going too far." He gave a helpless little laugh. "Breakfasts are important. We always ate a proper breakfast when the boys were home and when Mum was alive."

"Yes, we did. But it wouldn't have mattered then if we hadn't! We were so solid." She stacked the plates and put them in the deep sink. "And that sort of eroded. I lost my way somehow." She touched his shoulder. "Jack, I have to forgive Naomi. And I think you do, too. It's going to be easy to forgive each other. We're in the process of it, and you have to admit things

274

are going our way — being a big family again, coming here. Of course there will be hiccups, but if we just keep going . . . you know what I mean, don't you?"

He nodded slowly. "Jude. I don't know how to put this. There has been so much pain. Remorse. It has sucked me down like those awful old films of people in sinking sands." He gave an awkward laugh. "I've always been able to laugh things off — see the absurd in almost every situation. Especially those awful old films!" He bit his lip. "Now *I'm* in the sinking sands."

She said rallyingly, "Yet you were delighted to be on the case again when William sent you that new project last week."

"I think it was when I looked back at some of the old stuff and recognized the 'mole' that I realized what I was doing." He shrugged. "Darling, you have learned something from the last year — you can see the way forward already. I have got to do the same." He glanced at her, then away. "It's hard, Jude."

She was appalled by this new insight into his despair. She had thought they were doing so well; she had forged ahead, encouraged by his return to health, by the prospect of the whole family being together again. Kitty's simple analysis of their situation had been so comforting, and what she wanted to hear. She knew that it wasn't going to be easy; of course there would be times when the ghost of Naomi would haunt them. For an instant she hated Naomi Parsons, those legs, that long neck . . .

She pushed up the sleeves of her sweater and poured a kettle of water into the sink. She had not quite seen into the abyss of guilt and grief; had not seen it culminating in such hatred. She hid her horror with difficulty.

"You heard what the wonderful Kitty Davies said just now, Jack. The island will heal the mind."

"I feel I have to do something about it. Myself. Take myself in hand." He tried to follow her lead, levering himself up from the table and carrying the marmalade to the cupboard.

She said, "Well, step number one is fairly obvious, surely?"

He started to rearrange the cupboard. She had forgotten his habit of sorting — almost cataloguing — the most homely things: dishes in the dishwasher, crockery in the sideboard.

He made a space for the condiments and said, "Go on, what do you have in mind?"

"You do not lampoon your 'mole'."

"Jude, that's my job!"

"Not all of it. Think of the Fish-Frobishers. They made us laugh at ourselves."

"But this — this is important. Someone else might have to carry the can for all the computer-hacking and line-tapping that's been going on. There's no proof, you see — not to my knowledge, anyway."

She dried her hands. "In that case, I don't think William would publish, surely? The *Magnet* would be sued instantly."

"The man is dead. I'm not certain whether his family would sue."

"Ah. I see. So in a way it would clear others of suspicion. That's different, Jack. Quite different."

"Is it? I'm not thinking clearly any more. Is it different?"

She looked at him, surprised. He had never asked for moral judgement before. She said, "I think it is. Yes." She remembered how energized he had been from the moment William's thick package had arrived. "Yes, I am sure it is."

He closed the cupboard doors; he was smiling.

"Thanks, love." Some of the strain had gone from his voice. "I want to plod on — like you said just now, it's the way forward. And the only way I know is through my job." He took his plaid jacket from a hook near the door. "Shall we explore? I've brought a book about the birds, and the binoculars are in the bedside cupboard. Let's sally forth!"

They did so. The breeze was strong and the autumn warmth on the wane, but as they climbed to the top of the combe the scents of summer were still all around them, the colours too. They skirted the hotel and stood in the lea of a rock, fiddling with the binoculars, looking down towards Land's End and the Atlantic. And Judith said casually, "Who was this mole, then? Would I know him or her?"

"You might. Moss Jessup — d'you remember he was always on the edge of politics? Powerful-looking man. A bit like Robert: big, dark. Robert is brutally honest, Jessup was simply unpleasant."

She stared at a gannet as it began its long dive into the sea. She said, quietly, "I think I do remember him."

She had thought Lundy would be an escape from the outside world. She should have known better. Her weekend escape to Castle Dove had proved to be a microcosm of turbulent relationships, and Lundy was going the same way.

She said, "Oh, Jack. His widow was at Castle Dove. Her name is Sybil. She adored him."

He stared at her. "My God!" Unexpectedly he tipped his head and laughed. "Well, that's settled that. I'll definitely turn down William's latest project." He hugged her to him. "Look at that bird — he's just going into a dive — he looks like one of those suicide bombers: death and glory!"

They lunched at the hotel. It was full of birdwatchers observing and recording the big autumn migration. It had been going on for some weeks, they were informed: the puffins leaving at the beginning of August with their cousins the guillemots. They were told to look out for kittiwakes, who should have left the previous month but were still enjoying the north-west corner of the island. As she ordered sandwiches from the bar, Judith heard Jack's voice, stronger than usual, as he said incredulously, "One hundred and forty different kinds? All on this small island?"

"They have their own territories. The puffins use the same underground burrows they always have."

Information was bandied about with enthusiasm. The puffin was the island's emblem; they were shown coins and postage stamps imprinted with the clown-like parrot face. The "twitchers", as they called themselves,

278

liked nothing better than to talk about their sightings each day and to recollect — with the aid of battered notebooks — many others in the past. The more serious ornithologists were busy at their laptops, transcribing scribbled notes into statistical columns. A woman apparently on her own sat in a corner, and typed with head thrown back, eyes closed.

When they got back to Hausmann's cottage for a cup of tea, Jack said, "Did you notice that woman in the corner — yes? Did you recognize her? She writes metaphysical stuff. She is very popular. William wanted me to do a piece about her — fixed up an interview and a cameraman. Trouble was, she was almost too straightforward. He wanted something to ridicule, and she simply reports various phenomena."

"Wonder what on earth she is doing here?"

"Kitty might know. Paula Anderson. That was it — couldn't remember. She obviously didn't recognize me."

"Not surprised." Judith sipped her tea, thankful that lunch at the hotel had banished Jack's "black dog". "As far as I could tell, she did not open her eyes once while we were eating. Have another Welsh cake with some of Kitty's home-churned butter." She pushed a plate towards him and watched with satisfaction as he dealt with two cakes and poured himself more tea. The second part of Kitty's prescription was certainly being enjoyed. She grinned. "You know that Kitty Davies is going to take all the credit for your physical well-being?"

He looked at her, then spoke very seriously. "Jude, if you hadn't appeared on that Monday night, I would have let go. I had made up my mind." She was about to tell him sharply not to talk like that when he gave her one of his special smiles and added, "That part is all right. Now it's down to the island to do something with my mind!"

She smiled back, but spoke just as seriously as he had. "I know Kitty sounded like a tourist ad, but Robert thinks like that too. And maybe your Paula Anderson was writing down a special incantation to the spirits of Lundy!" She reached over the table and touched his arm; it was cold. "Come on, let's light the fire in the range. I'll make a hot-water bottle and you can lie on the bed and watch me braise some of that chicken for a casserole."

"I was hoping we could watch the sunset from the south lighthouse." But he made his way obediently to the bed and sat on it, slipping off his trainers.

"Sounds good. But a rest first."

"I've always liked controlling women."

She made a face at him as she tucked him under the duvet and put a hot-water bottle at his feet. It seemed as if there were tears in his eyes, and she looked away quickly. She collected the chicken pieces from the fridge and found onions and carrots in the vegetable rack. She wondered why she hadn't done the natural thing: cupped his face and kissed him, gauged his response and reacted to it.

The chicken pieces sizzled alongside the onions and immediately smelled good. It was so long since they had made love. She remembered that she had almost confided to Naomi that they had not made love since Christmas. Thank God she had not given her that satisfaction.

She turned the chicken and stirred the onions. Naomi could — perhaps — have been banished into the shadows if she had kissed Jack just now. But . . . she was still there. Judith scooped the contents of the pan into a heavy casserole and sprinkled plain flour into the pan, then smoothed stock into it, and knew again with a kind of sick dread that they had to bring Naomi into the open and try to forgive her.

It was getting dark when Jack woke up. Judith was sitting by the range with a bowl of vegetables on her lap, peeling and slicing and feeling pleasantly relaxed and comfortable. The sound of the birds was beginning to make her drowsy, and when Jack suddenly suggested they take that walk to the south lighthouse to watch the sunset, she almost turned him down. He registered her obvious reluctance.

"Don't forget, the clocks will be going back soon."

She turned her head to look at him and grinned, because his normally flat pale hair was sticking on end and his socks wrinkled around his feet.

"Anyone would think we lived in darkness all through autumn and winter. But OK, let's do it. We'll never get as far as the lighthouse without falling over a cliff in the darkness — that's a Lundy experience we do not want! But we'll find a bit of high ground and watch from there."

When they eventually ate their meal she admitted the expedition had been worth the effort. They had not gone far, retracing their steps of that morning and walking up the combe until they came to a suitable vantage point above the hotel. The breeze had strengthened, and they found a rock with a niche big enough to take the two of them and a view of almost three hundred and sixty degrees. They faced towards Land's End, where the edge of the sun was just touching the sea, and stood silently drinking it in. The intensely golden path on the water spread outward and looked to engulf the lighthouse, but then was lost in the rabble of enormous rocks that had been the graveyard for so many ships. Just out of its light were flocks of seabirds like clouds on the water, riding the swell as if it were a lullaby.

"I was going to try to paint this sort of thing when I was at Castle Dove." Judith gave a tiny laugh. "As if."

"It's worth trying, Jude. Over and over again. It's one of those journeys with no hope of arrival, but with its own peculiar satisfaction."

"Like Robert's landscapes, d'you mean?"

"Perhaps. I'm not sure about Robert. His journeys are so dark. But perhaps that can be said of all of us. I don't know, Jude."

He sounded lost again, and she held his arm to her side tightly and said, "Dancing in the dark, Jack. It can be marvellous. Candles and special outfits and romantic music." He responded by turning in to her as if to hold her close. She moved her head. "Darling, hang on! The sun is going — don't miss it!"

He turned back; it was indeed down to its last slice, the sea darkening, the beam from the lighthouse coming into its own. She felt him shiver.

"Come on, let's get back. Time for supper and a good night's sleep."

They held hands happily enough, keeping a sharp eye out for rabbit holes and loose stones. They both knew that they had seen a magnificent sunset and missed out on a personal moment, but as Jack said suddenly, "If we stay a full fortnight all the shenanigans will have happened at home! The gang might even have found some accommodation of their own!"

She nodded. "Yes. We've got plenty of time."

"And no urgency."

They went into the cottage, appreciating its warmth. Jack fiddled with the old-fashioned damper in the chimney breast and pushed the kettle on to the trivet. Judith reached for the mugs automatically.

He said suddenly, "I mean that, Jude."

"Mean what?" She looked round, surprised.

"About the urgency. There is none. Just to be with you is enough."

She stared. "Oh, Jack. I'm sorry."

"That was why I kept it from you. I knew that you would always see her if you knew. I told myself that I was not deceiving you, I was simply preserving our relationship." He controlled the quiver in his voice, and deliberately changed his tone. "Deception and preservation!"

She said gently, "Come and sit down, darling. I wish . . . I wish we could go back to how we were . . . of

283

course I do. But it's better that we know about each other. And about Naomi." She wondered whether this was true.

He sat down; he looked ill again, and her heart sank.

"I hated her, Jude. I'm no good at hating. I wanted her dead and out of my life for ever. And she died. But she's still there."

She held him and rocked him as if he were a child. She whispered, "Leave it all behind, Jack. We're in a magic place."

She knew that this sort of thing happened when he was tired; the sister had told her as much at Taunton only two weeks ago. But by the time they were both in bed she too was exhausted.

She cradled his head into her shoulder and remembered Jennifer and her introverted husband, Stanley. They had programmed their intimacies so carefully, and it had been mildly ridiculous until that evening in the orangery.

Judith put her cheek against Jack's pale hair and wept.

CHAPTER
SEVENTEEN

Kitty Davies said they settled into Lundy quicker than anyone else who had been in Robert's cottage, and what was more Lundy settled into them, too! They took this to mean that they were more conventional than most of Hausmann's guests, and during their occasional evenings at the hotel they socialized easily with the twitcher community, the fishermen and the dedicated conservationists.

Judith thought of their island life as being on two levels, and was deeply grateful for "Kitty's level", as she labelled it. It included the sense of solitude, of living with nature, of ceasing to measure time by her watch. Her eyes registered degrees of light and darkness, her nose — which Jack told her twitched like a rabbit's every time she left the cottage — kept her up to date with the coming of winter, though she admitted it also delighted in the morning smell of bacon from the hotel. The gulls assaulted all ears every morning, but were gentler during the daylight and evening hours. All the birds knew about the weather, too, and could accurately warn of a coming storm. Their cries mirrored human feelings beyond any other language. Plaintive nostalgia seemed their speciality at this time of the year, when the ever-present herring gulls said goodbye to the kittiwakes and the last of the auk family and settled on the cliffs like colonies of welcoming committees — awaiting the arrival of the winter birds.

Apart from Kitty the regular human residents of Lundy tended to keep themselves to themselves, but Jack struck up an acquaintance with the shepherd who looked after David Davies's considerable flock. Kitty told them he had arrived one summer years ago, intending to sit on a crag and write poetry. "It works very well with looking after our flock. They keep his feet on the ground and he does write some lovely stuff. I never quite understand it, but it's like music — you got to listen to it. Then you see it." She shrugged. "It's magic between two covers. But takes him ages. He doesn't mind that, he's very happy."

Judith nodded; she knew that she and Jack could allow Lundy to settle into them in just the same way. Already the daily phone calls and texts from Matt and Len, and the odd one from Martha too, had an intrusive quality about them. It was good to know they were together back in Bristol and the "deal" was going through. It was surprising — but not shocking — to hear that Toby was not going to join them after all. He was keeping the service in Perth operating until a good offer was finalized over there. Jack was of the opinion that Toby had no intention of returning to England. "He's had a steady girlfriend for a long time. And he loves Australia — big open spaces — plenty of air."

Judith understood that need, too. She had made sketches of several parts of the island, and was now experimenting with some of the Davieses' hens' eggs and a cache of powder paints discovered beneath the bed. She told Jack that egg tempura took more stirring than a dozen Christmas puddings.

She said absently, "Perhaps we could go to see Toby during their spring or autumn, Jack. I like the idea of viewing an enormous landscape from the air."

"You could take photographs."

"Yes. Work on them later. We've seen something like that recently — an exhibition. Where was it? D'you recall?" He shook his head just as she remembered. "It was at the Bristol College of Art. A collage piece."

There was a silence, then he said, "I do remember. Naomi told me. You went with her."

She stopped her gentle stirring, suddenly alert. He said, "Come on — don't look like that. We said we would be open with each other. She had enjoyed it, and she thought I would be pleased that you and she were still friends. Actually, I was horrified."

She recognized his facial expression and said fiercely, "You come on, Jack! Don't you see how manipulative that makes her? It was part of the game — she was playing both sides at once."

He said nothing, and she put a paint-smeared hand on his arm. "I thought we were so happy here, accepting what had happened and starting again."

"We are — oh, we are, Jude. And it's so great that you're working . . . trying things out . . . making a mess . . ." He laughed and rubbed at his arm. "I wish in a way I wasn't such a quick-fire artist — I love seeing you becoming immersed in making a painting."

287

"You send such a message, Jack. Straight from the shoulder." She laughed too, but she had noticed that he had not yet started on anything.

He shrugged. "Short-lived. Wrapping for fish and chips. Totally ephemeral."

"Not the impact. That will linger and grow for years."

"Sometimes. Perhaps." Jack signed. "I kept poor old Fish going when I hung about in Perth and then, quite suddenly, he became totally . . . irrelevant. I suppose if I'm honest, I was bored stiff with him."

"No, you weren't. You came over loud and clear when you handed him over to me!"

He looked up. "Our first contact, Jude."

"I know." She smiled across the table. "Come on. We mustn't get maudlin. Get your notebook and start on a script. I'll finish this, then I'll make tea and heat up some Welsh cakes — you can't have anything until you've scripted a strip — and that's not easy to say!" She was spluttering over her words, and as he started to laugh again she added sternly, "I mean it — remember, one line is better than two, and that includes scripts."

He grumbled, but fetched his notebook and settled at the other end of the table. She was silent, mixing methodically, watching the tempura settle into a wonderful shimmering aquamarine. She stood the saucer on the windowsill and went to the cupboard for the tin of Welsh cakes. She forced herself not to think of Naomi and the kind of games she had played; instead her mind flipped unexpectedly to Sybil and the time they had spent at the top of Lynmouth combe last month. She shook the griddle, and the Welsh cakes slid easily to one side and waited to be turned over. She used the fish slice and flipped, and then made tea. Had Sybil known what sort of man her husband really was?

Jack said, "How about Fish-Frobisher taking on a DIY job and managing to puncture a gas pipe?"

"Sounds very Fish-like. Make it a water pipe. They can cope with a flood, but an explosion is a bit much." She looked over his shoulder and took in some of the story. "I like the fact that he is doing it so that his wife can boast to her sister about his DIY skills." She watched while he conjured up an enormous spanner and a soldering iron. She said, "Have you done anything about Moss Jessup?"

"Of course not. I thought we'd settled that we wouldn't ruin his wife's memories."

"Yes. I was wondering whether she knew what he was doing. Ruining other people's lives. Putting other people under suspicion."

"I doubt it. You said she was besotted."

"True." She put the cakes on to the table and added two mugs of tea. "Shall we eat at the hotel tonight? Kitty's David will be there, and can tell us about tomorrow's weather." He nodded absently, still involved with his comic strip.

She nibbled one of Kitty's Welsh cakes and finished her tea. "I'll leave you in peace and go over — book two meals. Don't forget your tea, it will be cold."

"Oh Lord, I had." He drank deeply. "You were right, I must get back to work." He glanced up ruefully. "It's not easy, Jude."

"I know."

She breathed deeply as she walked to the top of the track and turned right into the path that led to the hotel. Below, the tide was out and several small boats had been pulled on to the dry sand. The evenings were dark early now, she must remember to bring a torch later.

David Davies was already on one of the bar stools, and several birdwatchers were scattered around the lounge comparing notes, looking at the photographs on their mobile phones. They lifted their hands in greeting, and David offered her a drink.

"Not now, David. I've come to book a table for later. It seems very still this evening — that's probably a sign of poor weather to come."

"Could go either way." The farmer covered himself. "Kitty says the cows are lying down but the birds are flying high. So take your choice." He grinned. "The post has only just arrived, the barman will be in with it any minute. The place is half-empty though, no shortage of tables. I think Kitty's cooking tonight — chef's in Porlock."

The barman appeared, holding a bundle of envelopes neatly separated with rubber bands. She took two letters from him, one for Jack embossed with the *Magnet* logo, the other in Sybil's handwriting. She tucked them into her pocket and thought how strange it was that Sybil had come into her thoughts only an hour ago. She dreaded reading the letter: it would probably be a diatribe against poor Nathaniel Jones, and

290

probably include some bitter allusions to Hausmann too.

Jack had closed his notebook and was sitting back, eyes closed. He took his letter and weighed it in his hand. He spoke as if to William Whortley. "I'm going back to it tomorrow, William — I promise. Not inspired at the moment." He opened the thick envelope and drew out just a single page. A photograph fluttered on to the table. He was suddenly all attention.

"Good Lord, listen to this, Jude. William says he's almost certainly got proof that Moss Jessup is our man. He actually wants me to start work and get something to him as soon as possible!" He screwed up the letter and threw it on the fire. "Good job we decided against doing it — William sounds almost voracious! This is the fox hunter in him!" He grinned. "He's not going to think much of poor old Fish-Frobisher and the water pipe!"

She put a hand on his shoulder. "Neither do you, Jack. If you did you'd still be sitting at the table with an open notebook in front of you!"

He looked at her, surprised. "I'm just a bit tired, love. That's all."

She let it go. "This is from Sybil. It's thick. Good job we're not cooking."

He laughed and went to the sink to swill his hands and face. She opened her letter and started to read. After the first page she sat up straight and reread it. Then she moved to the table under the lamp and spread out the next three pages and read them avidly.

"Jack. She did know. All the time she knew what Moss was doing. It sounds, my God, it sounds as if he was some kind of sadomasochist. She was all right with that for some time, and then when he got deeper and deeper into the phonehacking, she liked it less and less. She says she was glad when he died before he could do any more damage to her and to other people. She made plans, started work again — then she came to Castle Dove and met Nat and thought everything would be all right. But Nat backed off for some reason. She must have told him about Moss . . . told him the wrong way . . . she might have pretended that she thought he was clever. It was the sort of picture she painted for me. Pride?"

Judith looked up at Jack, who came to the table and sat down next to her. Then she went back to the letter. "Anyway, she was at a pretty low ebb when she heard from Moss's solicitor. The will is being contested. Moss was already married, and his wife is still alive. There are four children. Oh my God, Jack! He didn't want children with Sybil — because he already had four daughters!" She put the letter on to the table and stared at Jack. He put his hand over hers.

She felt her eyes fill. "Poor Sybil. What a swine of a man! How could he string her along? She fell for him because he reminded her of Hausmann! And then Hausmann showed her someone else who had loved her always. And *he* let her down, too! Oh, Jack! She borrowed my nightie and it was bad luck — and she still has it!" Her voice rose to a wail and she covered her face and gave in to tears.

292

Jack sat beside her and rubbed her back gently, then folded her into his shoulder. "She'll cope somehow. If we've learned anything in this past year, it is that people do cope. Somehow." He kissed the nape of her neck tenderly but with sadness, as if in farewell.

She lifted her head and gave a cry. "Jack! Oh, Jack! It was Sybil who showed me that I could not cope without you! And that is still true — it is true, Jack!"

He stared down at her, still sharing her sense of terrible loss. Then he could not look away. And neither could she. She felt his hands on her spine, tracing each vertebra until they reached her neck, and then his forefinger stroking gently as if feeling for the kiss he had placed there. She cupped his face.

"Jack. We *are* coping. I've been too frightened to see it! And you've caught my fear. You always caught my colds, didn't you? This is the same — an infection . . ."

He stopped her mouth with his. Even when she sobbed he still held her so that her sobs became his. And she held him as if she would never let him go again.

It was late when they sat down at their table in the hotel. Most of the diners had finished and retired into the sitting room to watch *News at Ten*.

The waiter came over to their table and looked at them disapprovingly. "Thought you'd let us down. Mrs Davies did the cooking tonight, and it's her special — steak and kidney puddings. She's gone home now, but she was going to bring two of them over for you tomorrow morning with the milk."

They apologized profusely. Judith wondered whether the sudden rush of heat showed in her face. Jack said easily, "Time is very difficult on Lundy. I suppose it's worse when the clocks go back?"

"It certainly is. The birds settle down for the night around five o'clock. No way of telling what the time is after that."

"You could always look at the clocks," Jack said.

"But you don't, not here on the island, do you?"

Jack thought about it, then agreed. "No, you don't."

The waiter glanced at Judith and rolled his eyes. "Unless you've booked a table for dinner, of course. We begin serving at seven o'clock. It's when most people feel hungry."

Judith smiled. "Which means that at this time of night, we are very hungry."

The waiter went off immediately, and Jack reached for Judith's hand. "He's made known his displeasure, but he can't keep it up in front of you. There are a lot of advantages to being married to a blonde bombshell!"

She twisted his little finger until he yelped apologies. Then she said, "You'll be able to make a start tomorrow — a proper start. Set Fish-Frobisher to one side, Jack. Concentrate on Moss Jessup."

His eyes lit up. "D'you mean it? When you read out Sybil Jessup's letter, the thought hit me like a bullet. Do you need to speak to her first?"

"Certainly not. It would become her responsibility then. She would become a woman scorned. No, Moss Jessup has been uncovered by the *Magnet*, and their cartoonist is going to show the world what he was really like. Nobody is involved in a personal vendetta against him — unless it is his victims, of course."

He smiled. "I might have guessed you would see it so simply, Jude. Thank you, darling. I think I can do something with this. In fact I know I can. Dammit, I've dreamed about this story even though I thought I could never do it."

"Oh, Jack." She tightened her grip on his hand. "You are a good man — you really are a good man."

He was surprised and then embarrassed. "Hardly, Jude."

"Darling, Naomi could never have manipulated the situation like she did unless you had been a good man. And that is that. I don't want to shut it all away and make it into a state secret, but I don't want it to haunt us any longer."

Their meal arrived, and Jack declared that he would have known at once that it had come from Kitty Davies's "fair hands".

"You haven't even tasted it yet," the waiter commented, placing the plates with exaggerated care.

"It's the aroma. It wafts." Jack looked him in the eye. "It's like that old advert for gravy — d'you remember? — two heads lifted in ecstasy as the scent of the gravy reaches their nostrils."

The waiter looked at him suspiciously. "Never saw that one. Course, that's your line of work, isn't it? Not that drawing comics is proper work. Getting up in the dark to clean this place is; going to bed in the dark after the final dish has been washed and put away and the breakfasts all laid up — now *that's* work."

The barman appeared with a belated bottle and interjected sourly, "Not done by you, though, m'lad. Off to sunny Spain in a week or so, aren't you? Go and finish up in the kitchen and stop worrying the clientele."

He turned to Judith and poured some wine, then grinned at Jack. "Started off when he was a student and decided it was the life for him, but once the dark nights arrive he's gone till the season starts next year."

He left the bottle with them and went back to washing glasses. Jack grinned at Judith. "I think, once I've finished William's project, Daisy, and Stargazer Fish-Frobisher, will have to get summer jobs on Lundy."

She was delighted. "Of *course!*" They smiled at each other, and then she sobered. "Oh, Jack," she said.

"That's about the eighth time you've said those two words. Is that good or bad?"

She smiled ruefully. "It's not the eighth time by any means. But it's a way of saying thank you."

They started on their steak and kidney, half-hearing the television and the responses from the residents; smiling, making their own comments, sometimes relevant, sometimes not.

Judith said, "I like her a lot. And she's good for Matt. I just hope Toby's girlfriend is as nice."

Jack picked up instantly that the first person she was talking about was Martha Gifford. "She's lovely. As for Toby's girlfriend, I might have met her. A couple of years ago when I was over there, a girl was working in

296

the office. Just a summer job, but she obviously liked Toby a lot."

"What was her name?"

Jack frowned and stopped chewing. "Named after a place . . . her parents had honeymooned there. Alice Springs. Her name was Alice."

"Oh, I like that!"

"Martha and Alice. Yes. A bit old-fashioned — which they are not."

From the sitting room came fragments of a weather forecast for the next day. Apparently the Indian summer would continue for the rest of the week.

The next morning Jack talked to William Whortley on his mobile for a long time. He then settled himself at one end of the table and started to make notes. Judith took milk and bread from Kitty and told her that Jack was starting a new piece of work. Kitty looked at his downbent head and smiled, nodding knowingly. "Magic worked, then?"

Judith smiled and nodded too.

She set herself up in the rock niche where she and Jack had wedged themselves on their first outing, and for the first time since taking up working again at Castle Dove she began to paint. She squinted at the sea, brush loaded and poised. She had always had to conquer her nervous fear of spoiling the whole image with that first application, and was certain that after so long she would scarcely be able to put her brush on to the outline sketch she had made of the south light. She started with the sea. The turquoise was exactly the right

297

shade. She tried the pointillism technique, hoping that the tiny blobs would produce the sparkle she wanted. She darkened the colour as she reached the horizon, peppering powder paint on to her brush until dark rocks appeared around the lighthouse. Time was going fast; she had left her watch at the cottage, but she knew it was late because she was suddenly hungry. As soon as the painted sea reached the rocky peninsula, she began to pack away. She needed to mix other colours.

A voice spoke behind her. "Please don't jump. I've just come from your cottage, and your husband said you might be by the sugar-loaf rock — but you're here." By this time Judith had turned and seen it was the woman writer from the hotel; what had Jack called her . . .? Paula Anderson.

Judith put her bag between her feet and held out a hand.

"I'm so pleased to meet you. I don't think I've ever seen anyone writing with their eyes closed before."

Paula Anderson laughed. "I see the print that way — and then I simply have to copy it down on to my laptop. I always feel it's cheating, somehow."

"I don't think it is. It's one of the exercises I did at art college, but it just seemed to make everything far more difficult."

The woman, middle-aged and very obviously shy, said, "I was looking at your work just then. It's beautiful. That wonderful colour . . . I wondered . . . I asked your husband whether you might consider illustrating my children's book."

Judith gaped. "Are you serious?"

"Of course. It's whimsical. Which might put you off." Paula scuffed with the toe of her shoe at the sandy soil. "It's a story about a family of puffins who can talk." She looked up, plainly embarrassed. "I went to Castle Dove for one of their weekend shows. Mr Hausmann spoke of your work. And your husband seemed to think — but of course I shall completely understand if you find it a bit too . . . unreal."

"I would love to do it . . . if you think . . . listen, I'll do some bird sketches and let you see them . . ." Judith was still so surprised that she laughed loudly. "I've never ever sold a painting, and here I am, forty-eight years old, and you are offering to . . ." She stopped suddenly. "I'm sorry. Perhaps you can't afford to pay me unless the book is a success, and I am quite willing to wait and see."

"We shall own joint copyright. There's not a fortune in children's stories, but the whole idea delights me, and I think it will delight you. Talk it over with your husband. But one thing — you must finish what you are doing before starting on my puffins — the Puffies. I cannot interrupt you in mid-flow." She scuffed the ground again; she reminded Judith of an Exmoor pony. "I'd better go. I am helping with the lunches today. Kitty Davies has a visitor — you know how it is."

She was gone as suddenly as she had arrived, leaving Judith staring at the marks she had made on the ground, hardly believing the short interview had taken place.

Jack confirmed that it had. He was almost fizzing with excitement, and kept telling her it was "all happening", until she began to feel nervous and pointed out she had never worked like this before, and why on earth had Hausmann recommended her? And what if . . . what if . . . her work didn't hit the right button?

He shut her up with a kiss, then held her close and told her how wonderful she was, and how much she deserved this, and that if she could draw a Fish-Frobisher strip and sell it to a canny old millionaire like William Whortley then she could do anything. Anything at all. And then he showed her the beginnings of "Maurice the Mole". The photograph that was still on the table where it had fallen showed an unmistakeable likeness to the large garden mole Jack presented to her. Half the animal's face was hidden by a mask, but it was obvious to Judith that the plump, well-fed yet squat creature with whiskers almost twitching from the drawings was indeed Moss Jessup.

She started to laugh. "Sybil will enjoy this — have you got a cloak and a dagger somewhere in the hallway?"

Jack kissed her. She put both her arms around his waist and pushed the two of them away from the table.

"What are you doing?" he asked.

"Trying to get you to dance!" she said.

He spun her round and steered her towards the bed.

"We started to dance the moment we came here — perhaps before then." He chuckled into her ear. Then he lifted her bodily and put her down on the bed. "Judith Freeman. I love you, and always will."

She took a deep breath. "Likewise," she said.

CHAPTER
EIGHTEEN

Hausmann arrived a week later. He appeared with Kitty, holding bread and milk under one arm and her ample shoulders in the other.

The weather had stayed warm — "mellow", as Paula Anderson called it — and both Judith and Jack had revelled in it, working with a sense of joy they both recognized and appreciated from a long time ago. Paula had insisted that Judith's painting of the south light should be the frontispiece for the new children's book. "You need my text for the chapter-by-chapter illustrations," she pointed out. "And they won't be ready for a few weeks yet. Plenty of time to complete your stunning sea and landscape. You are painting the place where it all happens. Puffins versus rats."

Paula had talked of the time when Lundy had been taken over by pirates, and the terror they had spread up and down the coasts of Devon and Cornwall and even as far as Bristol itself.

"The Puffies are in the same boat, their burrows invaded by rats. They have a meeting and decide to become pirates, and they recruit the gannets and the auks to help them." She spread her hands. "That's all there is, really."

She sounded deflated, but she had already inspired Judith.

"I can see them!" Judith enthused. "Their little parrot faces become suddenly stern and the black-and-white eyes full of cold menace! And the bit where the auks harry the rats into the sea and the gannets go for them! Great stuff!"

During almost ten days of "mellow fruitfulness" while Jack worked with all his old intensity and Judith mixed her wonderful colours and painted with growing confidence, the mainland world slipped further into the background. It was difficult to realize that home was half an hour away by one of the new Freeman helicopters; almost impossible to imagine Len and Matthew already part of the team patrolling the motorways. Martha's phone calls were reassuringly down-to-earth. "Judith, I'm really, really sorry . . . I broke that vase that is on the landing windowsill . . . can't think how it happened . . . Len wants to know if he can borrow Jack's navy-blue sweater . . . half-term is coming up, thank God . . ."

Judith said to Jack, "I am going to love that girl. She is sending sub-messages. I think they need us back home, Jack."

Jack looked up. "We're part of Lundy now."

"Not really. Winter is coming, and that is when Lundy can only manage to tolerate the non-migrants."

He nodded. "I know. It's just . . ."

She said, "We can do what we do anywhere, Jack. Anywhere at all. We're together again. We've learned to dance."

His face broke into a beam of delight. "We have, haven't we?"

It was the next morning when Hausmann came in with Kitty. She stood just in front of him, almost protectively, then stepped aside as if revealing a surprise.

"Look who is staying at the farm with Davey and me! Turned up last night just as the tide was starting to ebb — no phone call, nothing. Just the man himself, hungry as a horse."

Jack went to him with all his old vigour and shook his shoulders. Kitty rescued the bread and milk and put them on the table. Judith stared, shocked by his jack-in-the-box arrival, but also because this man who she hardly knew was so familiar.

Jack said, "We've expected you every day since we arrived — knew you'd have to check on the tenants at some point!"

"Oh, he's checked all right!" Kitty unloaded eggs from her pocket. "Phoned every day and wanted a call back if there was any change in Jack's condition, and I mustn't say a word because you needed peace, perfect peace!" She sighed. "And now, here he is, so I s'ppose winter is just round the corner." She met Judith's questioning glance and enlarged. "He spends most of the winter on the island. Painting like a demon."

"Ah. I didn't know that." Judith met Robert's dark, dark eyes over Jack's shoulder and smiled gently. "Lundy offers peace with solitude. Western Australia only offered solitude."

Robert cleared his throat and spoke. His voice was the same, deep and rough at the edges. "Not really. Australia was where I met another crazy man." He grinned at Jack. She could see their union of opposites. Dark and light.

She laughed. "Kitty, pass me two more mugs, can you? We need tea."

They sat around the table talking for over an hour until David arrived, wanting to know what had happened to breakfast. So then Kitty and Judith scrambled eggs and made toast for all five of them while they put David into the picture.

He looked darkly at Robert. "I might have guessed it. Half-Jewish, half-Welshman. Trying to make real life look like one of your pictures. Course it's all going to die away, that's what it's all about, you great lummock!"

Jack said, "All I know is he saved my life and arranged things so that Jude and I could . . . could —"

"Learn how to dance," Judith supplied. She smiled again at Robert. "We think we've done it, Robert."

He smiled back. "I thought you might." He turned to David Davies. "And you're a fine one to talk, half-Welshman and half-sheer-Lundyite! You and Kitty have helped me out often enough, and enjoyed doing it! You said to me once that we were all put on this earth to help one another."

"I think I said we were put here to get on with it!" David said sturdily.

Kitty nodded vigorously. "It's what God says too, Davey. You didn't invent that one!"

Jack clapped Robert on the shoulder. "You went a step further, then, Robert Hausmann! How often did you have to do the trip between Surrey and Cardiff?"

Robert suddenly grinned. "Not that often. Sybil admitted she had promoted her husband to some kind of wonder-man, and Nat thought she needed another year or two to get used to being without him." He turned to the Davieses. "Sybil lived in a house with Nathaniel Jones on one side, and my family on the other. She was very close to her father, and Nathaniel is like him. Gentle, formal in many ways." He turned to Jack. "You have no idea what Moss Jessup was like."

Jack nodded. "Actually, Sybil wrote to Jude. And on the strength of that and other evidence, I am uncovering the hacking mole. His name, of course, is 'Maurice the Mole', and he is sort of Pickwickian in shape."

Hausmann laughed. "Ridicule is a wonderful weapon. And if Sybil told Jude about him, then she obviously wants it to be used."

Kitty said, "How exactly did you get Sybil and Nat together, then?"

"She agreed to tell it to Nat just as she had told it to me. The whole story. It took time to persuade her. Even when she knew the contents of Jessup's will, there was still this lingering feeling of loyalty." He shrugged. "Relationships. Difficult."

David nodded vigorously, glanced at Kitty and growled, "I'll say!"

And Kitty came back smartly, "Too right!"

Judith looked around the table, smiling, full of deep affection for these people. When she came to Jack, the affection welled up into all the old tenderness. And more. Was that possible? Could the pain of this past year be giving something back — something extra? Her gaze settled on Hausmann, and she realized he was watching her.

She shook her head gently at Kitty and said, "Worth all the effort, though. Yes, Kitty?"

And Kitty's face, so like a russet apple, creased into a grin as she repeated, "Too right!"

Eventually David mentioned he had a farm to run, and Kitty remembered she was preparing cold lunches at the hotel. Hausmann, it seemed, had already offered to work in the garden. "He always sorts out the garden about this time of year." Kitty touched his arm gratefully. "Makes a bit of room for the winter stuff, stores enough potatoes for winter, that kind of thing. He's a good lad."

Hausmann barked a laugh, and for an instant Judith could see how he had looked when he was indeed "a lad". She had thought of him as being in Jack's age bracket, but of course he was younger, about the same age as Sybil; therefore so was Nathaniel — they had played together as children. It made his restless energy seem different; more youthful, an eagerness to help rather than to control.

She grinned at him, and then turned to Jack. "Let's all have dinner together tonight, shall we? You could join us, couldn't you, Kitty?"

"I certainly could — that lummocky boy from over Exeter way can finish off the desserts for me — give him something else to grumble about!"

After they had gone, Jack put away the crockery and cutlery — each piece in its proper place — and she cleaned the table ready for him to spread his work out at one end. Len phoned Jack from the hangar at Filton to tell him where he and Matt would be that day. Apparently, Martha had started her half-term holiday and was looking at the cottage on the Somerset Levels. The owners were considering the offer Matt and Martha had made them, and had left a key with the neighbours in case she wanted to do some measuring for furniture.

"Sounds as if they intend to accept the offer," Jack relayed to Judith.

Judith said guiltily, "I'd forgotten all about it. And I'd also forgotten about half-term! Lundy really has got inside us, Jack."

Jack nodded. "That's why Paula can write her stories here. She turns the clock back, closes her eyes and she's away!"

"Literally with the fairies!" They laughed as if it were a joke.

"Actually . . ." Judith was assembling her painting gear at the other end of the table, ". . . I'm beginning to look forward to seeing everyone again. Len and Matt, and Martha of course. But Sybil and Nathaniel as well. And Beattie McCready — Arnold's wife. I meant to ring her before we came here, and never did. And Bart and Irena, too."

"Who on earth are Bart and Irena?"

"Robert's brother and his wife."

"Of course. Robert bought the lease on Castle Dove for them, didn't he? She disapproves of him."

"He was drinking every night . . . he was disrupting her dream of a perfect hotel. But at some level or other, she is fond of him. And he of her. And he is close to his brother."

"Like Len and me. I'm looking forward to seeing Len."

She came round the table to kiss him. She said, "I love you. Don't work too hard, just let it happen."

"That's what is so good. It is just happening." He smiled. "Are you going to our rock corner? Will you be warm enough?"

"Yes. And another yes." She held the door against a sudden gust of wind. "I suppose our meal tonight is a farewell dinner?"

"Not in any sad sense, Jude. It's a celebration." He tipped his chair back and waved his left hand in the air. "We can dance together really well — but only two can tango. Now we're going to join the others. A sort of maypole effort."

She saw the smile lurking on his face, and said, "If I had anything in my hands besides my painting stuff I would now hurl it at you! See you soon!" And she let the door close sharply behind her and crouched below the level of the combe as she made for their first viewpoint of Lundy.

She worked until the sun clouded over and the wind stiffened her fingers. The clouds were most definitely scudding over her head from the Atlantic rollers. She thought about that word "scudding". It was exactly what clouds did — she must mention it to Paula. The Puffies would know all about scudding clouds; they became part of the "scud", beating their small wings against it as they dropped into the sea for a mouthful of fish. Slowly she packed her things away and pushed herself upright, ready to leave. And there, waiting for her to finish, was Hausmann.

She was not surprised to see him; something had been missing from the afternoon. She wondered why he was there; how long he had been there; whether she had been talking aloud to herself.

He came closer; he had the hood of his enormous parka over his head, and the wind was flattening one side over his ear and hiding his face.

"Jack was worried — apparently you never wear your watch — he's making tea."

She braced her knee against the rock face and wrestled her canvas bag over her shoulders. Then she smiled at the enigmatic face, so full of secrets.

She said simply, "Oh, Robert. What would we have done without you?"

She walked to him, put her head on his chest and wrapped her arms as far around the bulk of him as they would go. He became very still.

She said, "I love you too, Robert."

His arms encircled her; she felt his face against the top of her head, she was inside the hood of his parka; she realized how cold she had become, because she was suddenly so warm, so protected.

She said, "I should have said it that day . . . in the road . . . I'm sorry."

His voice was inside her ear. "I knew. I knew before we met that night at Castle Dove. You were part of Jack, and Jack loved me. It was logical."

She moved so that she was speaking into his ear. "It took me some time, Robert Hausmann!"

"Aah. Jude the very obscure." She felt his laughter in her own body, and closed her eyes, letting the essence of him flow through her. She took a deep breath, knowing suddenly what she must say.

"Listen, Robert. I think . . . I know . . . what you must do. You must paint all those people. In the camps. The ones who come to you at night and demand recognition." She felt his body jerk and held herself to him very tightly. "Don't you dare move away from me! You must do it. Because you will discover other things besides pain. You will discover something else . . . something good . . . Robert, listen . . . please . . ."

He twisted her suddenly and stopped her words with his mouth. It was scarcely a kiss; it was a protest and an angry protest. When he drew away her whole face felt

310

sore. He held her as if he knew she would fall without him.

She gave a small sob and he began to babble an apology. She slid her hands from his waist to his shoulders and then his neck and face. Slowly she drew him free of his hood and down towards her, and very gently and tenderly she kissed him.

She whispered, "Stop apologizing. Remember that the only thing we can share is honesty. And that is because of this love we have. Jack and I love you. And you love Jack and me!" She snuffled a laugh. Her face was wet, and the tears were not hers. "Come on. There's rain in that wind. We need tea and Welsh cakes."

He let her push him round, and they both began the descent to the edge of the combe. When they could see the roof of the cottage, he stopped and stared down to the beach far below them. She saw the hull of his boat pulled up out of reach of the tide.

He said, "Jude, I think I should go. Now. Before this wind works itself into the sort of storm we had last month."

She gave a small cry of protest. "Oh, Robert — please! Is this because I said . . . what I said?"

"I don't know. If it is, then it's not driving me away from you and Jack, it's urging me to go on. Shine a light into all that darkness? Learn to dance?" He drew her down into the heather. "I have done some work on the Holocaust, Jude. I always end up at some pub, trying to forget it."

"Is that how it was that first night at Castle Dove?"

"Yes. Worse still when I was in Australia." He looked sideways at her. His hair, free of the hood, was on end.

"Then there was Jack. And then there was you. Esmée. Nat. God — Bart and Irena too." He snorted a laugh. "And then that crazy couple in the orangery." He took her hand and gripped it hard. "It all meant something, Jude. Are all of us learning to dance? Is that why I've come back to the castle and my studio and those drawings?"

He waited for an answer and she said in a small voice, "Oh, Robert. I don't know."

"Of course you don't! And neither do I — and I thought I did, I've always thought I knew how to live. The places I must avoid, the people I must stay away from. And then . . . my God, I sent invitations to Esmée and Nat like some ridiculous matchmaker! And you turned up too! It was frightening. You were so ordinary, so practical, and yet — Jude, that bloody nightie, I have to tell you it was completely see-through!" She started to laugh. He went on, "I never thought you'd manage the Exmoor trek — my famous trek when everyone was so exhausted they would show their true colours!" He laughed too.

She said, "Well, it worked, didn't it? Robert, none of this means you have to leave now. Surely?"

He shook her hand and let his laughter die into a smile. "I haven't told you. I've left Nat and Esmée — or Sybil or whatever she calls herself now — at the castle. They wanted to come, but I talked them out of it." His smile widened to a grin. "I need to keep an eye on them!"

Judith stared back at him. She said, "I can't keep up with you — you are the most volatile person I have ever met. All I can say is — tea and Welsh cakes are obligatory. How does that sound?"

He pretended to give the question his full consideration. Then he nodded. "Perfect," he said. And he enveloped her in a bear hug.

It was as if Jack knew what had been said. The tea was made, the Welsh cakes lay in the griddle, and they sat around eating and drinking as if they had the rest of the afternoon and all the evening together. When Robert suggested that the two of them should come with him to help launch the boat, Jack nodded immediately.

"Changed your mind about the dinner party?" It was more of a comment than a question.

Robert grinned again; there was an assurance in that grin.

"Things to do," he said.

They trooped down the long combe to the beach. Two fishing boats were arriving, and Robert helped to pull them in and then recruited more help with his bigger boat. Judith and Jack stood back watching as he scrambled into the small well and started the engine, then grabbed the tiller.

Jack said into her ear, "I couldn't have been completely unconscious the last time I was here — I remember David Davies and Matt lifting me under the canopy."

"Oh, my love . . ." Judith hugged his arm to her side, reliving her own memories of that time and realizing how close they had come to disaster.

Robert waved and called something, and then the tough little boat got under way and began the short trip to the mainland, and Jack and Judith started the climb back up the combe, pausing now and then to look out to sea and wave. Below them on the beach the fishermen were unloading lobster pots. Above them smoke came from the chimney of the hotel.

Jack said, "I think we should go home too. Soon."

"Let's leave it with Matt and Len."

"Sounds sensible."

They paused to get breath. The wind had been minimal on the beach, but already the stronger gusts were bending the trees and the few birds which had ventured from their cliffs were being blown about the sky like rags.

He said, "Could be that we have to wait for the weather. A day or two, perhaps. It will give us time to clear up properly. I'll have a go at some of the wood. There's a chainsaw in the lean-to."

She did not ask whether his strength was up to such physical labour. She hugged his arm again. "Good thinking. I'll do a clean-up indoors."

He put his head against hers. "We're going to be all right, Jude." It was a statement, but then he added a question. "Aren't we?"

She answered in her most matter-of-fact voice. "I remember, in Paris, your . . . your sudden diffidence — yes, that is what it was, diffidence — somehow made me feel very secure, very safe." She rubbed her head against his. "I feel it now."

He held her close. She knew he was weeping, just as he had done then.

She kissed him. "I love you, Jack. But more than that. We really are two parts of a whole."

"Yes." He steadied his voice. "That's it. Exactly." He kissed her hair. "Robert said something similar."

She nodded. "Come on. By the time we've washed and changed it will be time to meet the others."

"Yes. Pity that Paula won't meet Robert. There are similarities there. She deals with her demons differently, but she has them."

They fell into step as they turned on to the track leading to the cottage.

She said, surprised, "You think so? We only talk of the book."

"Her childhood was cut off when her parents were killed in that air crash. D'you remember? I think it was seventy-three or four. A plane-load of people visiting graves in Germany? Charter flight?"

"Oh, how awful. She must have been about ten. Oh, Jack, how dreadful."

"Yes." They went inside the house and shut the door firmly on the wind. Jack kept his back to it as she began to shrug out of her jacket. "I wonder whether she will stay on here during the winter? She seems to need the actual place — to live the book, as it were."

Judith looked at him. "Jack . . ." She spoke almost warningly.

"If you think I'm matchmaking you are quite wrong!" But he was laughing, dropping his coat to the granite floor, taking her in his arms, swinging her around the table, stumbling against a chair.

The bleep from the phone interrupted them.

It was a text from Toby.

"Me and Alice getting married next Friday. All welcome."

They stared at it. Judith felt the outside world suddenly pressing in indefatigably. She stared at the message. The phone vibrated on the table, and it was Matt to tell them that Toby was at last making an honest woman of Alice.

"Lots to do. Coming over for you tomorrow, weather permitting. Got to juggle itineraries. Typical Toby, yeah?"

Jack said, "Yeah."

Judith waited to feel anxious for all of them. Instead she felt a tiny spurt of sheer excitement. They were all going to a wedding. They would meet Alice, who had obviously been part of them for some time.

Matt rang off, and for a moment they listened to the wind as it whistled down the combe. Jack opened his arms again. "May I have this dance, Mrs Freeman?"

She went to him but they did not move for a long time.

The room gradually filled with a sense of peace. And then at last they moved. She thought it was a slow foxtrot.

316

The Kissing Gate

Susan Sallis

Out of heartbreak comes a new life . . .

Gussie, Ned and Jannie are not quite siblings, but they share a fiercely close and affectionate family bond. In their bohemian Cornish home, with a famous and distinguished artist as their father figure, they glory in their unusual upbringing and their unconventional, loving family life . . . Until one day a terrible tragedy destroys the foundations of that family, and they have to learn to cope on their own.

ISBN 978-0-7531-9078-4 (hb)
ISBN 978-0-7531-9079-1 (pb)

The Promise

Susan Sallis

There were four of the Thorpe family in the Anderson shelter the night of the raid on Coventry. Mum and Dad, Florrie and little May. Jack was missing . . . he was one of those who did not return from Dunkirk.

When Daisy and Marcus, sixth formers in Coventry, are given a project on the bombing of the city in 1940, they go to talk to May, now living in sheltered accommodation but full of memories of the war. The two youngsters both have their problems — Marcus has to care for his alcoholic mother while Daisy's large and complicated family is full of tensions — and as their lives unfold they strike up an unlikely friendship and become involved in the strange history of May's missing brother and of a promise made all those years ago which still has its repercussions today.

ISBN 978-0-7531-8904-7 (hb)
ISBN 978-0-7531-8905-4 (pb)

The Sweetest Thing

Susan Sallis

A summer's idyll ends in tragedy . . .

Cornwall, 1960, and a whole new world for young Connie Vickers as she holidays with her brand-new fiancé William. But a strange encounter with a beautiful blonde boy on the beach leads to a terrible tragedy, the consequences of which are to affect Connie and William for the rest of their lives.

ISBN 978-0-7531-8678-7 (hb)
ISBN 978-0-7531-8679-4 (pb)

The Path to the Lake

Susan Sallis

Viv's marriage to David was not a conventional one, but when he died — in an accident for which she blamed herself — it was as if her whole world had collapsed around her. She escaped by running, mainly around the nearby lake, which was once a popular place of recreation but was now desolate and deserted. It became both her refuge and her dread.

But through the misery she made some unexpected friends — a couple in the village whose family needed her as much as she needed them. And gradually, as a new life opened up, she was able confront the terrible secrets that had haunted her and which could now be laid to rest . . .

ISBN 978-0-7531-8466-0 (hb)
ISBN 978-0-7531-8467-7 (pb)

Rachel's Secret

Susan Sallis

An engrossing and heartwarming novel from this beloved bestselling author

In 1943, two schoolgirls, Rachel and Meriel, best friends in the Gloucestershire city where they have grown up, amuse themselves by tracking down imaginary German spies. It all seems a harmless way of whiling away the long school holidays . . . until their game turns into a frightening reality, the consequences of which affect their whole lives.

Rachel becomes a reporter on the local paper while Meriel, a GI bride, goes to live in Florida. But the bonds that hold them together can never be broken, as the secrets and scandals which first surfaced in those far-off wartime days eventually come to light.

ISBN 978-0-7531-8162-1 (hb)
ISBN 978-0-7531-8163-8 (pb)

ISIS publish a wide range of books in large print, from fiction to biography. Any suggestions for books you would like to see in large print or audio are always welcome. Please send to the Editorial Department at:

ISIS Publishing Limited
7 Centremead
Osney Mead
Oxford OX2 0ES

A full list of titles is available free of charge from:

Ulverscroft Large Print Books Limited

(UK)
The Green
Bradgate Road, Anstey
Leicester LE7 7FU
Tel: (0116) 236 4325

(Australia)
P.O. Box 314
St Leonards
NSW 1590
Tel: (02) 9436 2622

(USA)
P.O. Box 1230
West Seneca
N.Y. 14224-1230
Tel: (716) 674 4270

(Canada)
P.O. Box 80038
Burlington
Ontario L7L 6B1
Tel: (905) 637 8734

(New Zealand)
P.O. Box 456
Feilding
Tel: (06) 323 6828

Details of **ISIS** complete and unabridged audio books are also available from these offices. Alternatively, contact your local library for details of their collection of **ISIS** large print and unabridged audio books.